Praise for the Yarn Retreat Mysteries

"If you haven't read this series yet, I highly recommend giving it a go. The mystery will delight you, and afterward you'll be itching to start a knitting or crochet project of your own."

—*Cozy Mystery Book Reviews*

"A cozy mystery that you won't want to put down. It combines cooking, knitting and murder in one great book!"

—*Fresh Fiction*

"The California seaside is the backdrop to this captivating cozy that will have readers heading for the yarn store in droves."

—*Debbie's Book Bag*

Praise for Betty Hechtman's National Bestselling Crochet Mysteries

"Will warm the reader like a favorite afghan."

—National bestselling author Earlene Fowler

"Get hooked on this new author . . . Who can resist a sleuth named Pink, a slew of interesting minor characters and a fun fringe-of-Hollywood setting?"

—*Crochet Today!*

"Fans . . . will enjoy unraveling the knots leading to the killer."

—*Publishers Weekly*

"Classic cozy fare . . . Crocheting pattern and recipe are just icing on the cake."

—*Cozy Library*

Praise for the Writer for Hire Mysteries

"Plenty of plot twists and an appealing heroine with a reluctant love interest. What's not to like?"

—Kirkus Reviews

"A sympathetic heroine coping with her own losses and colorful characters from a writer's group combine nicely with an intriguing plot involving class and abuse. Readers will look forward to future installments."

—Publishers Weekly

Books by Betty Hechtman

Yarn Retreat Mysteries

Yarn to Go
Silence of the Lamb's Wool
Wound up in Murder
Gone with the Wool
A Tangled Yarn
Inherit the Wool
Knot on Your Life
But Knot for Me

Crochet Mysteries

Hooked on Murder
Dead Men Don't Crochet
By Hook or By Crook
A Stitch in Crime
You Better Knot Die
Behind the Seams
If Hooks Could Kill
For Better or Worsted
Knot Guilty
Seams Like Murder
Hooking for Trouble
On the Hook
Hooks Can Be Deceiving
One for the Hooks

Writer for Hire Mysteries

Murder Ink
Writing a Wrong

But Knot for Me

BETTY HECHTMAN

BEYOND THE PAGE
PUBLISHING

Chapter One

It was Thursday morning, and the clock was ticking down to the arrival of my retreat group. I'd put on enough of these events to have a routine down. But just because I had a routine down didn't mean the retreats were the same. If there was one thing I'd learned, it was that each one was unique and full of surprises—not always good, either. For now, the six women and one man were just names on a list, but who knew what secrets would be revealed by the time they went home.

On the surface, it seemed like they were all coming for a weekend of yarn craft in a place that felt like a world away from their everyday lives, but there was always more to it.

It was hard to imagine that not too long ago, I hadn't known the difference between knitting and crochet. Now I knew far more than that one craft used needles and one a hook, and I had the finished projects to prove it. I had a certain sense of pride as I pinned on a red crocheted flower to the black sweater I wore over a pair of jeans.

My Aunt Joan would be proud, though the thought of her made my eyes well up. I pushed back the tears—they weren't me. She'd been the one to make an offer I couldn't refuse when I'd gotten to a dead end. It was either move back with my parents in their Chicago high-rise apartment with a view of Lake Michigan or come to Cadbury by the Sea and live in my aunt's guesthouse.

Who wants to move back with their parents, who both happen to be doctors, when they're in their thirties with a history of trying a bunch of professions that for one reason or another hadn't stuck? I admit I'd given up on teaching elementary school pretty quickly. Law school had ended after one semester and that had been my choice. But leaving the job making the desserts at the bistro hadn't been my choice. I'd loved the work, but the place had gone out of business. The temp jobs, well, the name said it all. It was a week here, working in a department store giving out samples of cologne, a few days there of handing out samples of a new gum on a street corner in Chicago, and two weeks with the job that I would have definitely stayed at. Working at the PI agency didn't even feel like work, but the boss, Frank Shaw, couldn't afford to keep me on. It might not have felt like work, but I couldn't afford to be a volunteer.

My aunt had helped me turn my talents as a dessert maker into a livelihood. I'd become the dessert chef for the Blue Door restaurant and the freelance muffin maker for the coffee spots in town.

The yarn retreat business had been my aunt's, but when she died shortly after I moved to Cadbury, her business, house and everything in it had passed to me. I'd discovered her death was murder and tracked down the guilty party. It had given me a little peace of mind and shown me that I had a talent for investigating that I'd put to good use since.

Much as I settled into life in Cadbury, there was still something niggling in the back of my mind. Would it last, or would I suddenly decide to take up my mother's offer for cooking school in Paris or detective classes in Los Angeles, or something else.

Not that I was thinking about leaving just then. It was more like a possibility or option in the back of my mind. At the moment it wasn't an issue—all my thoughts were on the long weekend ahead. I always went to the host site the morning of to bring over the tote bags I had made up for my people and to do a last-minute check.

I laughed at myself for calling it the host site as I gathered up the bin on wheels and went outside. *Host site* sounded so sterile and like a place with a lot of vending machines. At Vista Del Mar the only coin-operated things were the old-fashioned coin phones.

I always checked the sky when I went outside, and no surprise, any hint of blue was blocked by an even layer of clouds. As for the sun—I was sure it was up there somewhere. It was usually like that here on the tip of the Monterey Peninsula, making it always coffee weather, which was good for my muffin business. There was barely a hint that it was May, other than the length of the days and that even with all the clouds, the rainy season was over.

My house was on the edge of Cadbury, and it was more rustic than the places with neat lawns in town. Here the homes were small and cottage-like and most people either had ivy or native plants in place of a lawn. Native plants was the new way of saying weeds.

I didn't have far to travel—Vista Del Mar was literally across the street. As soon as I passed the stone pillars that marked the entrance to the driveway, the view changed. My street was rustic, but this was wild. Lanky Monterey pines stood guard with the spaces in between filled with dry golden undergrowth. The story was that if a tree died and fell over, it was left to decompose on the spot, and it was supposed to be true if some of the wildlife met their maker as well. Ever since I'd heard that, I'd kept my eyes on the driveway as I walked in.

The hotel and conference center had started out as a women's camp over a hundred years ago. The original buildings were all dark weathered wood with stone accents and were scattered over the sloping one hundred or so acres. The trees and dry grasses turned into a strip of sand dunes and beyond that lay the beach. I zipped up my jacket as the constant breeze carried a chill. The air had a hint of a salt smell, but the pungent scent of woodsmoke from fireplaces going in all the buildings predominated.

It was the perfect spot to get away from it all. Once you crossed those gates, the present world faded into the background. The definition of a retreat was withdrawing to a secluded space for prayer, meditation or instruction under a leader and Vista Del Mar was certainly the place for that.

The grounds were quiet at the moment. It was still too early for any guests to be checking in. The driveway forked off into a small parking lot and went on either side of the main building, which was called Lodge. It functioned as a combination hotel lobby and social gathering spot. It was built in the Arts and Crafts style, as were the other buildings, with a lot of dark wood and stone. An unmarked truck was parked next to the entrance. I walked around the men unloading stuff and went in through the open door.

There was a cavernous feeling to the large inner space thanks to the open construction. At one end of the main room a wooden counter marked the registration area. A door was open to the Cora and Madeleine Delacorte Café, which had recently been added, and the smell of freshly brewed coffee wafted toward me. The back of the room was set up with table tennis and pool along with shelves of board games. The door to the gift shop in the corner was still closed.

In between there were tables and hard-back chairs and a main seating area with couches and comfortable chairs arranged around a massive fireplace that had a fire set waiting to be lit. I pulled the wheeled bin up to one of the tables I planned to use to check in my people. I grabbed a couple of chairs and arranged the tote bags on them. I was just setting out a clipboard when a voice echoed through the barnlike space.

"What are you doing?" Kevin St. John demanded. I followed the sound to the massive wooden counter and saw that he seemed to be glowering at me. He was the manager of Vista Del Mar and as usual seemed overdressed for the rustic surroundings in a dark suit and white shirt.

"Was that a rhetorical question?" I said. I held up one of the blood-red tote bags with *Yarn2Go* emblazoned on the front. "I'm setting up for my group, like I always do," I added with a shrug.

"No, no," he said frantically. His usually placid moon-shaped face suddenly looked as if a storm had just hit. "Take all of that out of here. You're mixed up. Your group is coming next week."

He was still fussing when he came out of the doorway that led to the business area behind the counter and marched to where I was standing.

"I don't think so," I said. I had already pulled out a sheet from one of the folders. The date of the event was written across the top. I held it up for Kevin St. John to see. In my head, I always referred to him by his whole name, though when I actually addressed him, he insisted on being called Mr. St. John. We had a rather adversarial relationship. He didn't like me putting on retreats at Vista Del Mar, but he also had no choice, so he made it as difficult as possible, probably hoping I'd just give up.

He pulled the sheet out of my hand and began to shake his head. "This date is just wrong, then." He turned in a huff and rushed back to the registration area with me close behind. As soon as he saw that I was with him behind the counter, he started to shoo me away then relented. "Fine, I'll let you see for yourself." He went to a computer screen and started scrolling through something. He had a triumphant look as he prepared to point out my error, but then his face froze and he muttered, "It can't be." I took the opportunity to look over his shoulder, and there on the screen it showed the reservations for guest rooms and a meeting room for my group for this weekend.

"You have to change it," he said with a gulp. "What about moving it to next week, or maybe to another hotel in the area?" His eyes flashed panic. "You live across the street. Have them stay at your place."

"No, no and no," I said. "My group is already on their way. They specifically wanted this place this weekend, and you can't be serious about that last suggestion." Kevin had begun to pace with his hand on his forehead in the traditional worry pose. "I'm assuming there's a problem," I said. "Maybe I can help work it out." Just because he always looked for a way to give me a hard time didn't mean I had to be that way. I really wanted us all to get along.

"Yes, Ms. Feldstein, there is a problem," he said, almost spitting out the words in a condescending tone. He had stopped pacing and was glaring at me, obviously dismissing my offer of help. "I assume you've heard of Jordan." He didn't pause for me to respond. "He's holding his Find Your Greatness retreat here this weekend. He was specific about having the whole place. They're taking over everything. They're arranging all the meals and all the activities." He was silent for a moment to let it sink in.

Yes, I'd heard of Jordan. Who hadn't? He was the rock star of gurus. No linen pants and tunics for him. He was all about well-fitting jeans, work shirts with a red bandana hanging out of his pocket. His pitch was that he had the secret to being confident and self-reliant, which was a cure for whatever issues anyone had.

"I'll give you a refund with something extra," he offered. "The same for your people." His tone had turned to cajoling, but when I shook my head, he went back to snippy. "Then I'm just canceling your reservations. The rooms you have reserved had a flood—an act of God. There's a clause that says we can do that."

I looked at him and rolled my eyes. "Really?"

His shoulders slumped as he seemed to deflate. We both knew he couldn't pull something like that. One of the reasons he was so hostile to me was that I had a relationship with the Delacorte family, who were the owners of Vista Del Mar. They had given my aunt a sweetheart deal and it had continued on when I took over her business.

The Delacortes were considered the local royalty and owned lots of property in Cadbury by the Sea, in addition to Vista Del Mar. It had been assumed that Cora and Madeleine Delacorte were the sole heirs of the family fortune. But thanks to my meddling, the love child of their brother was uncovered. No one would have guessed it was the down-to-earth owner of Cadbury Yarn, Gwen Selwyn. She only reluctantly came forward. The Delacorte sisters ended up being glad to have some help with Vista Del Mar even though their new family members preferred to stay in the background. Kevin St. John didn't share their pleasure. He worried it was more people to interfere with his running of the place.

Cora and Madeleine Delacorte had led very sheltered lives and after finding out about their brother's secret life and meeting family they didn't know existed, they reconsidered their lifestyle and decided it was time to spread their wings beyond Cadbury and had gone on an Alaskan cruise.

Now that Kevin St. John had dropped the ridiculous threat, he changed to conciliatory.

"You don't understand," he said. "What am I going to do? Jordan thinks he has the whole place. If he sees your group . . ." He looked out over the counter as the delivery people continued to bring things in. I noticed that no one was asking Kevin where to put everything. It was as if they'd gotten instructions from someone else. The manager turned back to me. "You do understand the Jordan people have taken over the dining hall. There won't be any meals for your people. And none of the regular activities we usually have for all the guests. So, no marshmallow roasting or movie on Friday night and no special event on Saturday night. Your people would be barred from taking part in anything they put on."

As much as I said he was my nemesis, I did sort of feel for him. His life was being manager of Vista Del Mar. He was always trying to prove his worth and even more so now that he felt there were more people to impress. Having a Jordan retreat was a big deal for the place and if it blew up, a disaster for him.

"Here's a possibility," I said. "I have a very small group and we could keep a low profile. The Jordan people probably wouldn't even realize they're not part of their group. I can arrange for some of their meals at the Blue Door and have some brought in. Of course, since the rooms usually come with meals, Vista Del Mar would have to pick up the tabs. As for the activities, I can add some for my group and I could check the Jordan retreat's schedule, so we don't interfere with theirs."

Kevin's eyes shifted back and forth as he considered what I'd said. Eventually, he seemed to realize that he had no choice and grumbled something about us keeping out of sight. He waved for me to follow as he rushed back out into the main area of the big room and packed up everything that I'd just set up for my group. He grabbed the handle of my bin and led the way back to his inner sanctum behind the counter just as the door opened and the two men brought in several life-size cardboard cutouts of Jordan.

"The first thing is to get rid of those," Kevin said, pulling one of my red tote bags out of the bin. Kevin went to a stack of boxes against the wall, opened one and took out a handful of natural-colored bags that had Vista Del Mar written in black type and the silhouette of a cypress tree on the front. He removed the inserts out of all but one of them. "This is for you, so you'll know where they're going to be." He dropped the bags into my bin. "You can transfer the stuff for your people into these."

"They're so plain-looking," I said. But then I shrugged it off. There was no use fighting to keep my bags. If it would keep things smooth, it seemed a small concession to make. I put the new bags in the bin with the ones I'd already made up. It was my turn to grumble. Here I'd thought I was all set for my group's arrival and now I had to rush to redo the bags and make arrangements for meals. I'd have to come up with fill-in activities, too. I squeezed around the men bringing in another load of boxes for Jordan's retreat, barely avoiding running over their toes with the bin. In the short time I'd been there, they'd already hung posters with Jordan's favorite sayings and placed the cardboard cutouts around the large room. Each one had a slightly different pose and a different Jordanism.

There were always problems when I put on a retreat, but this seemed worse than usual. For a moment I wondered if I should have tried to move my group, but as I'd told Kevin St. John, several of them had specifically wanted Vista Del Mar. I couldn't blame them—it was a unique spot. I took a deep breath of fresh damp air and caught sight of a very grand-looking Monterey cypress tree. The constant breeze had shaped the foliage so it had a horizontal feel. I always said the cypress trees here reminded me of someone running with their hair trailing behind. I was sure I'd manage to work it out.

A flat-bottomed truck had just pulled in with what looked like prefab structures ready to be assembled. Wow, Jordan had brought along his own buildings. He really *was* taking over the place.

But then his retreat had a totally different purpose than mine. His people were coming there to fix their lives, mine were more interested in fixing a dropped stitch.

As I reached the end of the driveway and passed through the stone pillars that marked the entrance to Vista Del Mar, or in this case the exit, it was like stepping back into the world.

I was about to cross the street to my place when a red Ford 150 truck came barreling down the street and then pulled to the side, stopping so abruptly the tires squealed. The driver's door opened and Dane Mangano got out. His face lit into a smile as he approached me. I must have had a troubled expression because the smile faded into a look of concern.

"What's wrong?" he asked. It wasn't my nature to complain, but I told him about the mess with the overlapping retreats. "It sounds as if you handled it," he said. "You know how to stand your ground." His eyes lit up again and his mouth curved into a grin. "About this weekend. What about Saturday night—my place, dinner and . . ."

He lived down the street and was a cop for Cadbury PD. Honestly, there wasn't a lot of crime, and he spent a lot of time telling people to pick up after their dogs or urging tourists to drive slower. There was the occasional domestic abuse call or vandalism and even this lovely town on the tip of the Monterey Peninsula was not immune to murder.

There'd been an immediate attraction between us, but I'd learned the hard way that romance in a small town was different than in Chicago. We'd gotten looks and been teased the first time we went out to dinner. People were practically asking about wedding invitations. I couldn't handle being under that kind of scrutiny and we tried taking our dates out of town, but ultimately, I'd kept him at arms' length. Since I thought my time in Cadbury might be temporary, it seemed wrong to get all entwined in a relationship with him and then leave him hanging when I took off. But no one could say that Dane wasn't persistent. He'd ignored all my warnings about not staying and made a grand gesture about offering me his heart.

It wasn't that I didn't care for him and there was definitely chemistry. It wasn't just his looks, which were hot, but it was his character. I always said he had character to spare. His life had been light-years from my comfortable upbringing with two doting, though maybe too much at times, parents. His mother was an alcoholic and his father was completely out of the picture. Dane had been the one to take care of everything from cooking, shopping for embarrassing things for his younger sister, and taking care of his mother when she fell off the wagon again. All the while, he'd given the impression to the world that he was a bad ass. Even now he was the one his mother and sister turned to when they messed up.

And there was what he did for the local teens. His idea of being a cop was to stop trouble before it started. In a small town like this, the kids were bored and looking for mischief. To keep them busy, he'd turned his garage into a karate studio and offered them free lessons. He also cooked massive amounts of spaghetti for them and gave them big-brother-like advice.

Even with all of that, I'd been successfully keeping a distance—the standing my ground he'd referred to—but when he did the whole thing about offering his heart to me, my resolve had weakened, and we were sort of a couple, but without benefits. There had been lots of hot make-out sessions, but that was all. Until recently. What was the point of holding back? But after all this waiting, both of us wanted to make it an event—though a very private one. I know I was deluding myself that the whole town didn't know about our relationship, but I needed the illusion.

Then it became a problem of when. I baked at night. He often got the night shift. We'd been going in circles for weeks. The one night I got off, he had to work. The night he had off, I had baking to do.

"I have the retreat," I said, pointing at the bin.

He seemed undaunted. "Fine, you do whatever you have to with them and then we could have a late dinner."

I started to make an excuse, telling him about Jordan's retreat interfering with mine, but I stopped myself. "Whatever I have to do with my group will be done by ten o'clock," I said.

His face lit up. "All right," he said with a merry wiggle of his eyebrows. "I'll fire up the spaghetti sauce and get the candles and rose petals."

I said okay, but my voice came out in kind of a croak. I was so bad at the whole romance thing. When I attempted to flirt it came across like a comedy routine. Who knew what I'd do with candles and rose petals? Knock over the candles and set the rose petals on fire. I was afraid he had expectations that I could never live up to. Mostly, I was worried how it would change our relationship. It was my last holdout from commitment. He seemed to read my thoughts.

"It'll be fine. It's not like I'm going to throw you over my shoulder and carry you off because we spent a night together." He looked up and down the quiet street. "Looks like there are no gossipy eyes to see," he said with a twinkle in his eyes. "PDA okay?"

I rolled my eyes and opened my arms for a hug. I felt his breath on my neck as his arms encircled me. It felt too nice and could have easily led to something more, but I jumped back. He shook his head at my reaction. "Geez, there's nobody to see us."

He gave my shoulders a squeeze. "Got to go. I have to cook for the crew and go to work."

He climbed back in his truck and drove down the street. I watched as he pulled into his driveway and wondered what I'd just agreed to. I was already worried about the weekend and now this, too.

Chapter Two

I usually put together everything for the retreat in the guesthouse, but since I was just switching bags, I went right to the main house. Guesthouse/main house sounded pretty grand, but the guesthouse was a converted garage, and the main house was a two-bedroom cottage.

Whatever it was called, it had taken me awhile to move into it since the house still felt like it belonged to my aunt. Even when I moved in, it took a while before I could think of it as my place. I had gradually made changes like painting the walls and switching out some of the furniture. The kitchen was the only room I'd totally left as is. I loved it just the way it was. It was bigger than you'd expect for a small house and had room for a table. The counters were covered in vintage sea green tile with black accents.

I might be an expert at dessert and muffins, but I had no interest in cooking regular meals and survived on frozen entrées and instant oatmeal. There were also plates of spaghetti from Dane. Whenever he made a batch for his group, he left a generous plate at my door. He made the sauce from scratch and it was so delicious, I was tempted to lick the plate.

Julius was waiting by the door and started to swirl around my ankles as I came in. I pulled the bin to the table before I dealt with the black cat. Part of his greeting was a sign he was glad to see me, but there was also another motive. He left my ankles and moved on to the refrigerator, practically waving a paw for me to follow.

Of all the cat foods in the world, Julius had chosen one I called *stink fish* as his favorite. Actually, it was called Mackerel Delight, but my name suited it better. I found out the hard way that Julius would eat as much of it as I put out, but then throw it up in a stinky mess. The cat was also unrelenting in his demand for it, so I had come up with a plan to give him dabs of the pinky flakes of fish throughout the day. He never let me forget the plan.

I held my nose as I pulled out the heavily wrapped can. Even with all those layers and my nose closed, I could still smell it. When I finally reached the can, I gave him his spoonful. He'd almost finished it by the time I had rewrapped everything.

Much as I hated the smell, I felt it was the least I could do for him. I was pretty sure he'd been abandoned and then chased off Vista Del Mar by a golf cart driven by Kevin St. John before the cat had the good sense to show up at my door and invite himself in. When I heard that cats choose their humans, I was kind of honored that he'd chosen me. He was the first pet I'd had and I was a little uncertain at first, but now I knew that wherever I might go, he was coming, too.

Once he was done with his snack, he took off for a nap.

For a moment I wondered what to do first. I had expected to just bake some cookies to bring over and have some time to chill before my group arrived. But there were the cookies to deal with, the bags to redo and the meals to work out. Much as I'd given the impression that I was sure everything could be worked out so that the two retreats could go on simultaneously, I was annoyed that Kevin St. John had made it seem like it was my problem to fix. But I quickly realized that wasn't going to get me anywhere and pulled myself together to deal with what I had to.

The cookies were simple. I always kept rolls of butter cookie dough in my refrigerator. All I had to do was lay a piece of parchment paper on the cookie sheets, slice up the dough and put them in the oven. As soon as they were baking, I started on the tote bags.

The Vista Del Mar bags that Jordan was using were a noncolor and so dull compared to my bright red ones. I considered simply putting my filled bags inside the Jordan ones, but then I'd have to worry about my group pulling out the red ones, and I discovered the bland-colored bags had a divider, so my bags wouldn't have fit inside anyway. The simplest thing to do was to switch the contents into the plain bags.

Kevin St. John had given me empty bags to use and had included one loaded one. I was curious about the contents and emptied it on the kitchen table. There were a bunch of stapled sheets. The top one had *Elite Jordanaire* written in red across the top. There was a paragraph that seemed to be a welcome and said something about how special the group was. The rest of the page promised a weekend of learning the secrets from Jordan and completing challenges. The promise was that all the hard work would pay off and that by the end of the weekend their lives would be transformed. I flipped to the next page and glanced over the schedule. It seemed that every minute was full from the time they arrived that afternoon until they left on Sunday. And the days were long too: they started at six a.m. and ended after ten at night.

The timer pinged and I pulled out the cookie sheets. The smell of buttery sweetness filled the room as I slid them on racks to cool. I went back to looking over the Jordan pages and saw that the activities had names like Hot Coals Stroll, Hot Box Detox, and Dance Out Your Demons. And in between the challenges, as they were called, there were programs put on by Jordan. I saw that dance activity was listed on Saturday night when normally Vista Del Mar put on something fun that was open to everyone at Vista Del Mar. It was pretty clear that Jordan wasn't into fun. But I guessed if his retreaters were going to change their lives in a few days, they really had to work at it.

There was a note about the meals. They had to forage for their first one and prepare it themselves. The rest of the meals would be handled by different crews and a list of the assignments would be on a message board. It reminded me that I needed to make arrangements for my group. Luckily, I only had seven people to be concerned with. The obvious choice was to call the Blue Door. Not only did I make their desserts, but the owner, Lucinda Thornkill, was my best friend in town.

As soon as she heard the situation, she offered to handle the meals. The group would have some in the restaurant and other meals would be brought to Vista Del Mar. "Send the bill to Kevin," I said.

"Absolutely," my friend said. "He should do a lot more since it was his mistake. You are being very accommodating considering how difficult he always makes it for you."

"This may sound corny, but I believe in the golden rule, at least most of the time. Anyway, all I really care about is making the weekend good for my people," I said. I told her about Jordan's program. "Those people have no free time."

"I like your retreats better," she said. "Though it's probably good that I didn't plan to come to this one." She had come to a fair share of them. It was her chance to get away from it all for a while. The back of the Blue Door menu had a fairy-tale-like rendition of how she and her husband, Tag, had been sweethearts in high school and then reconnected many years later when she was divorced and he was a widower. They'd married and followed their dream of having a restaurant in the small seaside town. But the story left out a few details, like Tag had changed a bit since high school. He was borderline OCD and did things like follow the servers around and adjust the coffee cups they had just set in front of customers. Lucinda took most of it in stride, but every now and then she needed to get away.

We talked over the menus for the assorted meals. I was so used to them being provided in the Sea Foam dining hall that I was surprised at all the decisions I had to make. We agreed that most of the meals would have limited options to choose from and that everything would be delicious.

By the time I got off the phone, the cookies had cooled and were ready to be packed in a tin before I moved on to finish with the tote bags. I took a another look in the loaded Jordan bag that Kevin St. John had given me. Other than the thick wad of papers, there was just a pen and a pad of paper. It was a lot sparser than what I gave my group. The accommodations at Vista Del Mar were closer to a camp than a five-star hotel. The toiletries provided were unscented and the most basic, so along with a schedule and information about the place, I added some little luxuries like wonderfully fragrant toiletries, a lavender sachet to tuck under their pillows as a sleep aid and a fancy chocolate bar.

I left the stack of empty red bags on the table and packed the dull ones back into the bin and added the tin of cookies. It had taken so long that Julius had come back looking for seconds.

I'd found out that not only did cats pick who they wanted to live with, but they ran the show, too. I went through the whole ritual again of going through all the layers of bags and wrapping and finally got to the can of pinkish stuff while Julius did a victory dance around my ankles. As soon as I had some on a spoon, he raced me to his bowl. He ate it with such noisy relish, it seemed to be worth the trouble.

The phone had started to ring before I'd finished all the rewrapping. I assumed it was my mother. Our calls were always contentious. She'd gotten a little better, but she still didn't approve of my life. But then she was a cardiologist who spent her days fixing people's broken hearts and I spent mine making sweet treats that probably weren't exactly heart-healthy.

I grabbed the phone just as I finished wiping off my hands. I barely got out a hello.

"Case, you have to help me out." Only one person called me Case and I would have recognized his voice anyway.

"What's up, Sammy?" I asked. Sammy was Dr. Samuel Glickner, a urologist who was also my ex-boyfriend. He'd followed me out to Cadbury from Chicago, insisting it wasn't about trying to work things out between us, but rather for his chance to work on his real passion, magic, far from the disapproving eyes of his parents.

It was pretty sad that Sammy and I were both in our thirties and still not able to deal with our parents' disapproval, but that's what it was. He'd taken a leave of absence from his practice in Chicago and hooked up with a local practice. He spent his days working on bladders and such, and he spent his evenings perfecting his act. He'd talked me into being his assistant until he could find somebody else. The act had morphed into a mixture of comedy and magic, and he'd gotten a number of private party gigs at the fancy resorts in Pebble Beach.

Our breakup hadn't come from a fight or anything. Sammy was a great guy and probably perfect husband material. There just wasn't any chemistry, for me anyway. Frankly, I thought I'd done him a favor when I broke things off. He should have someone who got weak-kneed and saw sparklers when their lips met.

"The seal on the hot water heater broke and leaked all over the place. They're going to have to break up the floor and redo walls. I can't stay here. I know you said I couldn't rent your guesthouse, but this is an emergency. All my stuff is sitting out on the sidewalk. It would only be for a week or so." There was a moment of dead air before he continued. "It actually would work out really well. I got hired to put some touches on an escape room for Jordan."

There was more dead air and finally he said, "Case, are you still there?"

"I'm here," I said. I had balked at the idea of him living at my place for obvious reasons, but I really couldn't say no this time. It was an emergency and just temporary. "It's fine. Bring your stuff over whenever. I'll leave the key under the mat."

My phone made a noise letting me know I had another call and I signed off quickly with Sammy. If the other call was my mother, I was absolutely not going to tell her Sammy was moving in. It turned out not to matter. The call was from Frank Shaw, the Chicago PI I'd worked for.

"Feldstein, I haven't heard from you lately. Just wanted to make sure you're still breathing." I could hear the squeak of his office chair as he forced it back into sort of a reclining position. There was the rustle of paper as well, which probably was from his lunch. Frank liked hoagies, heroes, sub sandwiches—anything in a long bun with a lot of stuff in it. "So no dead bodies lately or mysteries you need my help on."

"No and no," I said. "It has been pleasantly uneventful around here."

"Oh," he said, sounding disappointed.

"But the quiet is about to end," I said. I could hear the chair make noise and I imagined that he'd sat up.

"Oh," he said, this time sounding alert.

I told him about my upcoming yarn weekend, and just as it seemed he was beginning to tune me out, I mentioned the conflict with the other retreat. "Do you know anything about Jordan?" I hesitated, wondering if I needed to add a last name, which I didn't know anyway. I was about to explain who he was when Frank answered.

"I know who he is and what he does," Frank said. "He's the sexy guru. Whatever they call their gatherings, the point is always the same. A weekend with him is going to change your life forever. The difference with him is that he's all about tight jeans that show off his attributes. And instead of harp music, it's the pumping beat of rock and roll. He's got some line that merely being in his presence will change your life. And he gets a bundle for it. I did some work for an attorney who had a client who claimed she was shamed when she wouldn't take part in one of his exercises and wanted a refund. The Jordan people argued that it came at the end of the weekend and she'd already gotten benefit from it or something. He claimed that just passing through his vibe pool would have changed her life. When the attorney said she'd go public with her complaint, they forked over the refund. The truth is they have people sign so many waivers, they're not liable for anything. You could get abducted by aliens and they'd still be free and clear."

" I suppose you found out a lot of inside dope," I said.

"I didn't get that far with the investigation before they settled. I'd have to look at my notes, but I'm sure there have been other incidents that they 'handled.' All those guru types have groupies. With the jeans and all, I'd guess he probably has more. From talking to the client I did the work for, I got it that the people who come to his weekends have a lot of money to spend and are expecting a solution. I didn't dig that deep, but I'm guessing she wasn't the first dissatisfied customer—or the last."

"How interesting," I said. "He charges a bundle for a weekend with no creature comforts, and they even have to make their own meals."

His chair sounded like it was being pushed back and the rattle of paper ended, which I assumed meant he'd thrown the sandwich wrapping away. All signs that he was done talking. I was going to end the call, but he beat me to it.

"You know where I am, Feldstein, if anything comes up and you need my advice." There was a click and the call was over. It was funny he was so impatient since he was the one who'd called me. But that was Frank.

He sure hadn't helped me to feel any better about sharing Vista Del Mar with Jordan.

Chapter Three

It was time to face the music whatever it was going to be. My last act before leaving was to give my appearance a touch-up, which meant combing my hair, a light touch of makeup and adding a few more touches from my stash of yarn adornments. The red cowl blended nicely with the flower I was already wearing, and it also added some nice warmth around my neck. I pinned a crocheted butterfly to my black fleece jacket. The butterfly was black and orange just like the monarchs that showed up to winter in Cadbury every year. It was actually my creation from a retreat I'd put on and I was very proud of it.

I grabbed the packed bin and left quickly before Julius could demand another treat. I dropped a key under the mat in front of the guesthouse for Sammy as I suddenly remembered the plans with Dane. It was too late to back out on either. Just another complication to deal with.

The Lodge seemed different when I walked in. There were more life-size figures of Jordan with a bubble spouting one of his sayings, like *Only you can live your life,* and *Your true destiny is waiting for you to grab it.* The figures had him standing in different poses. Some might say they were confident, but to me they seemed a little too *look at me, look at me* for my taste. The jeans and work shirt appeared a little staged, but as Frank said, they definitely showed off his attributes.

A table with merchandise had been set up adjacent to the door to the gift shop. Stacks of T-shirts emblazoned with *I'm with Jordan* and an image of his face sat next to a selection of red bandanas, mugs and books.

I turned to the registration counter expecting to see Kevin St. John, but Cloris was manning the space. She had recently turned in her white kitchen worker smock for a blazer and name tag. She was studying hospitality at a local community college, and even though she'd been considered kitchen help, she'd jumped at the chance to fill in wherever needed to get the experience. The Delacortes had been behind her getting promoted to assistant manager, though Kevin St. John kept referring to her as the manager's assistant and still had her fill in in different jobs. I liked working with her because she always seemed glad to take care of whatever was needed and had a calm sort of confidence. But not today. Her eyes seemed to be darting about and her brow was furrowed. When she saw me, the look got more intense.

She opened her mouth to speak, but I spoke first. "I know all about Jordan and his retreat. Kevin, I mean Mr. St. John, made a mistake. He thought my retreat was next weekend, but it's not."

She waved me closer, and when I reached the counter leaned toward me. "What a mess. These Jordan people have taken over everything. They put together a sauna on the grounds and are building something on the ground floor of Hummingbird Hall. They had their own food delivered into the dining hall and are doing their own prep." She let out a heavy sigh. "Mr. St. John put me in charge of the kitchen again. I thought I was done with the white smock, but I guess not. I'm supposed to keep an eye on things." She touched the blazer with pride. She'd really gone all in for her new position, adopting a conservative short hairstyle for her warm brown hair. "He's doing everything to cater to the Jordan people so they'll make Vista Del Mar the regular place for their yearly spring retreat. I'm sure you know he is having a fit about your retreat being held here."

"Don't worry. I'm not trying to make problems even though it's all on Kevin." She gave me a look and I added, "St. John." I told her I'd do my best to steer clear of the Jordan people and that I'd already arranged for my group's meals from the Blue Door.

"Be sure they send the bill here," she said. "Your group is going to be eating a lot better than his group. The meals here this weekend . . ." She shook her head in distress. "We always provide such nice meals, but this group actually has to forage for their dinner the first night. I saw the supplies they had delivered." She wrinkled her mouth in distaste. "One of his people said Jordan believes in food for fuel, not pleasure. Since I'm going to be stuck in the dining hall, I hope they don't blame me for the bad meals."

I assured her that they probably knew what they'd signed up for and if anyone said anything, she should just tell them it was Jordan's way. "My group's going to be here soon. I thought I'd meet them in the area by the fireplace." I gave the bin a tug and was about to move when I had an afterthought. "If Jordan's people have taken over the kitchen, does that mean there won't be the usual refreshments for my yarners?"

"Don't worry, I've arranged for coffee and tea service as usual." She glanced nervously around the large room. "Why don't you wait for your people in the café." The Cora and Madeleine Delacorte Café was a recent and very welcome addition to Vista Del Mar. The door was open and a chalkboard stood outside advertising their offerings.

She had picked up a clipboard and looked down at it. "Your group is so much easier. They have two groups: Elite Jordanaires and the Jordan Crowd. The Elites arrive today and get more time with Jordan. They are the ones to actually do the things they call challenges. The Crowd people get to observe." She shrugged in disbelief of what she was about to say. "Jordan claims they get benefits just by watching, though not the advance benefit the Elites get by the actual doing."

"No problem, I'll wait in the café," I said. "I'm sure that once the Jordan people start to arrive everyone will sort of blend together and it won't be a problem."

I picked a table by the window that had a view of the only green grassy area on the grounds. It was just before the entrance to the boardwalk that ran through the dunes. Now that my group's arrival was imminent I got jittery and looked for something to distract myself with. A group of people were huddled around a nearby table. I played detective and ascertained they had to be Jordan staff people.

It wasn't that hard. The Jordan people hadn't arrived yet and the three at the table had T-shirts on that said *Staff*. They were busy talking and taking no notice of me, so I checked them out and leaned a little closer to eavesdrop. Most of the talking was being done by a man with a shock of long light brown that flopped at an angle over his forehead. He seemed very dramatic, and his voice carried so I could hear him. He flipped through a list and kept talking about repeat retreaters. A rather prim-looking woman with straight-across bangs seemed less concerned with repeat retreaters than with someone named Megan who was late. A woman with chin-length white hair sat between them. It was clearly premature, as she looked about in her late thirties. She had a stern expression and seemed upset about the latecomer as well.

"I don't understand why she's still on the staff," the white-haired woman said. The other two shared a knowing smile.

"Really?" the man said. "You can't be that naïve. She and Jordan . . ."

Just when they were getting to the good part, I saw Cloris wave from the doorway before she brought my group to the table. I took a quick glance as they approached. I'd had groups of people that were all friends, but this group were all strangers. There were just seven of them this time, six women and one man. I'd had one male retreater who was a closet knitter and another who showed up by chance. I wondered what John would be like.

And there was something else. I'd done enough retreats now to know that not everyone was who they seemed. That people came with secrets and issues they thought a weekend away with yarn would work out. I tried to appear casual as I smiled at them, but I wondered if any of them was hiding something behind their friendly expression.

"I'll put their suitcases on the deck and they can grab them when they go to their rooms. I'll bring the keys here," Cloris said. I started to pull some more chairs around my table, but John beat me to it.

"I hope you didn't think I was implying that you were a weak female," he said. "These days you have to be so careful. I held a door for an older woman, and she seemed insulted and snapped that she wasn't that feeble."

"No offense taken," I said. "I'm always glad for help." I took a moment to introduce myself and explain the meal situation had changed. "Things will be a little different than originally planned. Vista Del Mar won't be providing your meals. But I've arranged for something even better."

"Fine with me, as long as there's dessert," one of the women said with a laugh. "I love pie." Her long black tunic barely hid her soft curves. "And none of that *don't eat the crust* for me."

"I thought we'd all get to know each other and have a drink." I held up a sheet with pull-off name tags. With such a small group, they wouldn't need them for long, but until everybody got who was who they would come in handy. It was first names only. They had a list of complete names in their folders.

"That's me," the pie lover said, reaching for one that said *Yolanda*.

The rest of them pulled theirs off and stuck them on their chests. I glanced back at the other table, and they were all looking at the doorway as if they were pointers. The woman with the white hair started making a *tsk* sound. "You certainly seem to be taking advantage of your position, Megan."

The woman in the doorway rolled her eyes. "Whatever," she said with a dismissive shake of her head.

The woman with the white hair continued. "I don't care what special privileges you think you have, but you should show more responsibility. And certainly even more so after what happened."

Megan let out a sigh. "It was an honest mistake. I thought I turned my phone off, and when it rang, I reacted," she said as she crossed to their table. "I said I was sorry."

"Hardly enough since it was a trust exercise," the prim-looking woman said.

"She was okay," Megan continued. "Jordan is always saying there's risk in everything."

I noticed my group was listening. "It should make you glad you're in my group. No risks, just rewards of spending time with yarn." I was going to ask for their drink orders, but one of the women tapped me on the arm.

"There's a mistake here," she said, pointing at her name tag. "There's supposed to be an exclamation point after my name."

"Oh," I said, surprised. "I thought that was a typo."

"No." She sounded adamant. "I added it to stand out." Inside I was nodding to myself. There was one in every group, and I was guessing it was going to be her. She had a head of thick hair that was hacked off in some asymmetric style. It had a reddish cast to the brown color, and just as I was thinking it had to be a wig, she read my thoughts and gave it a tug. "It's all me."

I was about to ask about the drink orders again, but Suzy! let out a yelp. "What's going on, my phone doesn't work. I need to post something." She held up the smart phone to show off the screen. "There're no bars, and no Internet connection."

Inwardly, I groaned. I always made a point to mention that Vista Del Mar was unplugged. No cell service or Internet. Not even TV. There was a row of vintage phone booths with landlines to make calls and the desk took messages and posted them on a board by the gift shop. But even with all my warnings, there was always someone who didn't understand what it meant.

I opened my mouth to explain, but John politely took over. "The point is getting away from all the electronics," he said. He repeated verbatim what I'd put on the information sheet about Vista Del Mar and again on the confirmation form I'd sent them.

"Well, nobody told me," she said, throwing her hair back with a groan.

I pointed out that it was clearly stated in her confirmation.

"Confirmation? What confirmation?" she said, looking at the

others and expecting them to agree, but they all said they'd gotten confirmations. Suzy! seemed to be getting more agitated and then she stopped. "Now I get it. This weekend was a gift from my son. He took care of everything and he got the confirmation. It was all a plot. They say I have an addiction to my phone." She let out a mechanical laugh. "Who has a phone addiction? Alcohol, drugs, cigarettes, but a phone? She smiled as she shrugged and looked around at the group for agreement.

No one said anything and Suzy! went back to fiddling with her phone as if it would magically begin to work.

"It might help if you turn it off and put it where you can't see it. Out of sight, out of mind." The woman who'd said that showed off her name tag, which said *Hanna*. "This might help, too." She held out a package of gum and took a chew to show that she had some. "I recently quit smoking. This weekend is supposed to help me over the hump. Vista Del Mar is strictly no smoking, so there's no chance to backslide, and I've found that yarn work helps take the edge off. I'm a high school science teacher, which means I should have known better than to start up again, but I was going through a rough patch." She smiled weakly. "But isn't that what people always say." Hanna was rather plain-looking by design. No makeup and dark brown hair that didn't need a lot of attention. Her only accessory was a pair of dangle teardrop earrings.

Suzy! defiantly refused the gum, but John took it. "It looks like we're in the same spot," he said to Hanna. "Maybe not the exact same spot. I'm in business affairs at Winkleman Brothers Studios. Everything in the industry is high-pressure. Now that grass, weed, marijuana, whatever you want to call it is legal, I was imbibing too much. My wife got me into knitting, thinking it would have a relaxing effect and keep my hands busy. I needed to get away from temptation." He popped the gum in his mouth and started to chew. Yes, he had the look of someone in the "industry," as he called it. Perfectly styled hair, high-end casual clothes and most important, expensive sneakers.

The small woman with bright eyes looked at the gum wrapper. "You could be replacing one habit with another." Then she turned to John. "And your wife didn't come?" She pointed to her name tag and introduced herself as Fern.

"She's dead, she died," he stammered. The whole group let out an uneasy *oh* sound before rushing to add their condolences. He seemed uncomfortable with all the attention. I knew they wanted to ask what happened since she must have been relatively young. I guessed he was in his forties and figured she was probably around the same age. I know I wanted to ask him what happened, but it seemed like an unspoken agreement that we'd leave it up to him to give out any details.

Suzy! continued to fidget with her phone, seeming unable to take Hanna's advice and put it away. It seemed to be making everyone uneasy and I was trying to think of how to handle it, when a tall woman with pretty features and long honey-colored hair pulled something out of her bag.

"Do you know how to crochet?" she asked, putting her hand on Suzy!'s arm.

"Sort of," the fidgety woman said with a half-hearted nod.

"I'm Daisy, by the way," she said as she held out a hook and a ball of cotton yarn. "Just start hooking and it'll keep your hands busy." Suzy! accepted the gift and with Daisy's help made a slipknot.

"You can just practice your skills for a few minutes, then I'll tell you how to make a washcloth." Daisy watched as Suzy! started making a strand of chain stitches.

"This is great," Suzy! said with a little too much gusto. "I can't thank you enough. You saved my life. I was getting into that panic zone. What was I missing on Facebook? Did something happen somewhere in the world I should know about? And emails . . ." Her eyes went skyward. "What if somebody is expecting an answer?" She was getting wound up and her gaze was going to her phone, which was still on the table. Fern made a grab for it and dropped it in Suzy!'s bag as Daisy urged her to take a deep breath and concentrate on her crochet work. Once Suzy! calmed down, Daisy spoke to the group.

"I wanted to take a short vacation alone, but not by myself. If that makes sense." She smiled as her gaze went around the group. "This seemed like a perfect situation." They all nodded and made agreeing sounds.

"I guess I'm the only one who hasn't spoken, the woman next to Yolanda said. "I'm Vonda, Yolanda's younger sister." She had a much different demeanor than her outgoing sister. No wild mane of frizzy curls, Vonda had a short trim cut. She was slender and her slacks and tucked-in shirt had a more structured feel than her sister's outfit. "I'm an assistant principal at a middle school," she said.

"I'm a hairdresser," Yolanda chimed in. "We always take a trip together. We take turns choosing where to go. This was Vonda's idea." She looked at her sister and her expression faded momentarily. "I like fun places, but Vonda has other ideas."

"Who says a vacation has to be just about a good time," Vonda said, sounding a little defensive. It seemed she realized what she'd said and quickly added, "I don't mean that we're not going to have a good time here. But there's a purpose. We're going work on our knitting and meet all of you."

There was an awkward moment and I stood up and asked for their drink orders.

"I suppose it's too early for wine, Suzy! said and gave me such an elaborate coffee order with so many details I suggested she place her order directly. The other six requested easy drinks. When I came back to the table, they were talking among themselves.

"I heard it takes twenty-one days to change a habit," Daisy said.

"That sounds about right." Hanna nodded. "I'm hoping go from gum to knitting." It was then that I noticed she'd taken out a pair of small needles with the beginnings of something purple on it. She began working the needles and took a deep breath, letting it out slowly. "And I'll have something to show for it when I'm done. She pulled out a folded paper and showed off the pattern to the others and they nodded appreciatively. "It's so nice to be with a group who understands." She glanced at Fern. "You seem to be the only one who hasn't said what made you come here."

Fern looked up from her drink and seemed pleased at the interest. "I'm a single mother with three kids and a career. Need I say more?" They all nodded with understanding.

"What's with all the cardboard figures of Jordan?" Daisy asked. I had been putting off talking about the other retreat other than mentioning the change in the meal plan, but now that Jordan had been brought up, it seemed like the right time to tell them.

"He's a hunk," Yolanda said. "I wouldn't mind if he came to one of our workshops and gave us a pep talk!" I glanced at the other table wishing Yolanda had said it a little quieter, but luckily they seemed intent on whatever they were doing and didn't seem to notice us.

I handed out the tote bags, explaining he was having a retreat at Vista Del Mar at the same time as ours and in an effort to not have our group stand out from theirs, both groups were going to have the same tote bags. I held up the Jordan group's schedule and said I'd made a few changes to my group's schedule so the retreats wouldn't interfere with each other. It was a better way to say it than to tell them Kevin St. John was hoping that Jordan wouldn't know our group was even there.

Fern picked up the schedule and glanced over it. "I hope we don't have to forage for our dinner," she said.

"No, no," I said quickly. "They'll be eating local grass, but you will all be having a delightful dinner at one of the best restaurants in Cadbury by the Sea. The Jordan group is having special meals and it seemed better to let them have the dining hall to themselves." I had decided not to let them think there was any sort of conflict between the two retreats.

"That's a relief," Fern said. "Foraging is pretty dangerous if you don't know what you're doing. There are lots of poisonous plants. Ever hear of deadly nightshade?"

No one seemed to know quite how to respond, and they put their attention on their drinks and the tote bags I'd just given out.

I glanced over at the other table. They seemed completely unconcerned with us. The woman they'd called Megan had joined them and she seemed to be getting a lecture by the woman with the white hair. Since my group was occupied looking through the contents of their tote bags, I tried to hear what the fuss was about.

"You have such an unprofessional attitude," the woman with the white hair said.

"And you are some kind of fanatic," Megan said. "Jordan thinks so, too." Her mouth curved into a smug, knowing kind of smile.

The man with the fob of hair patted the white-haired woman's arm. "You should let it go. You're overreacting. It's not really your place."

"Hah," the white-haired woman said with annoyance. "You know that saying, that we're only as strong as our weakest link. Someone around here needs to keep an eye on standards."

Megan's eyes flared. "You're just jealous because I'm closer to Jordan than you are."

It was getting a little heated and I was relieved when Cloris came in holding keys. "You're all staying in the Sand and Sea building," she said. She looked at me. "This might be a good time for them to take their things to their rooms." She gestured toward the door she'd come through and seemed to be trying to pass along a message there was something to avoid. "I'll be happy to take you to your bags and point you in the right direction," she continued. Her movements were a little frantic and I sensed she was in a hurry to get them out of there but trying not to show it. As soon as they were all standing, she moved them out the door that went directly outside.

I took a moment to clear the table, intending to follow them. As I was about to get up, I sensed someone close behind me. When I turned it was as though the cardboard figure had come to life, but without the upbeat expression. His brows were furrowed and he glared at me. "Who are you and what are you doing here?"

Chapter Four

I looked up at Jordan, trying to come up with something to say. I noticed that there were two muscly-looking men next to him wearing staff shirts. Bodyguards? He needed bodyguards? He leaned closer to me and spoke in a harsh whisper. "The insurance company sent you, didn't they? Or was it Eden or Saint Marco? Do they think I don't know that they've been sending spies? They can't stand that I'm number one."

I wasn't an expert on guru types, but I recognized the names as people I'd seen on PBS promoting some self-help systems. The "shows" were actually more like informercials. Neither of them had the presence of Jordan. Eden was a short balding man with a squeaky voice and Saint Marco was a tall bland man who claimed to have a system that could turn your life around in a week.

I was putting together my denial when Cloris came back into the café and attempted to intercede. "Is there a problem?" she said in her best customer service voice.

"It's this woman and those people." He looked at the door the group had gone out. "No one is supposed to be here other than the staff of this place."

I saw a light go on in Cloris's eye. "This is Casey Feldstein and she is practically staff. She handles yarn retreats. There was a technical error and one of her events overlaps with your weekend."

"Then they're leaving?" Jordan said.

I felt my temper flare and spoke without thinking it through. "No, we're not leaving."

Jordan whipped his gaze toward me, and it seemed as if he broadened his stance, in an attempt to seem all-powerful. "We'll see about that. Where's the manager?" His tone was agitated and one of his beefy escorts put a hand on his arm, appearing to try to calm the retreat leader.

I regretted my outburst, realizing it had only poured oil on the flame. I did not want him to go to Kevin St. John, as I knew it would turn out badly for me. Like it or not, Jordan had a lot more clout than I did. I looked to Cloris hoping for some kind of magical intervention, but she looked as panicky as I felt.

Then suddenly it was as if a lightbulb had flashed above her head with a solution and her whole demeanor brightened.

"I'm so sorry about the mix-up," she said to Jordan. Already I could see she was on the right track. Saying you were sorry for whatever was always better than being confrontational. Jordan reacted by softening a little, probably thinking he'd won and I was out. For a brief moment I had a sinking feeling that she was going to turn to me next and give me the I'm sorry speech followed by You'll have go, but she gave me the subtlest of smiles that gave me hope.

"Didn't I hear your assistant say that one of your presenters canceled at the last minute?" Cloris said. Jordan didn't acknowledge her question but one of the toned-up twins nodded in recognition. Cloris smiled sweetly, letting her gaze move over the whole group. "There might be a solution that works for everyone."

Jordan's expression darkened and he nudged one of his assistants, muttering they were wasting time and to find the manager. Cloris must have heard what he said and realized she better get to the point. "It was the person who taught your crowd how to make bracelets in a craft activity."

"They're called challenges, not activities, and they're survival arm-wear, not bracelets," Jordan said curtly. All three of them held up their wrists to show off brightly colored cord wristbands. He could call them what he wanted but they were bracelets to me. I couldn't get a close enough look to see how they were made, but it appeared they were woven or braided.

Jordan started to be dismissive. "We like to have our people leave with something to touch that reminds them of all they've accomplished over our weekend—but it's hardly an essential challenge."

"Casey's retreat is all about crafts. She's a craft expert. Suppose she took over for the person who didn't show?" She glanced in my direction for agreement, and I gave her a nod.

Jordan shrugged. "It's like the cherry on a sundae. Nice, but it's still a sundae without it."

"It's on your printed schedule," Cloris said, holding out the clipboard she'd had tucked under her arm. At the same time one of his assistants leaned in and said something about a mention of the arm things on the website. Jordan shifted his weight and stared at me.

"I get it—she does something for me and I let her people stay."

"Exactly," Cloris said. "Believe me, you'd be getting the better end of the deal. Casey only has seven people and you probably won't even know they're here. You, on the other hand, won't have people complaining they were cheated out of one of the promised *challenges.*"

"Is that a sample of what you do?" Jordan demanded, turning to me. I flinched as he reached out and touched the red cowl around my neck, wondering if he was going to grab hold of it, but instead he just fingered it lightly. He let out his breath as he seemed to be considering his answer. "Okay," he said finally, as if he'd just granted me a huge gift.

I forced myself to smile and uttered a thank-you. Inside I was annoyed at myself for bowing down to his supposed benevolence. All I'd gotten was what was rightfully mine and I'd just committed to teach something I knew nothing about.

"Sorry," Cloris said when Jordan and his entourage had moved on, taking the table full of staff people with them. "I hope that was okay. How hard could it be to make those arm things? And I'll make sure they pay you for taking over."

I gave her a pat on the shoulder. "It's better than how things would have ended if Kevin St. John had gotten involved, but now I need to use your phone."

Yes, my yarn craft skills had improved, but I wasn't the craft wizard that Cloris had implied. The phone call was to my helper, who was far more adapt at knitting and crocheting than I was, and I hoped that meant she'd know about the cord bracelets and would be willing to help with Jordan's arm-wear challenge.

Crystal Smith had been handling the actual yarn work for me since the first retreat I'd put on. In the process, we'd become friends. We were both about the same age, though in very different places in our lives. Things could have gotten complicated with Crystal after it turned out that she was part of the Delacorte family. But she wasn't looking to turn her life upside down or get in the middle of the running of Vista Del Mar. Mostly, she had continued helping her mother run Cadbury Yarn and trying to handle being a single mother to two teenage kids.

"Kevin really screwed up this time," Crystal said after I'd filled her in on the situation. I explained what Cloris had worked out and Crystal laughed. "I'm glad my *great-aunts* pushed for her to be assistant manager." She let out a sigh. "It still feels strange to refer to them that way. They were always the rich sisters who lived in that fabulous Victorian up on a hill. I never thought we'd be connected to them."

"But now it makes sense why your son has such a feeling for Vista Del Mar. He takes after his great-great-uncle."

"Cory is the one who's the happiest about the new relations," she said. "But to get back to the matter at hand, Cloris did a great job of working it out with Jordan. The ego of that guy, claiming that merely being in his presence could change your life." She stopped herself. "Maybe it's true, he does seem to have changed yours, more like gummed it up." There was a smile in her voice. "Politicians, rock stars and gurus, those guys are all the same. All that attention goes to their heads and other body parts," she said. She'd been married to a musician—well, Rixx seemed to think of himself as more of a rock god. Having a wife and two kids didn't go well with the image he had of himself and he ended up going off with one of his groupies.

"I know all about those bracelets," she said. "The band had them. They came in handy when they were on tour and the lock on somebody's guitar case broke. You can just unravel them and use the cord for all kinds of things. They're actually called paracord bracelets and the cord is really tough." She knew all about the origin of them. They were used in parachutes, and when the parachutes were taken apart, the cord was wound up to keep it orderly, and from there the bracelets had emerged. She was relieved when I explained they already had the supplies. "I'm sure we can handle the crowd if we work together. Of course, we'll have to make some ourselves first," she said with a chuckle.

When I finished the phone call and went out into the main part of the Lodge, it looked quite different. Several tables had been set up to register the Jordan people. One was deserted, but the other had a cluster of people around it. The cardboard figures of Jordan seemed to be watching the proceedings. After meeting him in person, I decided I preferred the cutout version much better.

I stood watching for a moment. The greeters were all smiles as they handed out badges and collected signed papers. It was the whole crew that I'd watched at the table. Even the one they'd called Megan was working side by side with them, and whatever hostility I'd seen seemed to have disappeared. Kevin St. John was all smiles as he circulated around the new arrivals. It was a lot more than he'd ever done for my retreat people.

Chapter Five

I took a deep cleansing breath when I walked outside. Disaster had been avoided for now. I felt an inner shiver imagining if Jordan had stormed Kevin St. John and demanded that my group leave. There wasn't a doubt in my mind that the manager would have insisted we go. Jordan's demands would have outstripped any fear of lawsuits, or repercussions from the Delacortes. I looked up at the sky and as usual didn't have a clue of the time of day by the light. Lucky we had watches inside of sun dials or nobody would have known what time it was. Mine told me it was getting close to three.

The grounds were a little busier as I noticed a couple pulling their suitcases up a winding path to one of the newer buildings that housed guest rooms.

My groups always stayed in the Sand and Sea building. It was one of the originals from the time it was a camp and I'd heard it had been where the counselors stayed. The path to it led up a slope through an area of tall golden grass. Like the Lodge, the Sand and Sea building was covered with weathered brown shingles. A column made of local stones held up the overhang in front of the entrance. By now, the group had spent some time in their rooms. I was always honest in the description of the accommodations, but I was beginning to think that nobody read them because there was always some surprise and maybe disappointment when they actually saw their rooms, which were spare, to say the least.

The rooms were small with beds that were the size of cots. The sheets were on the rough side and the bathrooms barely large enough to have a sink, toilet and tiny shower. The toiletries provided by Vista Del Mar were on the same par as the bathroom, which was why I added the nicer versions in the tote bags. There were no telephones in the rooms and the only source of entertainment was an ancient clock radio left from the time when installing meant plugging in.

But all that sparseness had a benefit. It sometimes took a while, but the simplicity brought peace of mind. No need for white noise machines; all they had to do was open the windows and let the rhythmic sound of the ocean lull them to dreamland.

I walked into the living room–like common area and imagined those young women camp counselors nursing a cup of hot chocolate in front of the fireplace, relaxing after their charges went to bed. The fireplace was the same, but by now the furniture had been replaced numerous times, though I imagined the comfortable style had stayed the same. My groups had gathered there for yarn craft on previous retreats, but it was also a nice place to settle in with a good book.

I thought I was there alone until I heard a voice. "It's so nice and cozy in here." When I turned, Hanna was eyeing one of the armchairs just as Daisy came in the door.

"I brought revised schedules," I said, waving a handful of pages. I'd taken out all the regular activities that Vista Del Mar usually provided and changed mealtimes and such. A lot of time slots were still labeled *To Be Announced*. Cloris had taken care of printing them up while I'd been on the phone.

I gave them each one and asked if they'd been able to find their rooms. Both of them nodded and I waited for some editorial comment on what they thought of them, but neither of them added anything.

I'd expected John to be the one most put out by the quality of the rooms. He seemed like someone who flew first class and who was used to plush towels and high thread count sheets that came with five-star hotels. He was unpacking his bag when I knocked on his door. I apologized for the rough muslin sheets, and he surprised me by saying the lack of luxury was a relief. "I was getting kind of soft. I like the idea of getting back to basics. You know, leave your everyday life behind for a few days," he said, glancing around his sparsely furnished room. "It makes the treats you put in our bags stand out even more." I noticed his chocolate bar had already been opened and some of it was missing. I assured him there were refills and gave him an updated schedule.

Vonda and Yolanda were sharing a room and I saw they'd come prepared with snacks and a small pot to make hot water. Since they had driven up from Los Angeles, it had been easy for them to bring their own pillows and the extras. They were laughing and talking as I was struck by how different they looked, but then I guessed it had to do with their different lifestyles. Hairdressers were artists of a sort and Yolanda gave off that sort of vibe. Vonda's was an authority figure as an assistant principal and it showed in her manner.

The door was open to Suzy!'s room, and she was pacing while peering at her phone. As soon as she saw me, she put the phone behind her back. She put her hand on her forehead. "I didn't know this would be so hard. Maybe I'll get some of that gum. I feel like I'm going to jump out of my skin. I can't seem to help it, but there is this tug that makes my finger want to scroll."

"It's toughest at first," I said. "Once we have a workshop, your mind will get off of it," I said. I reminded her of the phone booths if she needed to contact her family.

"It's not the same," she said, sounding agitated. "They tricked me. All my son said was that it was a nice getaway weekend. My emails must be piling up, and texts. What if something happens somewhere—I'm not going to know about it." I was glad to give her a schedule and leave. She was making me nervous.

Fern had the windows open in her room and was inhaling the cool damp air when I checked on her. She had already made her room seem homey. A knitting project was sitting on the bed with the needles stuck in a skein of an iridescent color of yarn. A book was open facedown on the night table, along with some framed photos. She saw me looking at the pictures. "I can't help it—I have to see their faces." She smiled at the photo and then did a twirl with her arms out. "But oh, how nice to be here all alone."

When I went outside, I felt rather than heard loud music pulsating from somewhere. It was so out of place on the grounds—where the usual sound was only the rhythmic rush of the waves—that I went looking for its source. I'd already figured that it was probably connected to Jordan's retreat, and I was curious what they were up to.

I passed the Sea Foam dining hall, and as I approached Hummingbird Hall, the volume seemed to increase. The building was the same Arts and Crafts style with dark wood, some local stone and lots of windows as the others in the area I called the heart of Vista Del Mar. This building was used as an auditorium when it was filled with rows of chairs, and when it was empty it became a big open space for activities like dances or mass yoga classes. The door at the side was open and I slipped in, staying in the shadow.

Jordan was already onstage wearing one of those headset microphones. The crowd seemed small, with only about thirty or so people sitting in a cluster at the front. Jordan had had a presence when I'd dealt with him, but it was nothing compared to what he gave off when he was in front of a crowd, even a small one. I watched with fascination trying to see how he connected with his people.

He walked to the edge of the stage and jumped off. He moved right into the throng, getting up close to them—really close, as in their bubble of personal space. "Ah, my special people," he began as he touched individuals on the shoulder or gave others a hug and welcomed them back. "You're the Elite Jordanaires—you're the most committed to wanting to change your life." He paused and seemed to be overwhelmed with emotion. "It means so much to me that you are so inspired that you joined this special group. I promise you will be transformed by the end of our time together." He put his fist on his heart and then waved his fist over the group as if he was offering them a special connection to him. They all cheered and tried to get closer to him, but he had begun easing back out of the crowd.

"We don't want to waste any time. We're going to get right to the first challenge. Accepting the gift of nature. Those of you who have been here before know the wonder of going out into a field and gathering nature's bounty. Lyla Konker is our expert in this," he said just as the white-haired woman came into the group. The vibe was completely different as she moved through them, handing out pieces of paper and pointing out a table to the side that had a display.

I lost interest as the white-haired woman started to speak and slipped back outside. For a moment, I felt a little lost. My whole routine of things I did at the beginning of the each retreat had been thrown to the wind. First there'd been my encounter with Kevin St. John and then dealing with Jordan himself. I hadn't even been the one to escort my people to their rooms, but at least I had checked up on them. Then it came back to me that I had never checked to see that the meeting room I'd arranged for the group was in order.

I dashed back across the center of Vista Del Mar and found the small building set between the ones that housed the guest rooms. It was actually a newer building but had been built in a similar style. All the buildings had names and this one was called Cypress and had two meeting rooms. Ours was the smaller of the two but had a fireplace and windows that brought in more light than the other one. I opened the door and rushed in, looking around. I let out a breath of relief when I saw that Cloris had come through and the counter was set with the coffee and tea service. A fire had been laid in the fireplace and just needed to be lit. The long table was surrounded by chairs. It seemed okay, but something was off, and I glanced around again. I shook my head as I realized what was missing. There was no tin of cookies next to the drinks or my bin on wheels. I went back over the earlier events and figured that I had left it behind the registration counter when I'd used the phone.

It was hardly the end of the world, but it upset me that I'd gotten so flustered. I was annoyed that I'd let everything with Jordan throw me off. I retraced my steps and went back across the grounds.

As I neared the Lodge, I noted a small bus parked in the driveway. I was relieved to see Cloris come out of the building. I dreaded having to deal with Kevin St. John to reclaim the bin. I waved toward her, but she seemed intent on stepping inside the door of the bus and didn't see me. It was only when she came back out that I was able to get her attention. I was a little stunned when I saw her face. I was used to her confident smile, but it seemed her expression was stuck in concern.

"What's the bus for? Did Jordan decide to relocate his people?" I asked, hoping to lighten her mood.

"I wish," she said. I'd reached her by then and she leaned in close to keep our conversation confidential. "Mr. St. John wants everything to go perfectly with them and I know if anything goes wrong, he's going to try to make it seem like my fault." She glanced around to check that we were still alone. "The bus is here to take his people to the Carmel Valley to forage for their dinner." Cloris showed what she thought of the idea by shaking her head with distaste. "The woman who works with him found the location; we just arranged the transport."

Just then the white-haired woman came out of the Lodge and joined us. Cloris shot me an uncertain expression, then shrugged and introduced us. I already knew her name was Lyla Konker from hearing Jordan introduce her to his people, but I smiled and acted as if I'd never seen her before in my life. She in turn barely acknowledged me. Up close it was even more apparent that the white hair was really premature. She had super straight posture and an expression that said nobody could live up to her expectations. She kept looking at her watch and seemed agitated. "Where are they? Jordan should have given them a lecture on discipline." She seemed most upset that the staff people weren't there yet. "They've done this challenge before and understand what an awakening it is to experience the bounty that is out there just waiting to be picked. She went on with what I imagined was part of the lecture she'd given them about the wonders of dandelions and burdock greens. How they were organic and loaded with nutrition. "After all, food is merely meant to be fuel," she said. "No need for any extras or dessert." She said the last word with a grunt, as if it was something awful.

Cloris looked at me and seemed apprehensive how I was going to react. After all, Lyla had just dismissed my whole field of cooking. But I simply smiled at her and tried to ease her agitation.

"I'm sure they'll be here soon," I said. "Your people are probably still getting acclimated to Vista Del Mar.

She glared at me in response. "This isn't some *whatever* sort of weekend. They have to push themselves and put in the work." She looked at me again. "I don't suppose you would understand that since I heard that you aren't even supposed to be here. What is it that you do? Run a knitting circle?"

"Oh, look, here they come," Cloris said, trying to distract her. I'm sure Cloris was worried that Lyla would keep hammering at me until I reacted. I'd been pretty good about letting it all go past me—first dealing with Jordan and now her—but you can only pull a rubber band so tight before it finally snaps. I was glad when her group started to pour out of the building and climb on the bus.

"Sorry," Cloris said. "She's a bit uptight."

"And strict and no fun," I said. "I'm starting to feel sorry for Jordan's group, but then I guess they must know what they're getting into." The door to the bus pulled shut and it started to back up.

"At least you're done with your part," I said.

"I wish. Collecting the stuff is just part of it. It's all timed out. The bags have to be checked and then they prepare what they gathered. I have to play traffic cop in the kitchen to make sure they don't set the place on fire or anything." She sounded wound up and tenser than I'd ever seen her.

"I'm sure you'll do a great job," I said, hoping to reassure her. I finally got to why I was there, and she went inside and retrieved my bin.

Cloris touched my arm as I turned to go. "Heaven help us both to get through this weekend. We'll have to have a wine toast after they all leave."

Chapter Six

Crystal caught up with me as I pulled my bin down the path to the Cypress building. She offered me a quick hug and we went inside. She was like getting a visit from a rainbow. As soon as she took off her jacket, I saw the colorful layers of shirts over her jeans. Her earrings didn't match and the way the curls in her short black hair bounced reminded me of Slinky toys. I still envied how she managed to carry off all that eye makeup. I shuddered remembering how it had turned out when I tried to emulate it.

She carried off the whole look with such ease that it never seemed like a costume, just like what she naturally wore. It was hard to believe that she had two teenage kids, but then she'd married young to the disappearing rock god.

"Wow, Jordan is sure full of himself," she said with an amazed shake of her head. She'd stopped in the Lodge and seen all the cardboard cutouts and his sound-bite sayings. "I know the type." Without saying more, I knew she was referring to her ex. I'd heard a lot about him, and mostly it seemed she was upset that she hadn't perceived what he was really like when she'd been with him. He still made guest appearances in her life due to the kids and I suspected that she had a hard time not falling under his spell again—and was annoyed with herself for doing it.

Crystal put her bin against the wall and pulled out one of the chairs, while I put the tin of cookies with the drinks. My helper looked over as I used one of those long lighters to ignite the fire. "Good, you have one of those," she said.

She had pulled out a soft-covered book and set it on the table. She started to flip through it. "You need a lighter to finish the bracelets." She stopped on one of the pages. "This seems to be the most basic one. You said they had the supplies. Did he say if they had a pattern?"

I shrugged and again wondered what I'd gotten myself into. "No problem if he doesn't. We can try making different versions and come up with our own." She went from the bracelets to asking about Jordan. What was he like? Was it true that you felt different just sharing the same space with him?"

"He's got charisma," I said. "Maybe I did feel different after I met him," I added with a smile. "Tougher maybe. He tried to intimidate me, and I didn't back down." I gave my head a confident shake. "But you can have his retreat as far as I'm concerned. I like the self-help ones that are gentle, that have meditation and yoga classes better. I get the feeling his theme is more like tough love. They have to forage for their dinner and then cook up all the weeds." I made a face at the thought. "My group will be dining at the Blue Door instead."

"Your dinner sounds tastier to me," she said, wrinkling her nose. Then our conversation turned into girlfriend talk and she asked about Dane.

"He's pushing for us to have our big night on Saturday," I said, getting all tense at the thought. "But that was before all the problems with my retreat popped up." I leaned on the back of one of the chairs. "I probably should try to postpone it."

"I'm sure you know best." Crystal knew when not to push, and she also knew about all my misgivings about getting too involved, though she didn't really understand. She would have been glad to dive into a relationship, but the pickings were pretty slim in the small town. "Back to the bracelets," she said. "I made a couple of them, though I didn't have a lighter to do the last step."

She got a flame on the lighter and was about to use it on the bracelet when she reconsidered and instead unraveled it and showed off the strand of the cord. "I'm not sure what you could escape with it, but it could be used to make a tourniquet." She picked up the other one and used the lighter to melt the ends together. "Not what I'd call exactly fashionable, but handy."

I heard voices coming down the path and she put away all the paracord materials. "Showtime," she said with a wink.

This group had the same tentative look my other retreaters always had when they arrived for the first workshop. They were still getting used to Vista Del Mar and the other people in the group were still mostly unknowns. Even Suzy! appeared a little uncertain. Crystal offered them all a warm greeting and I encouraged them to take drinks and cookies.

"These look homemade and delicious," Yolanda said, holding one of the cookies. She popped it into her mouth and her eyes half closed with pleasure as she ate it.

"Casey is Cadbury's premier baker. When she's not helping people like you have a yarn-filled weekend, she is busy making the desserts for the Blue Door. You'll probably get to sample them when you have your dinner tonight."

"Sounds good to me," Yolanda said. "Any chance there's pie?"

"There is," I said. "I'll make sure there's some left." Crystal finished the thought by explaining that my desserts were so sought after, that people ordered theirs even before they chose an entrée because the sweets always sold out.

Vonda seemed a little embarrassed by her sister's exuberance and gave her a sharp nod. Yolanda flashed her eyes in response. "She's always going on about food just being like coal for our bodies. Sure, it's what keeps us going, but there's so much pleasure connected with a good meal or a fabulous cookie." She took a bite of a second one.

I assured her she wouldn't be disappointed by dinner. Suzy! laid her phone on the table and kept looking at the screen. Her hand seemed on automatic pilot as it reached out to touch it.

"You'd probably do better if you just put it away," Hanna said before repeating what she'd said before. "Out of sight, out of mind."

Suzy! seemed uncertain, but Fern grabbed it and put it in Suzy!'s tote bag. "Sometimes you need help," Fern said, explaining her action to the group. The bags were on the table and Suzy!'s eye kept going to hers.

"What happened to your usual red ones?" Crystal said. "These are so dull-looking." She fingered the plain-looking natural-colored bags.

"I'll explain later," I said, not wanting to let my group know how I'd been forced to use the bags. I liked my Yarn 2Go tote bags much better. The fabric was nicer and the color caught your eye. I regretted letting Kevin St. John steamroll me into using the dull bags, but by now what was done was done. And my group didn't know what they were missing.

"The Jordan group seems to have taken over," John said.

I tried to smooth it over by saying it was a much bigger group than ours. "The people you saw are the tip of the iceberg—he calls them the Elite Jordanaires."

"And I'm sure they pay more, but our group has their rights," John said. "If you'd like, I could talk to Jordan. I have lots of experience dealing with people like him."

"Are you just saying that because you're a man and Casey isn't?" Fern said in a scolding tone.

John glanced around the table and let out his breath. "Am I going to be treated like a pariah all weekend? The evil man in your midst."

They all rushed to shake their heads. "I'm sorry," Fern said. "I've been a single mother with three kids for a long time and I've seen firsthand how people defer to men."

"I'm sorry for being insensitive," John said. He looked over the group. "You have to be so careful with what you say these days even when your intentions are good." He put his face in his hands. "It's hard when you don't have anything to take the edge off anymore."

Crystal and I traded glances and she stepped in. "We want to get down to why you people are here," she said brightly. She looked to me and I urged her to keep going.

She did a little pitch on herself and explained that she'd been working with yarn since she was a kid thanks to the fact her mother owned the local yarn store. "It's still my home away from home," she said and told them they'd get a chance to see the place for the yarn tasting. "You know, like wine tasting." They all nodded in understanding.

It was always a challenge to come up with a program for the retreat. Sometimes we taught them a new skill, but the theme of this retreat was getting away from it all and relaxing with yarn, so Crystal and I had come up with something different. We were calling it the Switch. Each of them had brought one of their works in progress, or WIPs, as they were called. It was something partially done that could be completed over the weekend. The idea was that they would switch projects. Crystal was explaining the setup of giving each project a number and then letting everyone pick a number out of a hat she had brought as a joke, when John interrupted.

"I didn't bring anything. I must have missed that in the description of the weekend." He seemed to shrug it off. "So, you can count me out."

"We thought something like that would happen. I brought some half-done projects just in case." Crystal glanced around the group. "Anyone else forget?" They all shook their heads and Fern shot John a scolding look. I looked at him too and tried to keep my expression benign, but I was wondering about him. He'd said he was recovering from a pot habit and had said that his wife had just died, so it wasn't so strange to think he might have forgotten about bringing a project. Still, I felt there was something off about him. I was curious to see how adept he was with knitting needles or a crochet hook.

The grab bag was held, and they all got partially done projects, which came with the needles or hook to finish them. It turned out they were all scarves, and the group spent the rest of the time looking over the project they'd gotten. Crystal's skills were definitely needed as the projects had come with problems. Daisy's had some dropped stitches, Yolanda's had difficult yarn, and Hanna had gotten a crocheted project and didn't know how. It was all tabled until the next meeting, and when we broke, they all went off to get ready for dinner.

I hoped that the biggest trauma of the weekend was John's forgotten project, which had been easily solved. But who was I kidding?"

Chapter Seven

The afternoon was fading, though it was hard to tell by the sky. With the cloud cover, the sun's location was invisible. There was just an overall diming of the light to hint that it was close to dinnertime. I had taken advantage of the little bit of free time to take a walk around the grounds to clear my head. As much as I tried to make the weekend a relaxing escape for the retreaters, it had the opposite effect for me. And I was even tenser than usual with the whole Jordan situation. To make it worse, I hadn't expected to have a number of people overcoming addictions. Suzy! seemed the most likely to explode since she was in the throes of withdrawal, and it hadn't been her choice. Hanna seemed pretty calm and past the hard part of quitting cigarettes. I wasn't sure where John was.

I was on my way to the boardwalk that wound through the dunes at the edge of the property when the bus with the Jordan people returned. Lyla was the first one off. And as the thirty or so people got off with their bags of weeds, she frantically waved her arm to hurry them as she pointed the way to the dining hall.

I was glad to leave that behind and get to the peaceful emptiness of the winding pathway surrounded by hills of silky sand dotted with low plants in assorted shades of green. I had purposely not gone to the beach. I needed something utterly safe. The beach had too many warning signs advising of strong currents and rogue waves that could knock anyone daring to walk out on the rocks into the water. The waves were powerful and rushed in from the open water. Most amazing to me was that the water truly was sea foam green.

The cool breeze and the scent of the sea worked their magic and by the time I came back to meet up with my group, I felt renewed.

As I approached the Lodge, Kevin St. John came outside. He'd always seemed the picture of calm with that placid moon-shaped face, but not now. "So they weren't going to know your group was here," he said. He rocked his head in distress and said that the barista had told him about the confrontation between Jordan and me.

"Did he tell you that we worked things out?" I said. I explained the deal I'd arranged with Jordan, and instead of calming Kevin St. John it made him more agitated.

"You didn't have the authority to do that," he said, sputtering. "I should have been consulted." I let him go on until he ran out of steam.

"Is the van coming?" I asked finally.

"Of course it is, Ms. Feldstein. I made special arrangements for it to carry your people around." He glared at me, and I understood that he was expecting a thank-you.

Why should I give him gratitude for something that was only necessary because he'd made a mistake. But then what was the point of withholding it? I got the words out, hoping they sounded more genuine than I felt. He took it as a win and smiled. Whatever it took to keep the peace. The van came up to the driveway and he went back inside muttering to himself about being ready to put out the next fire.

Suzy! was the first to arrive. I did a double take when I saw her. She was wearing a dun-colored T-shirt like I'd seen some of the Jordan people wearing. *Was she double retreating?* But when she got closer, I saw that just the color was the same. It had the Vista Del Mar logo and then a blank space where the Jordan shirts had the details of the retreat. She noticed me looking at it. "I had to do something," she said nervously. "So I went to the gift shop. It helped for a few minutes." She automatically reached to her pocket and pulled out her phone. "When we leave here, my phone will work, won't it?" she said with a look of relief. "Ha, my son didn't figure on that."

I didn't know if having her phone for a while would make it better or worse for her, but it wasn't really my business and I couldn't control it anyway. "Yes, you should get a signal," I said.

Fern was talking to Vonda as they approached, while Yolanda seemed more intent on taking in the surroundings. John's brow was furrowed, and he seemed to have something on his mind as he joined the others. Daisy must have slipped in unnoticed. It was only when I was looking over the assembled group that I saw her. Despite her height, she seemed to have the ability to blend in with the background, and I had the impression she was more an observer than a participant. Hanna appeared just as they began to climb into the van.

"Are you cold?" I asked, noting that her hoodie was zipped to the very top.

"I'm fine. I just spilled on my shirt," she said with a sheepish smile. "I was already late, so I didn't want to hold things up while I went to change."

The van had only gone a short way on the street when Suzy! let out a whoop. I looked back and saw her head down with the light of the screen reflected in her face. The rest of them were a mixed bag of checking their phones or looking out the window. It was an easy choice for me—I always chose taking in the passing scenery. No matter how many times I'd seen the same streets, I liked seeing how the wild part on the edge of town turned into houses with neat lawns and small apartment buildings with flower boxes of petunias. I never missed a chance to look at the driveway that led to the butterfly sanctuary. I also always laughed inwardly at how lofty it sounded when really it was just a bunch of pine, cypress and eucalyptus trees surrounding a small parking lot. But every year the orange and black monarch butterflies returned to hang out in those trees and spend the winter.

What was truly amazing was that with their short life span, it wasn't the same butterflies who came each year, but a different generation that somehow magically knew where to go.

We passed the butterfly statue with a placard that read *Winter Home of the Monarch*. From there, the driver took the scenic route that went along the town beach on one side and small motels and interesting houses that had been turned into bed-and-breakfasts on the other.

The main drag, Grand Street, lived up to its name. The two directions of traffic were separated by a strip of park. The stores and restaurants ran the gamut of styles from colorfully painted Victorians with fish scales on the side to old California mission-style buildings made of stucco with terra-cotta-tiled roofs. The town council was determined that the charm of the place be authentic instead of contrived. The natural beauty of the coast and the appeal of Cadbury, along with Carmel and the luxury resorts of Pebble Beach, attracted tourists from around the world.

The van pulled up in front of the Blue Door. It had originally been built as a residence and had been transformed into a restaurant. I led my group up to the long porch that ran along the side of the building. There were a sprinkling of outdoor tables near the door, which was of course blue.

The inside smelled delicious as always as I held the door while they filed in. Lucinda was waiting for us and as usual was dressed in something with a designer label. She was one of those people who didn't feel dressed if she wasn't wearing eyeliner and lipstick.

Several pedestal dishes with glass domes sat on the counter near the front. Yolanda eyed the one that held a pie with one slice left and her smile wilted. "Nooo," she said, dragging out the word in dismay as her sister gave her a dirty look.

Lucinda patted her hand. "Don't worry, we have a whole pie set aside for your group." She waved for the group to follow her.

"Everybody in town knows about Casey's desserts," she said as she walked them through the main dining area, which had been the house's living room. It had probably seemed like a nice-size space for a family but was very cozy for a restaurant. The tables were close enough together that you could practically take a taste of your neighbor's dinner. We passed Lucinda's husband, Tag, who was rearranging the settings on one of the tables. He was so intent on it, he didn't even look up.

The sunporch was tucked onto the back and had been set up so my group had the whole area. A table had been set up just for us with a crisp white cloth. As they all found seats, I let out a breath of relief with no worry that someone would pop up with a problem.

Lucinda handed out menus and I noticed several of them were checking out the back and the fairy-tale version of Lucinda and Tag reconnecting years after being high school sweethearts, getting married and realizing their dream of opening a restaurant. "I love this," Fern said, holding up the menu. "I sure hope something like that happens for me."

Lucinda smiled sweetly, but I knew she was thinking about the rest of the story that didn't appear on the menu. While she gave them a few minutes to look over the offerings, she pulled me aside. "I've seen pictures. That Jordan is certainly a hunk," she said, then laughed at her choice of words.

"Remember the old saying about pretty is as pretty does, well, he doesn't." I told her about my run-in with him and what I'd agreed to. "It was that or he would have gotten my group pushed out."

"To be continued," she said, noticing that everyone but Hanna had put down their menus, a sign they were ready to order. Suzy! was like a sleepwalker with no sense of anything but the screen she was staring at. When Lucinda asked for her order, she seemed dazed and pointed at Daisy, saying she wanted whatever she was having.

I was too keyed up to eat and just asked for a cup of soup. When the food came, they all appeared pleased with the plates set down in front of them. I left my soup untouched waiting for them to start eating.

"This is definitely better than the food at Vista Del Mar," Fern said as she tasted her entrée.

Her comment surprised me. "Then you've been there before?" I said and she nodded.

"The advertising agency I work for had a business retreat. It was supposed to bring us all together. We even had a bargain version of Jordan give a talk on how to be your best self."

John seemed more relaxed, and I noticed that he'd gotten a glass of wine. "My company has events like that too. With everyone working all over the place, we like to have something that brings upper management together." He smiled. "I'm afraid Vista Del Mar is too rustic for the group. Ours have all been at luxury resorts with lots of events and too much booze."

Vonda was focused on his glass of wine. "Do you think you should have that—considering the problem with marijuana that you told us about?"

John's expression hardened. "Forget I told you that. A glass of wine isn't going to turn me into an alcoholic."

I was glad when Hanna stepped in and started joking that they could probably sell anything they brought back in a doggy bag to the other group. "I saw what that they were eating." She wrinkled her nose in distaste.

"And we'd get a bonus for the pie," Yolanda said. She turned to the group. "But no way am I handing it over." She seemed so concerned about her pie that they all laughed, and once again her sister gave her a dirty look.

Yolanda was so worked up about the pie, I worried it would be a disappointment. But she gave me a thumbs-up at her first taste. Thankfully they all agreed. Since there weren't the regular events at Vista Del Mar for my group to take part in, I let them take their time with dessert and then had the van drive them around the small town before returning to the hotel and conference center grounds. The van dropped us off outside the Lodge. I peeked in expecting it to be full, but I saw no one. The gift shop and café were closed. A fire still crackled in the stone fireplace, but the seating area was empty. The relief guy was behind the registration counter. "They're having some kind of power session." He pointed in the direction of Hummingbird

Hall. "It should be breaking up soon." He let out a yawn. "Then they're back at it at six a.m."

"Glad it's not us," Daisy said when I reported back what I'd heard as I walked them back to the Sand and Sea building. They all seemed ready to go their separate ways. I heard Fern mention hanging out in the lobby and working on some knitting she'd brought with. Daisy asked about joining her. John wanted a night walk. Hanna seemed all in and went to her room. The sisters were talking to each other as they headed down the hall. Suzy! had gotten in enough time with her phone and had calmed down. But it was beginning to sink in that she was without it again and she seemed to be tensing up as she followed the sisters down the hall. They all seemed settled, or in the case of Suzy!, as settled as they were going to be, so I left.

I looked back at the outside of the Sand and Sea building. The light showing through the windows looked inviting, like a port in a storm. Most of the buildings were dark and blended in with the night. I could barely make out the outline of the trees as I walked on the path to the driveway. In the distance I heard voices and assumed the Jordan power talk had ended and his people were heading to their rooms.

When I got to the street I looked across to my driveway and was surprised to see a Cadbury PD cruiser parked in it with the doors open and lights flashing. I picked up speed, anxious to see what was going on. I heard voices and saw Sammy standing in the light from the headlights with his hands up. Just then another cruiser arrived and squeaked to a stop before the doors flung open and two uniforms got out. Two cop cars in the small town meant that something big was going on.

Sammy saw me and his body relaxed. "Talk to her. She'll tell you I'm not a burglar."

A third cruiser arrived, which meant it was probably most of the police department. Dane got out of the driver's side and asked the others what was going on.

"We saw this guy carrying boxes," one of the uniforms said. "We know that she's yours, so we went to investigate. He claimed he lived there, and we knew he was lying."

Did they really say that I was Dane's? The only way they would know that was if he told them. What else did they know? Poor Sammy looked like the blood was draining out of his arms from holding them up so long.

Now we were all standing illuminated by the headlights of the cop cars. Dane gave me a confused look. "Is he living here?"

Before I explained I made them let Sammy put his arms down. "There was a flood at the B & B where he lives," I said. "It was an emergency."

The cops all looked at each other with knowing nods and I heard a bunch of *tsk* sounds with shakes of their heads as they looked at Dane and me. There were mumblings of "can't take care of his woman" and something about a picture in his locker. Dane seemed upset by what they were saying, probably because he knew it would make me nuts.

They finally got back in their cars, and Sammy took the box inside that he'd picked up when they'd let him put his hands down. Dane waited until the other two cars had backed out before he approached me. "You've got Sammy living here now? Are you getting cold feet and looking for a reason to back out?" he said.

"Your woman?" I said, glancing in the direction the cars had gone.

He started to say something, but a figure dashed across the street and ran up my driveway. Cloris threw her arms around me. "Please, Casey. I need your help."

Chapter Eight

I'd never seen Cloris like this. I knew dealing with the Jordan retreat was getting to her, but this was different. She seemed completely undone.

Dane eyed her with concern. "Anything I can help with?" Dane asked in his cop voice. She surprised me by violently shaking her head and then pressing her lips together as if to silence herself.

"I'll talk to you later," I said, shooing him away, and he went back to his cruiser. Cloris waited until he'd backed down the driveway and driven off. She was shivering and I didn't know if it was from whatever she was upset about or the fact that the staff blazer didn't offer much protection from the chilly night air. "Let's go inside," I said, putting my hand on her arm in a supportive touch.

I was anxious to hear what the problem was, but I also wanted to give her a moment to calm down. She'd always been the one offering me hospitality and I was glad to reciprocate and said I'd make coffee to go with the cookies I'd baked earlier. Julius had been hanging in the window watching everything going on in the driveway. He sensed someone new and jumped off his perch and came over to investigate.

I let her collect herself while I brewed some coffee. I brought the mugs and a plate of cookies and joined her at my kitchen table.

She took a couple of sips and bit into a cookie. "I'm sorry for interrupting whatever that was," she said. "But you're the only one I could think of talking to." She was starting to get worked up again and I suggested she take a couple of breaths. Meanwhile the suspense of what she had to say was killing me and I wanted to let her spill it. I assured her it was okay and encouraged her to talk.

"Remember I told you I was worried about having to deal with the foraging meal. Someone got sick from their dinner," she said. "It wasn't my responsibility to check what they gathered." Cloris put up her hands as if to emphasize that she wasn't involved.

"My job was really in the kitchen," she said. "I saw the tote bags were hanging on the back of the chair and helped with the arrangement to inspect the contents." She rocked her head with dismay. "It was chaos in the kitchen. Those Jordan people insisted on running everything. All I saw were some huge pots of rice and beans. I had to deal with the groups coming in to prepare what they'd gathered, and I was mostly a traffic cop."

"Did you see what they'd collected?" I asked.

"It seemed like a lot of green stuff. I didn't look too carefully." She shrugged. "I was just helping them turn it into their dinner. The Jordan people had a program about foraging before they went out. The bags were all checked before they came in the kitchen." The upset was showing in her face again and I pushed another cookie on her.

She took a deep breath and let it out as she prepared to continue. "They were back at it in Hummingbird Hall. A woman stumbled into the Lodge and threw up all over the place. Mr. St. John had me take her to the ER. The doctor thought it was stomach flu until I mentioned the foraging. He asked if there'd been any mushrooms." Cloris shrugged. "I said I didn't know. They were pumping her stomach when I left," Cloris said. "It wasn't my job to check the stuff. Jordon is blaming us and insisting that no one hears about what happened. Mr. St. John is beside himself and saying it's all my fault." Cloris looked like she was going to cry. "All I did was hand out frying pans and blender carafes."

She sat up a little straighter and seemed to have pulled herself together. "I know you worked at a detective agency and know about investigating. Please, can you find out what happened?"

When she said it like that, how could I say anything but yes.

Before Cloris rushed off, I got some more information from her and had scribbled down some notes. The sick person was a member of the staff, and her name was Megan Sills. That was the woman the staff people had been so annoyed about earlier in the day. I also remembered being in the café and seeing her upset that her phone didn't work. I thought about calling Frank, but it was hours later in Chicago, and I could figure out what to do on my own. I'd just wait until the woman recovered and find a way to talk to her and work backward.

For now, it was time to change hats. Figuratively speaking. I never wore one of those puffy white chef hats when I made the desserts and muffins. It gave me an inner chuckle to picture it. I gathered up everything for the muffins I was planning to make and hauled the shopping bag to my yellow Mini Cooper.

I gave a glance to the guesthouse as I backed out of the driveway, wondering if I'd made a mistake letting Sammy move in.

Then it was off into the night. It was a short drive and there was barely any traffic since everything closed early. The lights on the marquee for the movie theater were already off, meaning the last showing of the night was almost done.

Grand Street looked a lot different than it had when I'd brought my group for dinner. There had been cars parked along the curb and people on the street. I glanced at the empty sidewalk and thought it could be considered desolate or peaceful, depending on your frame of mind.

Lucinda and Tag were getting ready to leave when I came in. The chef had already left, which was a relief. We had a territory issue about the kitchen: we each viewed the other as an intruder in our space.

"Everything good?" Lucinda asked. She was putting on her coat, with some designer label of course, and Tag was fidgeting with the place setting for the next day. All I could really see of him was his unnaturally thick head of brown hair and the immaculate white shirt as he bent over the table.

"With my group, yes," I said.

Lucinda stopped in her tracks. "Did something happen with the Jordan people?"

"It seems that one of the Jordan staff people got sick after eating the foraged meal. They're playing pass the blame. Jordan pushed the blame on Kevin, and he's passed it off onto Cloris. She came over just before I left asking me to find out what happened. The unsaid part is she wants me to get her off the hook."

"Kevin St. John makes such a big fuss about being manager of the place. Doesn't he realize that means the buck stops with him."

"It's more like he views himself as the lord of the place. It's pretty tacky that he's trying to push it off on Cloris. As for the incident, according to Cloris they foraged for greens and there could have been mushrooms."

"Uh-oh," Lucinda said, shaking her head.

"Exactly, but Jordan had an expert who put on a program to tell them what to hunt for and was specific about what to avoid. As a double check, someone looked through the tote bags to make sure it was all safe to eat." I paused for a moment. "I heard all of that from Cloris."

"So, you're saying that it's secondhand news?" my friend said, and I nodded. "But it was an accident, right?"

"It would appear so, though the staff didn't seem very fond of the victim." I set down the bag of muffin ingredients as the bag was heavy to hold. "That I heard firsthand."

"What are you going to do?" Lucinda glanced toward Tag, who was finishing up rearranging all the settings. He always got impatient when he was done and wanted to leave. I knew enough to give her the short version and told her I was going to talk to the victim, probably the next day.

"Good luck," Lucinda said and went to the exit.

Tag joined her at the door and gave the dining room a last cursory glance. "Everything is ship shape," he said, nodding toward the tables. "Let's make sure it stays that way."

I nodded without saying anything. What did he think I was going to do, dance on the tables? I took my shopping bag and went back to the kitchen, relieved as I heard the outer door close. Once I deposited the bag, I went back through the empty dining area and turned on the radio to my favorite soft jazz station. Alone at last and I felt the tension go out of my body. Just thinking about making desserts and baking muffins did that for me.

I always did the desserts first. Tonight it was bread pudding. It had been Tag's suggestion as a way to use up the leftover bread. It was easy and fast as well. The hardest thing was tearing the bread into little pieces. I poured the custard mixture over them and sprinkled dried cherries and slivered almonds on top and put the pans in the oven. Yolanda's love of pie had inspired me to whip up some apple and cherry pies. The air was filled with a mixture of delicious baking smells when I moved on to the muffins.

Instead of the usual sweet cakey things, I was trying biscuits baked in muffins tins, or as I was calling them, Biscuffins. The name would be my secret. I had long ago given up on the clever names I'd come up with for the muffins after the town council objected. They really needed to focus on something more important, but the head guy was a stickler and had gotten the rest of them to agree to outlawing cutesy names for anything. So there was no Ye Olde Taffy Shop or What the Fishmonger Found. The saltwater taffy place was called the Taffy Shop and the fish store was called—what else, the Fish Store. So instead of Biscuffins, they would be Biscuits in Muffin Cups.

I was just settling into measuring the flour when I heard a knock at the glass on the door. I had been unnerved when it first happened, but now I accepted that everyone knew I was there baking and felt free to drop by.

I was pretty sure I knew who it was before I even got close to check the window in the door. In the beginning I'd grabbed a frying pan as weapons. You have to understand, I was from Chicago and a late-night knock at a business door was ominous. But here in Cadbury my overreaction was ridiculous. I could just make out the figure on the porch since Tag always made sure the outside lights were off when they left, which meant the porch was mostly in darkness.

"Hi," I said, opening the door.

Dane held back for a moment while he checked my hands. "No weapons," I said, holding them up.

"Safety first," he said with a smile. "You almost clocked me a couple of times."

"You're never going to forget that, are you?" I said.

"No. It's too much fun to tease you about it," he said. He was wearing his midnight blue uniform that was covered with accessories, including a radio clipped to his shoulder. He shut the door behind him and followed me back to the kitchen, sniffing the air. "Something in the oven smells good."

That was the extent of his small talk, and he went right to what he really wanted to know. "What's going on with Sammy staying in your guesthouse?" His smile faded. "If you want to back out of Saturday night, just tell me."

"No," I said, maybe a little too emphatically. "I just want to get it over with now." He seemed taken aback by what I said.

"Wow, I didn't know you felt that way about it. It's supposed to be something good. Something we both want," he said. I realized what I'd said had seemed a little harsh and I wanted to get the spotlight off of me, so I brought up the cop's comment about me being Dane's woman.

"Our relationship was supposed to be on the down-low," I said, and he laughed.

"The only person who believes that is you. This is a small town and people have nothing to do but mind other people's business. The fact you were trying to keep it quiet only made it more interesting to talk about."

"And the picture in your locker?" I said.

"One of the guys stuck it in there as a tease." Dane shrugged. "I liked it, so I left it."

"Do they all know about our weekend plans?" I said, suddenly upset.

"No," he said. Then he chuckled. "But that's probably because they think we're way past that."

I reacted with a stormy expression, and he reached out and pushed a tendril of hair off my face. "You have to stop being so afraid to commit. I'm not going to die of a broken heart if you decide you've had enough of Cadbury. I'm pretty tough," he said with a soft smile. It wasn't the first time we'd had this conversation. He'd kept pressing and well, the truth was I more than liked him. He'd used the other word, but I'd held back. I was convinced I was being altruistic, no matter what he said about being tough. I didn't think he understood. There was no guarantee I wouldn't tire of Cadbury and decide to leave, alone. Not to mention that we came from such different worlds.

His father had been just one of his mother's flings and never a part of his life. His mother had an alcohol problem, which he'd been dealing with since he was a kid.

I'd been brought up with two parents who hovered a little too much, but my life was stable. I'd always had a safety net to fall back on, even though I'd never taken advantage of it. I'd always been there to catch myself when something didn't work out.

"What are you really afraid of?" he said. He was acting all caring and serious and it was freaking me out. I didn't want to talk about what I was really afraid of. I didn't want to *think* about what I was really afraid of. So, I did what I always did when I felt cornered, I changed the subject.

"Want to hear what Cloris was so upset about? Something happened at Vista Del Mar."

Even though most of his cases had to do with cleaning up after dogs and an occasional rowdy tourist, he was still a cop, so he was instantly attentive, for a moment at least. Then his expression sagged, and he shook his head. "I know what you're doing. It's just like your attempts at flirting." He rolled his eyes at the thought. I'd be the first to admit that my attempts at batting my eyelashes or twirling a strand of hair bordered on comical, but I'd thought I'd done a better job at trying to pivot the conversation.

"Aren't you even curious?" I said.

His copness clicked in, and he nodded. "Okay, tell me," he said.

I gave him some background, telling him about Jordan being this rock and roll sort of guru and what I knew about his weekend activities. I threw in a little editorial comment about how it wasn't something I'd enjoy.

"Are you going to get to the point?" he said finally.

I cut right to the dinner plans and that someone had gotten sick afterward. He started to put up his hands as if it was no big deal, but then I added that the ER doctor seemed concerned there might have been mushrooms in the foraged food.

"Accidents happen with mushrooms," he said. "It sounds like a stupid idea to have a bunch of people gathering plants for their dinner. Stupid, but not criminal." He gave me a knowing smile. "Now, back to our plans. I have the rose petals and candles all ready."

I hesitated and Dane let out a groan. "I was just building up the suspense," I teased. "Yes, we're on for Saturday night. Nothing is going to interfere. And I'm sorry I made it sound like it was like taking a bitter pill. There's just been a lot of buildup," I said.

Dane stepped closer, putting arms around me, and after taking a joking look from side to side to check that no one was watching, kissed me. He put a lot into it, and suddenly I remembered what Saturday night was all about.

His radio squawked and he pulled away abruptly. "Sorry I can't stay and help. Looks like there's something happening out on the mean streets of Cadbury," he said with a wink.

Chapter Nine

It took me a few minutes to collect myself after Dane left. He'd done an excellent job of reminding me of the chemistry between us. I started chiding myself for making such a production about our Saturday night plans.

I pulled the bread pudding and pies out of the oven and set them to cool while I finished up with the muffins. Since they were something new, I did a taste test and was relieved they were delicious. I did a bit of cleanup, put the bread pudding in the refrigerator, and the pies under glass domes before packing up the biscuffins. My final chore was to drop them off at the coffee places in town so they'd be ready for the morning rush.

The only hint that Sammy was in the guesthouse was his BMW parked on the street next to my driveway. Julius barely got a greeting from me before I collapsed on my bed and only managed to take off my shoes before I fell asleep.

• • •

The cat was better than an alarm clock. I awoke to him sitting on my chest, nudging my face to remind me it was time for his breakfast.

He got his stink fish, but I didn't even have time for a cup of coffee. I took a shower like I was driving through one of those self-serve car washes and dressed quickly before heading across the street.

Normally, my retreaters would have just gone to the dining hall during the serving hours for their breakfast and I would have met up with them when it was time for their first activity. But with Jordan taking over the dining hall, I had to be at Vista Del Mar to deal with their meal. I had saved some of the biscuits in a cup for my group, and Cloris had promised coffee and tea, but the rest was coming with Lucinda.

A table was supposed to have been set up in the Lodge for the meal. But when I checked the social hall, it hadn't been set up and for the moment no one was manning the registration counter. I knew where the tables were kept and was considering how I could drag one out when Cory Smith came in to report for work. He was Crystal's teenage son and the one that had caused his grandmother to push for her place on the Delacorte family tree. The tall lanky teen had already been working part-time at Vista Del Mar before he knew his connection. He just loved the place, which as it turned out might have been in his genes. Edwin Delacorte was his great-grandfather and the one who had bought the property and cared for it. He would have certainly been happy if he saw how Cory felt about the place.

He worked as sort of an all-around helper and was able to arrange his high school classes around his job. He immediately offered his assistance, and when I told him about needing a table, helped me get one. We set it up under the window that looked toward the boardwalk and sand dunes. He pulled chairs around it.

"I don't suppose you could lead a nature walk?" I said. I was thinking of the empty time after breakfast. Because Vista Del Mar wasn't holding their usual activities for the guests, I was looking to create some of my own.

"It would be my pleasure," he said. He was at the age where his body parts didn't exactly fit together and words like gangly came to mind. But there was something courtly about him and he almost bowed when he said the words. I gave him a quick hug and told him what time to pick up my group. I thanked him again for his help with the table and his smile went up to his eyes.

The door by the driveway opened and Lucinda came in rolling a metal cart. It was well before the Blue Door opened, so Tag had come along.

"Sorry," she said under her breath when she reached me. "Just remember that his intentions are good."

He was already adjusting the table and placing the chairs at an even distance. I'd expected something casual, but they'd brought a tablecloth, dishes, silverware—the works—and that was before they began with the food. Tag commandeered another table and arranged a buffet of eggs, potatoes, bacon, fruit, and toast. Lucinda added pitchers of juice and I set up a plate of my biscuits in a muffin cup.

Tag didn't like my arrangement and was moving them around when I sensed that someone had stopped next to me. I figured it was one of my people and was going to ask them to give us another minute, but when I saw the dun-colored Jordan T-shirt realized it was one of Jordan's group. She seemed to be savoring the fragrance of the food.

"That looks great. A lot better than what we had."

"You already ate?" I said.

"Breakfast was at six a.m. and I was on the cooking crew." She held out her hand. "I'm Diana Gladwell, and you must be part of the group Jordan told us to ignore." I introduced myself while she continued to intently look over the food and the setup. "I can see why Jordan told us to steer clear of your group. That's all completely against what our retreat is about."

I asked her what their breakfast had been. "Oatmeal with no add-ins, ten almonds, a half of an orange and a cup of hot water with lemon." She saw my surprised look. "Jordan is all about food being fuel and nothing else. I suppose it works since some of the people have weight or food issues." She saw that I didn't understand what she meant.

"Most everybody comes to one of Jordan's retreats with a specific issue and the challenges, as he calls them, help people deal with whatever it is. Not everybody gets it the first time," she said. "Or the second," she added with a woeful smile. "This is my third go-round."

She was being friendly, and I realized it was a chance to find out more about their plans. "Then you probably know how the weekend goes," I said. I had seen the list of activities on the packet of Jordan pages Kevin St. John had given me, but maybe I could learn about them in more detail.

"Oh, yes. The first two times I came I was part of the hoard before I understood the benefit of being in the Elites."

"Hoard?" I said.

"There are two groups for the retreat. What I call the hoard is really referred to as the Crowd. They're not even here yet," she said, gesturing to the mostly empty Lodge. The Elites come a day early and have a special time with Jordan. For the rest of the weekend, they sit in the first rows of all of Jordan's programs. They actually take part in the challenges while the hoard watches. They're supposed to get benefit by osmosis." Tag and Lucinda had finished with the setup and told me they were going for a walk.

Diana gave another longing look at the food. "You'd think with all the extra cost of being an Elite, they'd throw in some better food. But we're supposed to be grateful for the chance to be in a small group with Jordan. The hoard has team leaders and only gets to interact with Jordan for the talks."

I hadn't thought about the cost until she mentioned it. I wasn't sure she'd tell me, but I asked how much anyway. I was shocked when I heard that it was over a thousand dollars a day for the Crowd and over two thousand dollars a day for the Elites. Now I understood her grumbling about the food. She seemed open to talking and I asked her about the previous night's dinner without mentioning anything about someone getting sick.

"You mean the meal we had to forage for," she said. "It was the first of the challenges and supposed to open our eyes to what was right in front of us. It was my first time doing it," she said. "I was pretty nervous."

"You mean in knowing what to gather?" I asked.

"Jordan has an expert who did a program before we went out. She talked about the plants to pick and the plants to not pick. Then it was off to a field in Carmel Valley."

"And then you just ate what you'd collected?" I asked.

"We had a choice of what to do with what we'd gathered. We could make a stir-fry, use it in a sushi roll, or add it to some apple juice and make a smoothie. There was a pot of rice and beans available, too. Plain brown rice and black beans with no sauce or seasoning. Jordan believes in the pure taste of the food."

She gave the table of food another hungry glance, just as the bell outside the dining hall started to ring. "Time for our first activity," Diana said. "Exercise." She gave me a wave as she jogged off to the door.

My group arrived and attacked the food. We had the whole big room to ourselves. Neither the café or the gift shop was open, nor was anyone manning the Jordan merchandise table. I was so intent on managing the meal that I was unaware of the surroundings until they were finishing up. When I glanced around, I saw that all three doors were open and a flood of people had come in and were lined up at the registration desk. Kevin St. John was observing, but two people I recognized as Jordan staff people were checking the people in. The line snaked out the door into the driveway. This had to be the hoard, as Diana had called them.

After they got their room assignments, some people started to wander over to our table, probably smelling the food. Kevin St. John rushed out from the business area and blocked their way, giving me a dirty look.

"If they expect meals like this, they're in for a surprise," I said to my people before telling them about the Jordan group's morning menu and his philosophy about food.

"So, you mean they aren't having any pie?" Yolanda said with a teasing laugh.

"Pie?" I said, rolling my eyes. "Hardly."

Suzy! seemed sullen as she looked at her phone and then put it away, only to take it out again.

"Withdrawal is the hardest," Hanna said.

"Self-control is important," Vonda added. "You need to simply put it away and leave it put away except if you want to use the camera."

"You sound like someone from the other retreat," Suzy! said in a curt tone. "I don't really have a problem with my phone. My son just overreacts."

John ignored her comment and gave a comment on the food. "Worthy of a high-class resort," he said. "I was expecting camp food, so this is a nice surprise."

"I just think it's so nice that we're all eating together," Daisy said. "And like John said, it's delicious food." She gave the hoard a look. "I don't get why people go to those kinds of events. It seems like punishment."

Fern leaned into the table in a conspiratorial manner. "I spoke to one of the Jordan people and she said the weekend is supposed to be tough. Everybody comes with a problem they want to fix, and the attitude is no pain, no gain. It's like they have to suffer to overcome whatever's bothering them. And they pay a fortune for it." She added a disbelieving shake of her head.

"I certainly prefer our retreat," Hanna said. "This is much more affordable and a nice way to get away from it all. Working with yarn is so therapeutic, and when you do it in a group everybody talks to each other."

"Well said." John made a toast with his coffee cup.

I heard a sound I couldn't quite describe. It was kind of like breath being sucked in and I felt the energy in the large room suddenly change. Everyone else at the table felt it too and we all looked at the line of people. Jordan had just come in through the other door, the one that went out onto the deck. He was flanked by his two assistants. The jeans, work shirt and red bandana looked the same though were probably a fresh version of them. It seemed like there was a glow around him, and when I looked more closely I saw one of the assistants had something that was backlighting the jeaned guru.

The line fell apart as they clustered around him. I suppose they'd heard the same thing I had, that merely sharing the same space with him could alter your life. I didn't know if that was true, but he gave off something. I guess that was the definition of charisma. The assistants made sure that nobody got too close.

He looked in the direction of our table and seemed to be examining it. He turned to one of the muscle-bound men and a moment later that guy approached me.

"What's all this?" he demanded. I went through the whole story in case he didn't know who I was. I explained having to arrange meals for my group. He listened with a stoic expression, though I saw him eye Hanna's plate. He left and went back to Jordan. A moment later, the same man waved over Kevin St. John.

The two men had their backs to me, and I had no chance to read their expressions. But as the manager approached our table, his moon-shaped face was locked in a tense expression that seemed to get grimmer the closer he got. I went over to him, determined to deal with the problem out of earshot of my people. "Okay, what is it?" I said.

"Jordan is 'asking' that you don't feed your people in here. It's disruptive to his message and to his retreaters." Kevin looked down and I saw that he was reading from something. "It will have to be out of sight and scent of his group."

I was going to argue, but decided to give the manager a break when I saw who'd just come in. It could only mean trouble.

Chapter Ten

Kevin St. John's whole body stiffened when he saw Lieutenant Theodore Borgnine glancing around the large room. He was built like a bulldog or a fireplug with barely any neck to speak of and his herringbone jacket was rumpled as usual. His salt-and-pepper hair was cut in a bristly buzz cut. Most cops were known to hide behind a benign expression, but not him. His lips seemed locked in a scowl.

Cloris was with him and she looked haggard, to put it mildly. I had the feeling his appearance was connected to the Jordan staff member who'd gotten sick the night before. I hated to think it, but it probably meant she had died.

Poor Cloris. All her training in hospitality at the local community college hadn't prepared her for this. Our gazes met for an instant and her eyes were wide with distress. The manager let out an exasperated groan as he pushed past me and went to join them. As soon as he did, they all went through the door to the business area behind the massive wood counter. I would have liked to follow behind him to be support for Cloris, but I was pretty sure it only would have made it worse. Plus, I had my group to attend to.

They were unaware of what had just transpired when I rejoined them. I told them that Cory would meet them outside in half an hour for a special nature walk I'd arranged. They all seemed agreeable, and I said we had a workshop in the same meeting room before lunch.

I was looking over the leftover food when one of Jordan's assistants showed up. He took a power stance. "Jordan insists this food be removed now." I started to say that my people were done and that it would be packed up, but he interrupted me and said he was supposed to take care of it. Before I could object, he'd grabbed the platter that had the remainder of the eggs and loaded the rest of the food on it. And then he was gone. I wondered if the food was for him and his associate or was it for Jordan?

By the time that Lucinda and Tag returned from their walk, I had everything packed up and back on the cart. Lucinda was grateful, but Tag seemed uneasy and immediately noticed that a platter was missing. It didn't help when I explained what happened and told him to add it to the bill. He kept going on about leaving with fewer dishes than they'd come with. I finally got a hold of a paper plate from the café and that seemed to calm him even though he kept repeating it was only a placeholder.

"There's been a change in plans," I said. I had waited until Tag was taking a load of things to their van before I talked to Lucinda. I was afraid more changes would set him off. We talked over the options for the upcoming meals. Lunch was no problem as I had arranged a tour of the area and they'd have lunch on the road. For the upcoming meals, they'd have to be served someplace else.

"That Jordan is a piece of work," my friend said.

"Yes, he's a pain, but I just want to avoid confrontations and he's got his own problem now," I said. Lucinda was all ears waiting to hear what had happened. "I'd hoped to be able to talk to the woman, but I'm guessing . . ." I looked at my friend and told her about the lieutenant's arrival. She nodded with understanding.

"He wouldn't be investigating if she was on the mend." Tag was standing in the doorway waving for her to come. "Got to go. He has it timed when we should get back and heaven help me if it's even a few minutes off," she said.

• • •

"Feldstein, slow down," Frank said. I'd rushed across the street and called him. It wasn't just to share the news. I was hoping for a repeat of what he'd told me before about an investigation he'd been involved with regarding a problem with someone at a Jordan retreat.

I took a deep breath and made an effort to speak slowly as I got to the point. Someone connected to the Jordan retreat had died. I left it hanging as I heard some rattling coming from Frank's end and could almost smell the garlic from the salami in his favorite Italian sub sandwich.

"Give me a minute," he said. I knew it was partly to think and mostly to get a bite in of his sandwich. I wondered if I should tell him that I could hear him chewing. It didn't so much matter for me but would for a paying client.

"After I talked to you, I looked through the notes I had from the investigation we did. No one wanted to talk besides the woman who hired us. The staff people all said the same thing, that they'd signed nondisclosure agreements and couldn't say anything. I couldn't find any information on deaths connected with the retreats. I was finally able to find a former employee who basically said they'd been lucky. Jordan somehow managed to blame any accidents on the people involved in them, either saying it had happened for a reason or that it was a life lesson that nothing was without risk. Mostly there'd been just some falls and burned feet. The whole self-help business is unregulated and worth billions of dollars. Jordan can promise whatever transformation he chooses and if people aren't satisfied, he tells them they weren't ready and to come again."

"But this time somebody *did* die," I said.

"My guess is that they'll try to pass it off as an accident rather than negligence," Frank said.

"I don't think that will help get my friend off the hook," I said. "They'll still try to say it was her fault somehow."

"It might be different this time. You are on the scene and can ask around. I bet you can uncover something to take the blame off your friend."

I thanked him for his confidence in my skill and he chortled. "It's only because you learned from the best."

"Hey, I only worked for you for two weeks," I said.

"When you learn from a master, that's enough." He was trying to sound serious, but I knew he was being facetious, at least sort of anyway.

"Sure, whatever you say." There was more rustling sound and the squeak of his chair, a sure sign Frank was done with the call. He told me to keep in touch and then there was a click as he was gone.

I used the free time to do a few chores around the house and baked more cookies for the group. When I headed back to Vista Del Mar a van was dropping off more people at the Lodge. The hoard, as Diana had called them, was certainly a bigger group than the Elites, but then she'd made it sound like the bigger group was more like just an audience. I checked their faces as I went by. There were more women than men and they seemed to be a mixture of hopeful and nervous having been promised they were going to transform their lives. I was instantly grateful that my retreaters had lower expectations.

I followed the path to the Cypress meeting room and was distressed to see that the room hadn't been set up, though my group must have stopped there on the way to their nature walk. Their tote bags were sitting in a pile in the middle of the table. I set down the tin of fresh cookies and was considering what to do when I heard a group coming down the path. I grabbed a quick look and saw Jordan was in the lead and the rest were all wearing the staff T-shirts. They filed into the other meeting room next to mine. Was this a meeting where he told them what had happened? I wanted to hear what he was going to say. The other room was considerably larger and I worried they would go to the back of it and shut the door. I knew a glass against the wall was supposed to make it easier to hear, but all I had were paper cups. Of course, there was an app that would help using earphones, but there was no service to download the app and no earphones either.

It was my lucky day or they were unconcerned about privacy. They didn't even close the door. I was able to position myself just out of the doorframe, where I could grab a peek. Jordan gathered them at the front of the room. I pulled out of sight just as I saw him scanning the room, but I could still hear.

"You might have noticed that Megan isn't here," he began. There were some shuffling noises and I imagined that they were looking around to check out what he'd said.

"I'm sorry to report that she died." He stopped and there were instant gasps. Someone called out asking what'd happened to her. Jordan didn't answer immediately, as if he was taking a moment to collect himself. When he began his tone was even but had just the right emotional note. "She got sick after dinner last night and died this morning. It seems she ate something from the foraging that caused a reaction, maybe an allergic reaction." There was another pause and I assumed he was looking around at all of them. "There's no reason for the rest of you to worry. She was the only one affected. Just a tragic accident." There was another pause and this time it seemed as if he was using it to emphasize the seriousness of what he'd said. "We don't want to burden the retreat group with the sad news, so please keep it to yourself. We'll all miss Megan tremendously. She was a light among the group. Since she was only assisting, everything can continue on as planned. Whenever there's a death there's a police investigation, and some of you may be contacted by them. It's perfectly fine for you to just say you don't know anything."

The words made it sound like a suggestion, but his tone made it seem more like an order. He finished by suggesting they have a moment of silence to remember her.

I heard chairs scrapping as the group broke up and I slipped back into my room, hanging just out of sight. Jordan was the first one out the door, without even a glance toward my open door. He walked with a self-confident strut.

Two women were talking as they straggled behind the rest of the group. "Well, it looks like Jordan is rid of her, finally. She was such a bubblehead and so careless, I can't believe he kept her around so long."

"He looked the other way. I think he kept her around because she knew too much about him," the other one added before they got too far away to hear.

Crystal rolled in and saw me hanging just inside the doorway and smiled. "What's going on? Are you trying to hear the Jordan message?" she joked. "I passed him on the path. He's sure got 'it,'" she said.

"That wasn't one of their workshops," I said. "He was telling the staff that one of them had died."

Crystal stopped moving. "What? Someone died?" She looked at me. "What happened?"

I gave her a quick update of what I knew. "Cloris is beside herself, feeling she's going to get the blame." Crystal pulled her bin all the way in, and I followed her to the table. "The woman who died certainly wasn't well-liked." I told Crystal about the comments I'd overheard in the café and what the two women had just said about her.

"She was probably a groupie, though I suppose she'd be called a devotee or follower," Crystal said with a shrug. "Jordan's not really different from a rock star."

"I'm sure you're right. She probably had something going with him."

"All it takes is putting a guy in front of a crowd and people hang their fantasies on him. Take it from one who knows firsthand," Crystal said, shaking her head with regret. "Rixx seemed bigger than life, but then I was too young to know better. And someone like Jordan probably seems to have magical powers to fix your life." Crystal had set the bin against the wall. "There's another side to the coin, though. When you're a public figure, you're vulnerable to accusations. Who knows what she could have claimed and if it was even true?"

I suddenly became aware of the mess in the room. "I have to do something about this before the group gets here. It's not their fault that housekeeping screwed up and they shouldn't have to suffer."

Crystal offered to straighten up the room while I went off to deal with the rest. I was able to flag down someone pushing a housekeeping cart that had supplies for the many fireplaces and she agreed to take care of it immediately. The café was busy with the new people who'd just checked in, but I got the counterman's attention and picked up a hot pot of coffee and one of hot water along with tea bags and accessories.

When I returned, Crystal had straightened all the chairs and taken the pile of bags and spread them around the table. The fire was lit and beginning to give off a warm glow. I set up the refreshment area and was just taking a last check to make sure everything was in place when I heard voices approaching.

My group sounded upbeat, and I was able to pick out Cory's voice as he explained that the meeting room buildings had been built many years after the original structures. It was wonderful how despite him being all arms and legs that were too long for his torso and features that were out of proportion for his head, he sounded very confident. I guess knowing that he had ownership in Vista Del Mar did that.

He did a salute to his mother and then stepped aside as they came in the room. They all thanked him, and he smiled with pleasure before he left. They all had a glow from the brisk air and seemed energized by the walk. They gladly helped themselves to the refreshments and took them to the table. I'd noticed that after the first workshop, people seemed to stick to the same seats and this group was no different.

"There's something wrong here," Suzy! said. She sounded a little on edge, but I was getting used to it and was going to dismiss it, but she waved the bag sitting by her seat. "This isn't mine," she said.

"It's my fault," Crystal said. "I was trying to straighten up and I just put a bag in front of each of the chairs.

"Here's Hanna's," Fern said, grabbing one of the bags. "Smart move to put your name on it. I like the decorations." She held it up to show the rest of them how Hanna had drawn a filled-in circle with some spokes around it that made it appear to be a sunflower. She'd drawn a more delicate flower on the other side of her name with a long stem and leaf.

Hanna took the bag with a smile. "It's a habit. That's what happens when you're a teacher: if you don't stick your name on it, it disappears. I like to add something extra to catch my eye. I draw better flowers than frogs."

The rest of them started going through the bags to figure which was theirs and began inking their names on them along with putting some sort of mark that would stick out.

Once they had the bags sorted out, I figured we could get started, but they seemed more interested in talking. The retreat was to please them, so I didn't get in the way.

The walk had been a success and Cory had taken them on the boardwalk that paralleled the beach all the way to one of the posh resorts in Pebble Beach. Suzy! had gotten a signal for her phone, which had put her back to square one of withdrawal now that it was gone. John had passed an area where someone was smoking marijuana and felt compelled to confess that he'd hung in the spot and taken a few deep breaths. "It's like an alcoholic finding a glass with some wine left in it," he said.

"That's what that smell was," Yolanda said. "I thought it was a skunk."

"I noticed something when we came through the Lodge," Daisy said. "There seem to be a lot more of the Jordan people, but there was this guy that seemed to stick out. He was wearing a rumpled herringbone sport coat and had cop written all over him—like a real-life version of that TV character Columbo. Is there something we should know about?"

I inwardly laughed at the mention of Columbo. I'd watched the show but hadn't put the character together with Lieutenant Borgnine until now. Lieutenant Borgnine did seem sort of like something concocted by a Hollywood screenwriter. I had wondered what I should tell them. One of Jordan's staff people dying wasn't really my group's concern, particularly since there was no threat to them, but now that it had been brought up, I kind of had to say something.

I tried to gloss over it saying that I'd heard that someone in Jordan's staff had gotten sick the preceding night and gone to the hospital, where she subsequently died. "It's probably just a routine investigation. And no need for you to worry. I can't imagine the police would even want to interview any of you since you didn't interact with them."

"Somebody died?" Suzy! said, swiveling her head with a frantic expression, as if the grim reaper was hanging around looking for another pickup. It had taken an extra moment for what I'd said to sink in because she was fidgeting with her phone. "Some gift my son gave me. No phone service and now a dead person. If he wanted to give me time away from it all, it should have been at one of those places we passed today. I don't have a problem with my phone. I just need to be in touch." She looked around at the group. "We all do. What if there's an Amber Alert?" She waited for them to nod in agreement, but they just viewed her with concern. When she didn't get the expected response, she seemed uneasy. Fern was next to her and urged her to put the phone out of sight.

"You better tell us exactly what occurred," Hanna said, sounding concerned.

"It's nothing to be worried about," I said, realizing I needed to reassure them that what happened to someone in the Jordan group had nothing to do with them. "They had to forage for their dinner, and it might have been something she picked up," I said.

"I bet it was a mushroom," Fern said. "It's really hard to tell the good from the bad. I heard the poison ones even taste delicious."

"You certainly seem to know a lot about them," John said.

"I got interested when I read a newspaper story about a family that was foraging for them and picked up the wrong kind by mistake.

They were experienced people, too. They didn't die, though. I think they just got sick," she said.

"You still read the newspaper?" Daisy said with a smile.

Fern fluttered her eyes with consternation. "Yes, it's more trustworthy than all the stories you get online." At the word *online*, Suzy! got a forlorn look and Fern patted her hand in an effort to cheer her.

"Do you mean they just sent their people out there to gather weeds and then eat them?" Vonda said with a shudder. "That sounds very careless."

"They had precautions, and someone checked what they'd gathered. But it really isn't our concern," I said. "You're not collecting your own food and I guarantee all the mushrooms the Blue Door serves come from a produce buyer." I hoped that would end it, but they started talking about the dangers of retreats like Jordan's. Fern seemed very knowledgeable about bad things that happened at programs put on by motivational gurus, as she called them.

"One of them made the group dress up like homeless people and took their IDs, phones, and money away," Fern said. "Then they dropped them all at a mall and they had to get back to wherever the retreat was being held. One of the women jumped off a balcony in the mall and committed suicide."

There was a communal sound of sucked in breath except for John, who didn't have an emotional reaction. Was it just a guy thing not to react, or was he really that cool about it?

"We've really gotten off what you're here for," I said, looking to my rainbow-hued helper.

"Why don't you take out your projects so I can offer any help you need," Crystal said. The mood changed and they all took out what they'd gotten in the switch. John was the first to ask for help. There was a dropped stitch a number of rows back. My helper used it as a lesson to demonstrate how to pick up a stitch and then handed it back to him. It wasn't just that he was a man in a group of women, but he seemed out of place with a yarn group somehow. I was curious to see what he did next. He took a moment and then began to knit somewhat hesitantly. It clearly wasn't second nature to him, but it was also clear that he did know how to knit. Crystal gave a crochet lesson for the person who'd drawn the crocheted project, but they all paid attention. Just when they'd settled into finally knitting and crocheting, it was time to stop, and I brought up the outing I'd arranged for them.

"That's right, we're going off-site," Suzy! said. "That means we'll have cell reception." She sounded excited but got scolding glances from the group. "I'm telling you I don't have a problem with my phone. One of the Jordan staff people told me you could get a signal if you went outside the grounds and up the street. But I've been good when we're here and never tried to go out into the street. That means I'm in control," she said. Her expression changed as she thought of something else. "I wonder if she's the one who died?"

Chapter Eleven

The van was waiting when I walked them back to the Lodge. I had been tempted to go on the trip with them. It seemed appealing to just be one of them while the tour guy I'd hired drove them through the 17-Mile Drive with scenic stops along the way, ending with a tour of the Carmel Mission. Lunch would be at a café in Carmel.

But now that Megan had died, I wanted to use the time to find a way to get the blame off of Cloris. I waited until the van drove off and then I went into the Lodge. Lieutenant Borgnine was standing near the registration counter, holding one of the tote bags, which I assumed was evidence since it didn't seem his style. His gruff expression got gruffer when he saw me.

He wasn't a fan. As my ex-boss Frank had pointed out, there had been an uptick in murders since my arrival. Not my fault, but the lieutenant might have felt there was a connection. But even more than that, I had kind of bested him at solving said murders. Cops really don't like that.

But cops like baked goods and the lieutenant was partial to my muffins, so we had kind of a mixed bag relationship.

"Ms. Feldstein," he said as I approached.

"Lieutenant Borgnine," I said with a little bow of my head. My gaze rested on the tote bag.

"New accessory?" I said, holding back a smile. He reacted just as I'd expected, kind of sputtering and then running his hand through the bristle of his salt-and-pepper hair.

He ignored my comment. "Does your presence mean you're holding a retreat this weekend?"

"A small one," I said. His eyes were moving back and forth, and I could tell he was thinking about something.

"What did they think of the dinner last night in the dining hall?" he asked. I held back another smile. He was trying to be crafty and find out if my people had been in the dining hall without saying anything about what had happened.

"I already know someone died," I said. "And I'm sure you know that my group had dinner off-site."

There was just the hint of a quiver to his mouth as he tried to hide his consternation that I'd seen around his question. "Okay, then. Your group isn't involved, so I'm sure there's no reason for *you* to be involved." He sounded matter-of-fact, as if that would make it so. "It's just a routine investigation. There's no killer on the loose for you to attempt to hunt down. It appears that it was just a tragic mistake." He looked me in the eye clearly hoping for some kind of acknowledgment from me.

I nodded and it wasn't a lie. Cloris had asked me to find out how it happened, not nab a killer.

"So, what do you know?" I asked, hoping my agreement would get him to talk.

"There's no reason for me to share," he said. "Since you have no stake in it, there's no reason for you to care."

I tried to think of something to say and considered noting that he'd just made a rhyme. I gave up mentioning that quickly as it probably would have just irritated him. Besides, my goal was to get Cloris off the hook. "Then you're sure there was no negligence with the Vista Del Mar kitchen or staff?" I said. He seemed to grit his teeth and I quickly added that if it was a problem with the kitchen, it could affect my future retreats.

"That's still to be determined," he said tersely. He saw me looking at the tote bag and put it behind his back. "I'm sure there's someplace you need to be. I don't want to keep you." He used his free hand to wave me away to emphasize what he'd said. It was clear I wasn't going to get anything more out of him, so I started to walk away. "What's with those biscuits you tried to pass off as muffins?" he said. "Mrs. Borgnine gave them a thumbs-up because they're not sweet, but couldn't you at least throw in some raisins?"

• • •

I went back to the Cypress meeting room to straighten things up. They'd left their tote bags, but all had added their names. I took them out of the pile in the middle of the table and hung them on the back of the chairs. There were scraps of yarn and some crumbs to clean up, along with some abandoned drink cups.

"Hi, there," a man's voice said. I looked up from what I was doing as a guy in a Jordan staff shirt stopped in the doorway. I remembered him from the group in the café. It was hard to forget his weird haircuts. It was mostly short, but the top was long and flopped over his face. "This is so much nicer than that room they gave us to use as a lounge." His eye went to the counter with the thermal coffeepots and open tin of cookies. "And you have refreshments, too." His face took on an uncomfortable look. "You're with that *other* group. We're supposed to pretend you're not here." He'd started to pull back but had a longing look as his eye went back to the counter with the drinks and cookies.

"Come in. Help yourself," I said. I'd barely gotten the words out when he changed course and walked into the room, going directly to the counter. He sighed when he got a clear view of the cookies. "They smell wonderful. Homemade?" He had taken one and popped it in his mouth before I had a chance to reply. His eyes went skyward with pleasure as he finished it off.

"Yes, they're homemade," I said, getting a better look at him. There was something stylish about the way he wore the staff shirt tucked into a pair of cargo pants with a fleece jacket on top.

"Mind if I have another?" he asked. "They're delicious and, well, the food at our retreat . . ." He stopped himself and then rolled his eyes. "We're not supposed to say anything negative, but what the hay. You're not part of our group." He shrugged and smiled. "I know that Jordan is all about food just being fuel, but who says you can't make it taste good, too." He took one of the paper cups and filled it with coffee, then poured in sugar and cream.

"Then you weren't a fan of the foraging?" I said, realizing he could be a good source of information.

"Maybe after what happened, Jordan will give it up," he said. Then he looked stricken. "Scratch that. We're not supposed to talk about it." He drank the coffee and took another cookie, as if keeping his mouth busy would keep him from saying anything more. But the way his eyes were moving around and the expression on his face, I could tell he wanted to say more.

"I know someone got sick," I began. "And they died." I left it at that, thinking it might make it seem okay for him to give me the whole story.

"Well, if you know that, there goes the plan of keeping it hushed up." He looked as if the information was bubbling up inside of him and ready to gush out.

"I tried to tell Jordan the foraging was a bad idea, but he was looking for activities to add for the Jordanaires—that's what he calls the Elite group."

"There's an elite group?" I said, playing stupid, figuring it would keep him talking.

He nodded. "They are the real participants in the retreat. The rest of the people are just observers. They come a day early, have some extra time with Jordan. The foraged dinner is supposed to be a benefit." He'd finished off the coffee and went for a refill. "Lyla sold Jordan on the idea that it fit in with the idea of being self-reliant and he was looking for another activity for the special group." His expression made it seem like he didn't agree. "She started out coming to the retreats as a participant and worked her way into becoming part of the staff."

"You don't sound like you're a fan of hers," I said. He settled in and was ready to gossip.

"You have no idea what a pain she is. She's rigid and exacting and always looking to tell Jordan how someone on the staff isn't up to her standards." He shook his head again. "That's what makes it so odd about what happened. She had a whole setup of checking bags and marking them. I don't know how she could have made a mistake."

"What do you mean?" I asked, hoping it would inspire him to offer specific details.

"I told you she's rigid. There's a whole ritual of how the foraging is handled. Before the group goes out, Jordan gives them a pep talk about the wonders of being self-reliant when it comes to food. He tells a story how he was hiking the Pacific Crest trail and realized he was running low on food, and he looked to his surroundings and discovered there were all sorts of sources of nourishment available. Lyla follows with a PowerPoint displaying the plants the group should look for and more importantly what they should avoid. She always has samples of the deadly stuff to show them. Everybody gets a sheet with pictures of the good plants and the deadly ones. As a double check when the group gets back, she goes through each tote bag to check what's been gathered. She puts a check mark on the bag and hangs it back on the person's chair. Then each table has a turn to prepare what they have." He made a face. "By the way, the staff has to gather their own meal too. Well, except Jordan—he goes on a juice fast for the weekend. Personally, I just grabbed a few dandelions and some lamb's quarters and planned to fill in with the stuff the kitchen had."

"What kind of stuff?" I said.

"The choice was to make your foraged stuff into a stir-fry, sushi roll or smoothie," he said. "There were some power greens to add for the stir-fry, rice and seaweed paper for the sushi, and unsweetened apple juice for the smoothie." He glanced at the cookie tin. "And the ever-present pot of beans and one of rice."

"And only one person got sick?" I said. "I heard it might have been from a mushroom."

"Really?" he said. "That's different than what Jordan said. He made it sound like she had an allergic reaction." He seemed to think over what I'd said. "It figures if someone was going to pick up a bad mushroom, it would be Megan." He glanced up at me. "She kind of stuck out from the rest of us."

"Did she start out as a participant like that other woman you mentioned?" I asked.

He nodded. "She came in the big group but somehow managed to work her way into the Elite group. Jordan seemed to take a special interest in her and then she came to some retreats as an invited guest. Finally she was added to the staff. She always gave off the vibe that she thought she was special."

"She sounds like a groupie who'd moved into the inner circle," I said. I really meant that she'd latched on to Jordan, but decided it was better to be a little more vague.

"Yeah, that kind of says it." Our eyes met and he gave me a knowing nod.

"How did she get along with the rest of the staff?" I asked. I was concerned that all of a sudden he'd realize I was asking too many questions and clam up, but he seemed glad to unload.

"She wasn't well-liked, to put it mildly. We all agree with Jordan's message." He glanced at the cookie tin and hung his head with a guilty look. "The main theme of his message is helping people. The food thing is a little hard to take. We need our strength and energy to deal with the retreat people. But Jordan is insistent that we eat the same as the retreaters." He looked down into his coffee cup. You won't tell on me, will you?" I shook my head and he seemed relieved. "Jordan was smart enough to keep her as an assistant only. She was the kind who seemed more concerned about not breaking a fingernail than helping with the challenges." He rocked his head. "And don't get me started on how she was about her phone."

"I have somebody like that in my group," I said.

"It's less of a problem here because there's no signal, so no worry that she'd 'forget' to turn off hers when she was supposed to be working."

I told him about hearing that someone on their staff had figured out how to go out on the street and get a signal. He nodded with recognition. "Yeah, that was probably her."

I decided to push a little further. "Do you think she might have had something on Jordan?" He appeared surprised by the question and the way his eyes lit up made it seem like I'd touched on something.

"Wow, you're really turning this into a mystery story," he said.

There was a clatter outside the door as a woman walked past and then looked in. She was wearing a staff shirt and seemed upset when she saw her fellow staffer hanging with me.

"Tyler," she snapped. "What are you doing? She's with the other group."

Chapter Twelve

I was sure that Tyler would have told me something juicy about the victim and Jordan if that other staff person hadn't shown up and spirited him off. He seemed into gossip, but she seemed like a real stickler for following Jordan's orders. When they left, I grabbed the coffeepots and took them back to the café. It was more efficient than trying to get someone from housekeeping to do it. The barista promised to have them refilled and back in my room before the afternoon workshop.

I was about to leave when Dane came in. He was all dressed in his police blue and smiled when he saw me. "There you are. I was looking for you." He held up a brown paper sack. "I brought lunch."

"That's convenient, because I'm hungry." I considered suggesting we go into the main part of the Lodge. The Jordan people were all in the dining hall and not likely to see us. I was sure whatever they were eating wasn't close to as good as what Dane had brought. I could smell the Italian dressing coming from the sub sandwiches.

Before I could speak, Dane took my arm and led me to the door of the café that led directly outside. "How about a picnic on the beach?"

"I get it. You're afraid Lieutenant Borgnine will see us together," I said. The cop frowned on Dane spending time with me when he was on duty and had punished him by giving him the worst shifts. He probably frowned on his spending time with me when he was off duty, too, but that was beyond his control. Borgnine assumed that I had finagled inside information from Dane when I was poking around in the cases where I'd uncovered the guilty party.

Dane seemed unconcerned as we crossed the grassy circle and stepped onto the boardwalk. The sand on either side was filled with plant life, including tall bushes. The sky was its usual flat white and the cool breeze made me glad that I'd worn one of my wardrobe of fleece jackets. Dane, the tough guy, wore no jacket.

There were just a few people walking along the water when we arrived at the beach. The sand was like silk, and I took off my shoes, letting it surround my bare feet. The closest anyone came to going in the water was walking along the edge of the wet sand. With all the rocks and currents, it was too dangerous.

Dane sat so that our shoulders were touching. It was the only way our words didn't get blown out to sea. "Okay, what's this about?" I said. While it was nice that he'd shown up with lunch, it was a definite surprise and I had a feeling there was a reason behind it.

"Can't a guy just show up with an amazing sandwich?" He had taken them out and ripped open the bag to make a table. The Italian dressing had seeped through the white paper wrapping and my mouth was watering. The smell alone made me understand Frank's devotion to the boat-shaped sandwiches. But much as I wanted to dive into all that cheese and meat, I wanted to find out why Dane was there.

"This is about tomorrow night, isn't it?" I said, turning to him. "It's the comment about getting it over with, isn't it?"

"Well, yes," he said. "I was hoping to stir up a little enthusiasm, good anticipation."

"It's just become such an event," I said. "It would be different if we'd just met and, you know, spent the night together."

"Now you tell me," he said in a teasing tone.

"You do understand it isn't anything about you. It's all me and my problem." I let out a sigh.

"In case you haven't noticed, you have already made commitments. You own a house and you have a cat. You have friends in Cadbury and are famous for your desserts and muffins. So, much as you might like to think you could just pick up and go, you have ties—and a lot of sweets-lovers who'd be brokenhearted if you left." His tone was light, but there was warmth behind it.

"You seem to think you're one of the monarch butterflies, just here to eat some milkweed and wait for the weather to warm up before you fly away."

My mother's words haunted me. How many times had she said that at my age she'd been a wife, mother and doctor and what was I? Just a butterfly stopping by?

"I am not," I said, putting some space between us. "I thought this was about lunch. You do know that Lieutenant Borgnine is on the grounds poking around and could show up at any moment and see us," I said. I looked behind me back toward the archway over the boardwalk that marked the end of the Vista Del Mar grounds, half expecting to see Cadbury's top cop.

"It's not a problem. He actually suggested I buy you lunch," Dane said.

I swiveled to face Dane. "He what?" I said with an incredulous laugh. Then I had a thought. "I get it. He wants you to pump me for information."

Dane shrugged and smiled. "He did suggest I talk to you about what happened."

I started to rock my head with amusement. "This is a switch. You coming to me for information. Aren't you going to bat your eyes and twizzle a strand of hair?" I joked.

"I was hoping I wouldn't have to resort to that," he said with a grin. "So, tell me everything you know."

"Why don't you tell me what you know first," I said. "I'm sure that the lieutenant gave you some details." I tried to make it sound like I didn't want to repeat what he already knew, but Dane saw through it and laughed.

"Is that something that PI in Chicago taught you?" he said.

"No, I figured it out on my own." The breeze rippled the sandwich wrappings and Dane secured them. He glanced in my direction and shrugged.

"What can I say, I'm putty in your hands even though he told me not to give up any information." He went over the basic information, telling me that Megan had died of apparent organ failure and the ER doctor had said it seemed likely it was from something in the foraged meal. Borgnine was checking around Vista Del Mar. He'd managed to collect the victim's tote bag, which still had residue from the foraging, including a mushroom stuck to the inside of the bag. The foraging expert had identified the mushroom as a death cap, but insisted it had to be the victim's fault. She had inspected all the bags and there was no way she would have missed the poisonous mushroom. Jordan had stonewalled when Borgnine spoke to him. He had no idea how it could have happened, and it was obviously an accident, making sure to mention that both participants and staff signed waivers acknowledging that there were risks involved in the retreat. The other staff people had all said they didn't know anything and had been tight-lipped when asked about the victim. "Borgnine wasn't happy that he couldn't get any more out of them and . . ." Dane looked at me.

"And he thinks there's more to get?" I said.

"Yes. He's sure they're holding back," Dane said. His demeanor had changed to cop.

"The only reason I got involved is that Cloris is worried that she's getting the blame for what happened," I said. "She was in charge of the kitchen for the foraged meal." I thought over what I'd found out and there was no reason not to share. He was interested when I told him about Jordan's assistants confiscating the leftovers of our breakfast and the story that Jordan claimed to be on a juice fast for the weekend. But he was even more interested in the details about Megan and her possible connection to Jordan, along with the fact that she hadn't been well-liked.

"That's more than what Borgnine heard, particularly about the victim. What about negligence?" he asked.

I shrugged. "I know they checked through the stuff, but not exactly how it worked."

He gave me his best smile and half closed his eyes in his sexy pose. He was way better at that kind of thing than I was, but I also knew what he was doing. "Do you think you could get the details?"

he asked.

"I was planning to anyway, so I could help Cloris." I left it at that, not saying if I would share, and he made a face.

"Okay, would you get the details and tell me about them?" he said finally.

"You can tell the lieutenant that you succeeded and won me over with your simmering stare and I'll pass along what I find out."

"You're not supposed to know that the information is for him," he said.

"So you mean no gloating," I said with a smile. "Okay, as far as I'm concerned it's for your ears only."

"Thank you," he said. "It'll pay off in the long run. The lieutenant will owe me one, so maybe no Christmas duty this year." He gave me a hug. It was hard with all the paraphernalia of his uniform, but I cuddled into it. It felt so nice neither of us wanted to let go, but we forced ourselves to pull away.

"Those sandwiches aren't going to eat themselves," I said, grabbing one and handing it to him. "Let's eat."

• • •

I might not be able to gloat around here, but I could certainly tell Frank. As soon as lunch was over, I headed back across the street and called up my ex-boss.

"Take a breath, Feldstein," Frank said. I'd been so excited to tell him that the local cop was finally acknowledging that I could get information that he couldn't, that my words were tripping over each other. I did as ordered and took a moment to collect my thoughts. I could hear music in the background and thought to ask Frank if it was a good time to talk.

"Sure, I'm stuck at a kids' piano recital, waiting to see if one of the dads shows up so I can drop some court papers on him." Now as I listened more closely, I could hear it was a halting rendition of "Fur Elise," which got softer. "I have to sit through three more kids before the one I care about plays," he said in a bored voice. "I hope in your excitement you didn't give it all up to that lieutenant."

"I'm not exactly dealing with him directly," I said. "But I did do what I learned from you." Frank suddenly sounded more interested now that it was about him. "I got more than I gave," I said, and I heard Frank chortle.

"I did teach you that, didn't I? Good work." Then he asked what I'd found out. He wasn't surprised that Jordan had stonewalled the lieutenant. "I'm sure he's hoping the cop will just chalk it up to an accident and let it go."

I heard the music again and Frank explained he was keeping tabs on who was performing. "What about the victim?" he asked. "Did you find anything more about her?"

"She wasn't very popular, and it seems like she might have had something going with Jordan."

"I bet Jordan didn't mention that," Frank said with another of his chortles.

I felt something brush against my leg. Julius was circling my ankles. He'd been off napping somewhere and must have just noticed that I'd come home. As his circling became more insistent and he added a couple of plaintive meows, I realized what was going on. I had inadvertently trained him to expect stink fish at his demand.

This was not the moment to try to break that habit, so I lodged the phone between my shoulder and my ear as I attempted to continue with the call.

"Do you have a plan?" he said.

"I was so wrapped up in thinking about the wonder of Lieutenant Borgnine needing my help, I kind of stopped there." I dropped the dab of stink fish in the cat's bowl. "My first concern is still the same, getting the blame off Cloris. I guess I'll start by finding out what exactly happened in the kitchen," I said.

"Just a thought," Frank said. "Be sure to consider that it might not have been an accident."

"You mean like murder?"
"The cop would probably call it homicide."

Chapter Thirteen

Whenever I left the Vista Del Mar grounds to come home, I found the transition abrupt. As long as I was wrapped up in the wild grounds and cut off electronically it was like the outside world had ceased to exist. But as soon as I'd crossed the street and gone up my driveway, my phone had gone into a pinging frenzy, reminding me I was back in the modern world.

I'd been so intent on calling Frank that I'd ignored all the notifications. I finally had a look. It was mostly junk, though there was one from Vonda registering a complaint that Suzy! was trying to get the driver to make unscheduled stops. Vonda had said she was an assistant principal so I took her message more as tattling on Suzy! than a request for action. Also, there was nothing from the others, so I let it be.

Now that I knew I was sort of working with Lieutenant Borgnine—though I'm sure he thought of it more like working *for* him—I decided to use the time to do some research.

I brewed myself a pot of coffee. Dane had been the one to push me into using the real stuff instead of envelopes of instant. He was still incredulous that someone who made all the desserts and muffins as I did had settled for frozen food and powdered coffee.

The smell alone of the freshly made coffee was a reminder that he was right. I grabbed a cup and took it to the bedroom I'd turned into an office. Julius gave up cleaning the residue of stink fish off his whiskers and followed me. Whoever had said that cats weren't companions hadn't met Julius. I knew nothing about his origins other than he'd been wandering on the grounds of Vista Del Mar raising the ire of Kevin St. John before he'd made his way to my front door. Once he'd moved in, he'd showed no desire to go very far away, and when I was home he was always close. I usually awoke with him entwined around my head or sleeping on my shoulder.

The office was filled with reminders of my aunt's expertise with yarn. My favorite was a crocheted lion that sat on my desk. I didn't think I would ever get to her level of skill, but I'd learned enough about knitting and crochet to begin to turn all the yarn she'd left behind into scarves and small afghans. It was always cool here on the tip of the Monterey Peninsula, but not really wool scarf weather, so I'd sent them as gifts to both my parents and Frank. I'd also made a cat mat for Julius that sat on the small leather love seat.

I was extra proud of the throw I'd crocheted in a burnt orange super bulky yarn. For a person who had trouble sticking with things long term, it was an achievement.

Now that I knew for sure that it seemed pretty clear that Megan had eaten a poisonous mushroom and I knew what kind, I got lost in staring at my computer screen. What I read sure put me off any future plans of mushroom gathering. Death caps were abundant in California and could be easily confused with edible mushrooms. I examined photographs of them and of hedgehog mushrooms, which were edible, and I couldn't tell the difference. But the creepiest part of what I read was that the poison mushrooms tasted delicious, and people felt fine after eating them, at first anyway. It could take hours for any symptoms to show up, but meanwhile the toxin was injuring their liver cells. And then when symptoms showed up, they caused dehydration, which could cause kidney failure. In a five-year period, five people in California had died from the mushrooms and fifty-seven were sickened.

When I finished with that, I moved on to seeing what I could find out about Jordan and his retreats. There was a website filled with photographs and positive sound bites from attendees testifying to how their lives had changed. One person said the challenges had swept away the power of fear. Someone else had called it boot camp for their spirit. When I looked beyond the content that Jordan had controlled, I found a blog written about self-help retreats, and there were some specific comments about the Jordan weekends. There had been some injuries like falls and burns and the writer had questioned if there was negligence in how the incidents had happened and in how the injured were treated. Someone from the Jordan organization had left a comment saying that everyone was informed there were risks involved with taking part in the challenges and signed a waiver agreeing to it.

I figured that the lieutenant knew all that already. What he wanted I could only get from talking to people. I'd already made contact with the woman who'd been to numerous retreats, and Tyler, the guy on the staff, seemed pretty willing to talk. I had gotten lost in all the reading and was surprised to see how late it had become. I needed to get back to greet my retreaters when they returned.

I felt myself smile when I saw that the sun had come out. Not a big deal most places, but here it was. There were a lot of variations of cloudy skies—the most common seemed to be sort of a flat white. But blue sky and sunshine was a treat. Julius had already located a spot of sunlight on the kitchen table and was basking in it as I headed to the door.

As I headed down my driveway, Sammy's BMW pulled to the curb, and he got out. He was wearing his white doctor coat and seemed in a hurry. He stopped when he saw me. "Hey, Case," he said in a cheerful voice. "I left work early. I promised Jordan that I'd work on his grand finale." He started to walk and I followed him, asking about what exactly he was doing for Jordan.

"At the end of the weekend, he has his people go through a bunch of escape rooms. Normally he has a magician who puts it together, but the guy quit with no warning. He asked Kevin St. John if he knew anyone local. Lucky for me I did those close-up magic shows at Vista Del Mar." Sammy puffed himself up. "The manager recommended me." He fidgeted with the key. "It's something I've never done before. Their people put most of it together. I just have to fine-tune the illusions and make sure everything works." He got to the door and unlocked it. "Thanks again for letting me stay here. This way I can pop over there whenever." He was so sincere in the way he looked at me with those puppy dog eyes that all my worry about making a mistake faded away.

I continued on my way and was relieved when the pinging of notifications on my phone stopped as I stepped back onto the Vista Del Mar grounds. Everything seemed quiet as I went down the driveway toward the heart of the grounds. The sunlight made the buildings seem a little less dark. The flat white sky took away all the shadows and made everything feel more two-dimensional and seem blended together. The sunshine made everything stand out. I forgot how much I missed it until a time like this when it returned. I didn't want to go inside and continued on the walkway that went past the Sea Foam dining hall. It was empty and the lights were off, but I heard an amplified voice coming from somewhere. It was too distorted to make out the words and I kept going toward Hummingbird Hall, figuring that it was coming from the auditorium. The voice grew more distinct and I began to catch a word here or there. The door had been left open. There was no one to stop me, so I slipped into the shadows at the back to listen.

Jordan was on the stage addressing the crowd. This time the whole place was full. There was something about him that made me stop and watch him. He prowled the stage staring out into the audience, who seemed mesmerized. Then he jumped off the stage and moved into the group clustered in the front. I knew now they were the Elites and the ones in the back were the hoard. He was up close to the front group, but he looked over the whole crowd with a hawk like stare and seemed to be picking out individuals. It sounded crazy, but when I saw him look toward where I was standing, it was as if he was speaking to me. That is, until one of his staff people came over and checked to see if I had a badge on. Then I was shooed away.

As I went out the door, he was telling them they had to face down their fear, which would take away its power. It wasn't just what he said, but how he said it. He was a magnetic speaker and I was sorry not to be able to hear more. The person who helped me leave stood in the doorway to make sure I walked away.

Cloris was behind the counter at the Lodge and she waved me over when I went inside. She was trying to be professional, but there was a little franticness in the way her hand moved. "Did you find out anything?" she said in a whisper.

"I'm working on it," I said. "Do you know exactly why Kevin St. John is trying to pin the blame on you?"

"I was supposed to make sure everything went okay and he said I was careless about the foraged stuff. I had nothing to do with going through the bags. My job was strictly watching as one of their staff people collected the bags so the contents could be examined. When the woman with the white hair finished looking at each one, she put a check mark on it and hung it on the back of the chair." She seemed a little exasperated. "It was just supposed to be the three of us in there, but people started coming in and hanging around the tables they were using."

"Then what happened?" I asked.

"I went into the kitchen. The tables had numbers and each group came in the kitchen with their bag of stuff and I helped them make their meal. The Jordan people had already made a big pot of beans and rice. I offered them frying pans if they wanted to make a stir-fry. There was seaweed paper covered with rice so they could make a sushi hand roll. Then there were several blenders with some juice so they could make smoothies. All I did was direct people. One of the housekeeping people helped clean out the frying pans and blenders between uses."

"What about the woman who died?" I asked. Cloris's features collapsed into worry.

"Honestly, I don't remember what she did. I was so busy handing stuff out that I didn't notice to who I was handing it. What could I have done anyway? I had no way of knowing she'd collected something poisonous." Her face filled with regret. "I should have paid more attention. The woman with the white hair is insisting that the woman's bag wasn't checked and it's my fault because I was overseeing. They were pulling out chairs and sitting as I was trying to deal with the bags."

"Are you sure the woman with the white hair looked in her bag?" I asked.

"They were all brought to that woman. Her name is Lyla. At least I think so." She began to glance from side to side a little frantically. "Maybe that's what happened," Cloris said. "What if she missed a bag?" She put her hand over her forehead. "Then it would have been my fault. I should have seen that there was a bag with no check mark on it."

It was hard seeing Cloris so unglued. She had been the one to handle things with seeming ease, whether it was making up a plate of food for me when she'd worked in the kitchen or keeping things smooth with the guests when she'd started working in registration. It made sense that somehow Megan's bag hadn't been gone through. "But if it had a check mark, then it would have been examined, right?" I said.

She nodded. "Yes, that's it. We need to see her bag."

"That might be a problem," I said. I remembered seeing Lieutenant Borgnine holding a tote bag, but he'd put it behind his back when I'd tried to look at it. I'd only caught a glimpse and had no idea what was on the outside other than the Vista Del Mar logo. It had to be Megan's and it was probably locked up somewhere as evidence. "But I'll see what I can do."

Our talk was cut short as the Jordan people began to filter in. Cloris swallowed back her panic and gave her blazer a tug to straighten it as she became the cool professional and I moved on.

There was a mood of excitement and I picked up tidbits of conversation. They were all about Jordan and the talk he'd just given. They seemed supercharged and at the same time a little nervous about their next activity. The schedule I had was rather vague and I wondered what exactly it was.

Most of the people seemed to be just passing through the cavernous room, stopping just long enough to check the message board.

I noticed a woman veer off toward the seating area. She was holding a bag rather surreptitiously and took a seat in the shadows. She glanced around as she dipped into the bag and slipped something into her mouth. Then she pulled out a cup and took a sip. I gathered by her expression that whatever she was having tasted pretty good. I realized she was the woman I'd spoken to before. I remembered that her name was Diana and she'd been to previous retreats.

"How's it going?" I said in a friendly voice as I entered the area with a couch and chairs around the massive stone fireplace.

She jumped at the sound of my voice and tried to hide the bag and cup before she glanced up at me. "You're with the other retreat," she said, sounding relieved. She took the bag and cup from behind her and kept them next to her legs so they were mostly out of sight.

"I'm sorry, I know that Jordan's philosophy about food is probably correct and certainly a lot of the people on the retreat need to come to grips with their relationship to food, but I guess I'm weak. I couldn't manage on the lunch they served—watery vegetable soup and a piece of bread with a slice of tomato and half a piece of cheese." She showed me that she had a couple of protein bars and a cup of coffee. "Going cold turkey on no caffeine left me with a headache."

"Don't worry, I won't report you," I said with a smile. The pinched look about her face eased and she almost smiled. "I guess you knew what to expect since you said you'd been to a retreat before," I said. "I'm just curious why you keep coming back."

She went to grab another secret bite of something, and I heard her suck in her breath suddenly as if she'd been caught. When I looked around, I almost laughed. One of the cardboard figures of Jordan was positioned so it appeared he was staring at her. Even though she seemed to recognize that it was just a fake figure, she slipped the bag out of sight.

"I've never been one of the Elites before. I hope being part of the group that does the challenges instead of just watching others do them will make a difference. The other times I've gone home all fired up, and then after a few days of being back in the real world all my intentions to be different faded away.

She was being so honest, and I really wanted to say something supportive even though she wasn't my responsibility. "I'm sure this time will be the charm," I said with a hopeful smile.

"I'm a little nervous about doing the challenges," she said. "It helps if you have somebody to talk to. But all the people here are on their own path and are totally self-absorbed. I knew one of the staff people from before. We'd hit it off right away. We both felt like outsiders and seemed liked kindred spirits. You'd think that since she was on the staff, she'd feel like one of the group, but she seemed convinced they didn't like her. I was hoping to get some reassurance from her today, but then she disappeared."

"What do you mean disappeared?" I asked, trying to keep my causal demeanor.

"Not disappeared really. When I didn't see her at breakfast or the morning session, I asked around. The staff people mostly just shrugged it off, but finally one of them said she'd gotten food poisoning from the dinner last night." Diana seemed disconcerted, as though she had something on her mind. "I just don't understand how she got sick and I didn't. We foraged together and took the same plants. Neither of us was really into it and just grabbed some burdock, dandelions and a few handfuls of lamb's quarters. We went to the kitchen together. We'd both decided to make smoothies with our finds. Most of the people went for the stir-fry since it seemed like a meal." The woman put her head down. "We both wanted the sugar in the juice. We even joked about our weakness."

"Then what happened?" I asked.

The woman shrugged. "Someone from the kitchen staff handed Megan a blender carafe with the juice in it and she dumped in the stuff from her bag." The woman stopped for a moment, as if trying to remember it. "Megan was busy talking about Jordan and their special relationship and wasn't paying much attention. She poured it into a tall plastic glass and waited until I made my drink. We toasted each other when we got back to our table and then drank them down. It makes no sense that she got food poisoning and I didn't."

"Did they say what happened to her?" I asked.

"Just that she wouldn't be back."

That was certainly an understatement.

"Wasn't somebody supposed to check what you gathered?" I asked. She nodded and told me what I'd heard before about the bags being left on the backs of the chairs. I mentioned I'd heard something about check marks on the bags. She held up her tote bag and showed me the check mark.

When I asked about the other woman's bag she couldn't say for sure. "It must have had a check mark. We left them on chairs next to each other and the woman with the white hair is a fanatic." She started to go on about another challenge the woman with the white hair was handling. It involved sitting in a sauna to sweat out your fear. I was only half listening, more concerned about what she'd said about them gathering the same plants.

"What about mushrooms?" I asked. She gave me an odd look.

"Neither of us wanted anything to do with them."

"Then Megan didn't gather any?" I asked, hoping she wouldn't suddenly wonder why I was so concerned.

"No, like I said, we stuck to burdock, dandelions and lamb's quarters. They're all really safe." She drank some more of the coffee and massaged her temple. "The headache is going away already." The furrow in her brow seemed to have released, and as she started talking about her worry about the upcoming challenge, I realized I was filling the need for someone to talk to. I let her go on with an occasional nod to make it seem like I was listening, but I was more intent on what she had said about the foraged meal. According to her they hadn't collected any mushrooms.

I zoned into the one-sided conversation for a moment. She seemed to be worried about a trust challenge and an accident in the past.

It reminded me of what I'd read online and I asked for the details of the challenge. She described something I'd seen before. People were blindfolded and had to let go and fall backward, trusting they would be caught. I asked what had happened to the person who had the accident. "I guess they were okay," she said with a shrug. "I just remember Jordan saying something about it. He turned it into a teaching moment, saying that life was full of risks and that we couldn't let fear win even when things didn't work out. He said we needed to step over it and keep going forward."

"I can see why you're worried," I said.

"That's what's coming up next," she said. "But it's going to be on the beach. If anything goes wrong, sand is a lot softer than a floor." By now the room had emptied out, and as she looked around her expression tensed up. "Time to go," she said, taking a deep breath.

Chapter Fourteen

It was late afternoon when my group returned. The fire was glowing and the room was cheerful and inviting. The sun had long since disappeared, replaced by a white sky mottled with gray, though the clouds were all for show. Despite the bits of gray there wasn't any rain ready to fall at this time of year.

I thought they'd all be in a good mood from the outing, but I heard some grumbling as they came down the path to our meeting room.

Vonda's lips were pursed, and she gave Suzy! a dirty look as they came into the room.

"I just asked the driver to pull over for a few minutes while I posted some things on Facebook. It doesn't mean I'm an addict." Her phone was in her hand and she shoved it in her pocket.

"I saw a police car parked on the street. Are they still investigating what happened to that woman? Didn't you say it was an accident?" Hanna asked. "It sure detracts from the peace of this place seeing the police hanging around."

"It's a small-time police department. They probably overreact when something happens," Fern said. "In a town like this most of their calls are probably about teenagers being rowdy."

"You sure seem to know a lot about everything," Vonda said to Fern. It didn't seem like a compliment, and I suspected that Vonda thought that as an assistant principal she should be the one in the know.

"What can I say—I'm curious and I read a lot," Fern answered, giving Vonda a dismissive shrug. It was time for me to step in and smooth things over. There was no reason not to tell them the truth. "I heard that Jordan and his people weren't being cooperative and the police are still looking for information," I said.

"And the cops are probably suspicious of why the Jordan people aren't talking. Maybe there's more to it than it seems," Daisy said.

"I would ascertain that Fern is probably correct. Not much happens in Cadbury and someone dying from eating wild food connected to a retreat put on by a well-known guru type is more interesting than dealing with rowdy teenagers," Vonda added.

John came in at the end of it. He had an envelope tucked under his arm and was holding a plastic cup of wine. Hanna looked at the dark red liquid and gave him a disparaging frown. "Considering your problem, do you think you should have that?"

His eyes flared as he glared at her. "It would be a lot worse for all of you if I didn't," he said, pulling out a chair and sitting.

"Is something wrong?" Fern asked with concern. "Maybe it would help if you talked about it."

"It wouldn't," he said firmly. "Consider the subject closed." He picked up the cup and drank off half of it.

There was a moment of awkward silence. "The Jordan people were on my plane," Daisy said, trying to change the subject. "He was in first class and a couple of women who were in the back with the rest of us kept going in the front. The flight attendant had to tell them to stay in their seats."

My ears perked up. "What did they look like?"

"It was that woman with the great-looking white hair and a younger dark-haired woman who had an air of entitlement," she said.

The woman with the white hair was Lyla, and I was betting that the other one was Megan, though I kept that to myself and ended the line of conversation by asking them what they thought of the cookies.

I had baked another batch during my stop home and added dabs of cherry preserves to some and chocolate wafers to others. Yolanda was the first one to speak up and give them her approval. I suggested they spend the time working on the switched projects. They seemed okay with going ahead with them without having Crystal there for help. The only issue was that Fern had decided to alter the pattern of the scarf that Vonda had brought. "I thought we were supposed to stick to whatever the original instructions were," Vonda said in a sharp tone.

"Nobody said anything about rules," Fern said, showing the rest of the group how she'd added a section with an open space between the knitted stitches. This was all on me and something Crystal and I hadn't considered when we came up with the idea. The only thing to do now was take a vote. Vonda was overruled and seemed disgruntled.

• • •

After the hassle over serving breakfast to my group in the Lodge, I'd arranged for dinner to be set up in the living room–like lobby of the Sand and Sea building. Friday night was a busy dinner time at the Blue Door, so Lucinda had agreed to deliver my group's meal early. I had met her at the Lodge and was helping her wheel the carts with the food to the building. Plates and a table were being supplied by Vista Del Mar. I was beginning to feel like a traffic cop. As we pushed them up the path, a group of Jordan people were coming toward us.

The smell of food wafted toward them and they clustered around us. I recognized Diana among them. "Don't get your hopes up, that's not for us," she said to the others.

They all seemed to deflate at once and I heard one of them urge the others to chant "food is just fuel" and move on.

Diana hung back. "I did it," she said, seeming bright-eyed and animated. I wasn't sure what she was talking about and my smile must have seemed blank. "The challenge I was so worried about. I let go and someone caught me."

I congratulated her. Her smile waned a little. "But that was the easy one."

"But you did it," I said. "I'm sure you'll do great with the next one." I realized I was doing Jordan's job of pumping her up, but since she seemed to have latched on to me, I wanted to help her if I could. It seemed to work. She hugged my arm and thanked me multiple times before she rushed off to catch up with the others.

"What was that about?" Lucinda asked after the Jordan follower moved on to join the others.

"She's with the other retreat and we've talked a bit. She needed a little encouragement. The Jordan retreat is more like boot camp," I said. "The activities are called challenges and accomplishing them is supposed to help them fix their lives. There's no fun or even the pleasure of a good meal. It's a 'no pain, no gain' kind of philosophy." We moved closer to the building and I explained that Diana had been with the woman who died at the foraging meal. "According to her, they ate exactly the same stuff and she said they deliberately avoided mushrooms, but she was probably confused. Lieutenant Borgnine took the dead woman's tote bag as evidence and I heard that there was a mushroom in it and it was identified as a death cap."

I considered whether to tell her that Lieutenant Borgnine had asked for my help, indirectly anyway, but I decided to follow what Dane had said and not tell anyone, including Lucinda. I did mention that I was trying to find a way to get the blame off of Cloris.

"Good for you," my friend said. "It's ridiculous for Kevin St. John to try to make it seem like she was responsible." We wheeled the carts around to the back entrance, which had no stairs, and went on into the main room. A table had been brought in along with chairs. Serving platters, plates and silverware sat on top of the table. "Tag would be pleased," Lucinda said. "He's still fussing about the platter we didn't get back." She glanced around the common room. "It's very cozy with the fire going and all. It's something you should consider for your date with Dane," she said.

Lucinda pulled out a tablecloth and we began to set up the table. She knew all about our big Saturday night plans. "I can't believe that you and Dane have abstained so far. Who holds out anymore," she said. Then she smiled. "Except you do."

"Don't make it sound like I'm some kind of ice queen," I said. "It's going to change how he views me. And by the way, he's arranging things and has promised candles and rose petals."

"He can't be that old-fashioned that he's going to want to stick an *A* on your shirt."

"I think you have to be married to be an adulteress," I said. "And no, he isn't so old-fashioned as to view me as compromised." I laughed at the thought. "More like it opens the door to a kind of commitment." I repeated the idea that it would have been different if it had happened when we'd just met. "Then it would have been just casual, just sex. Now it has more slapped all over it."

"Like love?" she said.

The word made me uneasy and I just shrugged it off and said that I really needed to concentrate on how to help Cloris.

• • •

Lucinda had returned to the Blue Door to help keep Tag out of the customers' way by the time my group filed in for dinner. It was lucky that the Jordan people were all off doing something, because they might have lost control if they'd seen the meal of fried chicken tenders, coleslaw, corn, mashed potatoes and some of the bread pudding I'd made the night before.

Friday evenings, Vista Del Mar usually put on camplike activities for the guests like roasting marshmallows and a movie in Hummingbird Hall, but that was all canceled since the Jordan group had taken over the whole place. I'd come up with a night hike followed by a wine or hot chocolate toast in the Lodge after.

I was pleased when they all agreed and seemed glad to move around after the heavy meal.

To add to the feeling of being out in the wild, the grounds were purposely kept on the dark side with just small-wattage lights along the roadway that wound through the place. The buildings seemed to float in the darkness with only the glow from the lights inside to show they were there as I led the way through the grounds. We left the center area behind and followed the roadway as it wound through the assorted buildings. Because everything my group had done had been so close to the main area, they were surprised to see how big the grounds really were. We backtracked the same way we'd come, though in the dark I don't think they even noticed.

When we neared the Lodge, I took them across the grassy circle to the boardwalk. It was surrounded by the silky sand the area was known for. Though there were bushes and plants growing in it, enough of the sand was exposed to reflect light back from the clouds in the sky. It wasn't bright enough to see colors, but bright enough to easily see where we were going. The boardwalk wasn't actually a boardwalk. While it appeared to be made of wood slats, it was made of recycled plastic bottles. I'd planned to take them on the route that meandered through the dunes, but as we got close to the spot to turn off, there was loud rock music along with screams or yells coming from somewhere.

"It's coming from over there," John said, pointing toward the beach. The words were barely out of his mouth when there was a crescendo of shouts. Without me saying anything everyone started to move forward on the route to the beach. The music and shouting grew louder the closer we got. We picked up speed and rushed across the street. It was lucky there was rarely much traffic because I wasn't sure how carefully anybody checked before going across.

A crowd was huddled around something glowing. As I got closer, a figure started moving over what I realized were glowing embers. The hoots and shouts got louder as the person continued over them, moving quickly in time to the rock music. When the figure stepped off the end, a cheer went up and they were greeted by hugs and high fives. And then it was repeated with someone else.

"It's fire walking," Daisy said, pushing in front of me for a better view.

"Is that what it's called?" Vonda said. "It's not for me."

"Actually, I think Jordan's version is called Hot Coal Stroll," I said, remembering what I'd seen on the schedule. I didn't care what it was called, I was with Vonda—not for me. Now I understood why Diana seemed so nervous. Falling into someone's arms was tame compared to putting your bare feet on glowing embers.

We had stopped a distance away since I figured we wouldn't be welcome.

I noticed a tall lumbering figure approaching and got ready to argue that we had every right to be there. I probably had my fists balled up, expecting to do battle when I heard my name, well, a version of it. "Hey, Case," the voice said. There was only one person who called me that. He thought it was a nickname, but it seemed to me just taking away one syllable, actually one letter, didn't create a nickname, but I had let it go too long to say anything.

"Sammy?" I said, sounding surprised. "What are you doing here?"

"I'm working for Jordan. Right now I'm Dr. Samuel Glickner, ready in case anyone gets burned," he said.

"But you're a urologist," I said. "It doesn't seem likely they'll get burned in your area of expertise."

"I learned general medicine before I specialized," he said. "Besides, it's just first aid, but my real job is as a magic consultant. The grand finale is a setup called Escape Your Fears. It's got some cool illusions. You should see it," he said.

"Too bad you weren't with the group last night," I said.

"Did something happen?" he asked, sounding concerned.

"How about somebody died." I told him about the foraging and Megan getting sick and then dying. "It seems she ate some poison mushrooms."

"That is close to my area of expertise," he began. "The toxins attack the liver and can affect the kidney." He asked a lot of questions about the foraging, and I mentioned the bags were supposed to have been checked by an expert. He repeated what I already knew that there was no immediate reaction from eating a death cap. "I don't know if I could have done anything," he said.

The noise continued in the background, but suddenly there was a yell that sounded more like pain than triumph. Sammy picked up on it immediately. "Got to go, Case." He turned and yelled, "Doctor on the way," as he rushed toward a woman hobbling toward Jordan.

He was a sweet goofy guy who seemed to think I could do no wrong. It was too bad there just wasn't a spark between us anymore, at least on my end. Sammy seemed more than content with the chemistry he felt, but for me it was just flat. When he'd showed up in Cadbury claiming he was just there to work on his magic away from his family, I'd made it clear that our relationship was over and there was no chance of it being revived. He knew I was friends with Dane, but he didn't know the details, or he chose to ignore them. Either way, I didn't want to push it in his face that I was going to spend the night with Dane. I would leave my car in the driveway and then slip down the street to Dane's. Another problem presented itself. What if my mother called my landline Sunday morning and I wasn't there to answer? If she got worried, the first thing she'd do was call Sammy. I'd have to make sure I called her first. This simple sleepover had become way too complicated.

I waved for my group to follow and led them on back to the grounds. With all the Jordan people on the beach, we had the Lodge to ourselves. With the warm light given off by amber glass shades on the table lamps and the fire going in the huge stone fireplace, the interior felt cozy and bright after the night walk. Cloris was behind the counter pacing. She looked up as we walked in. When I'd mentioned the drink choice, they'd all voted for wine. Hanna had given John a concerned look, but he insisted it was fine. I got wine from the café for all of them and then helped them get set up with the board games before I went over to talk to Cloris. It was only when I saw that I had an extra glass of wine that I realized Daisy wasn't there.

"Did you see what they're doing on the beach? Is everything okay?" Cloris said quickly.

I said that it seemed to be going okay and I watched someone cross the coals with no problem, and I assured her that Sammy was at the ready for any problems. I didn't mention that he was already working on somebody. She relaxed enough to take a breath before leaning toward me. "What about the bag? Have you found out anything? I keep going in circles reliving the situation with the bags. Trying to figure if there was a way a bag was missed." She put her head down. "If that's what happened, I have to take the blame."

"I promise, I'll see what I can do," I said, and she let out a gush of air.

"Thank you so much. I know I can count on you. I feel terrible being unglued like this. It's so unprofessional. They even covered it in one of my classes at the community college. When you worked in hospitality, you had to stay cool and seem in control no matter what. Thank heavens my professor can't see me." I'd seen enough wellness-type retreats at Vista Del Mar to know what to do. I urged her to take a deep breath and hold it for a moment and count to five as she let it out. It took repeating it a few times, but she seemed improved. I went back to my group.

"This takes me back," John said, looking at the Monopoly board he'd pulled out from the shelf at the back of the cavernous room.

Daisy had just joined them and grabbed the glass of wine I'd left her. Her face was bright from the chill damp air and she seemed more animated than before. She had noticed me talking to Sammy and asked who he was. I didn't go into the details of our relationship, but instead mentioned that he was a doctor who was there for the other group.

"It's good they had medical help," Fern said.

"It's not as dangerous as it seems," Hanna said. "The best way to understand it is the difference between reaching in the oven and touching a metal pan or touching the top of the cake in the pan." Her gaze swept the group.

"I get it," I said. "I've felt the top of a cake more than once to see if it springs back to the touch, meaning it's done, without getting burned. Not the same when I've made a mistake and my finger hit the pan." Fern winced in sympathy and said she'd done it, too.

Hanna started to explain the different way that heat traveled, but wood was a poor conductor of heat and the layer of ash was even more protection. It also had to do with moving quickly.

"You seem to know a lot about it," Daisy said.

"I'm a science teacher," Hanna said with a shrug. "It's the kind of stuff that fascinates me."

"Not for us," Vonda said, glancing at her sister.

"Speak for yourself," Yolanda said. "I might like to do something daring."

Vonda shook her head. "You're just showing off. You'd put one toe on those coals and be screaming your head off."

"I would not."

"You would too," Vonda said. Yolanda had gotten up and seemed ready to go to the beach to prove her point.

"Sorry to have to stop you," I said. "But Jordan is adamant that we stay out of their activities."

"Saved by the rules," Vonda said with a knowing nod.

Yolanda seemed dejected as she sunk back into her seat. "Say what you want, but I would have done it." She looked at the rest of us. "My sister thinks she can speak for both of us."

"Here, you can be the iron," Vonda said, pushing the game piece on her sister.

"No," Yolanda bellowed, pushing the tiny iron back at her sister. "I want to be the little Scottie dog."

Hearing the sisters fuss made me glad I was an only child.

Chapter Fifteen

The Monopoly game was in full swing when I left. I still had baking to do, but I decided to stop by our meeting room before I left the grounds. Everything had been off and I wondered if housekeeping had cleared away the old coffeepots and used paper cups.

I noticed the light was on in the room the Jordan people were using as I opened the door to my group's room. I had barely turned on the lights and noticed that housekeeping hadn't been to the meeting room when Tyler stuck his head in the door and called out a greeting.

"She's the one with the cookies," he said, and I saw he was talking to a dark-haired woman in a staff shirt who was standing behind him.

"Really?" the dark-haired woman said. "Please tell me you still have some." The two of them came in the room and I saw Lyla step behind them into the doorframe. The white-haired woman shook her head.

"You two are so weak. I should tell Jordan about you. The staff is supposed to go by the same rules."

I was suddenly not sure what I should do, but Tyler gave the white-haired woman a dismissive look as he said, "Are there any left?"

"I was just going to see," I said. There was still a layer of cookies in the tin, and when I checked the coffeepots, they still had something in them. I invited them to help themselves, realizing they might drop some useful information.

The woman in charge of the foraging shook her head with contempt as she stayed in the doorway.

"You can tell on us if you want to," Tyler said. "But Jordan's not going to get rid of us any more than he did when you told him that Megan didn't demonstrate proper responsibility." He gestured toward the counter with the coffee. "I bet there's some chamomile tea. Just pretend you collected the flowers yourself."

She reluctantly came all the way into the room. I went to introduce myself, but she stopped me. "I know who you are," she said in an unfriendly tone. "The instructions were not to interact." She gave the other two visitors a dirty look. She examined the room and her gaze stopped on the table with the tote bags and works in progress.

"I'm BB," the dark-haired woman said to me as she grabbed one of the cookies with a chocolate wafer on top. "The bliss of sugar," she said, biting into the cookie. "And chocolate, too."

Lyla made her way to the counter and looked through the tea selection. Even though she'd brushed me off, I made another attempt to talk to her. "You're the foraging expert, aren't you?" I said as she flipped through the array of tea bags. She gave me a sideways look with a shake of her head.

"If you're going to ask me about the incident last night, forget it. I've said all I'm going to say." She went to the door, and instead of going into the room next door she disappeared up the path.

"Don't mind her. She's an absolute fanatic. She's beside herself over what happened and angry that the foraging experience is under scrutiny," Tyler said.

I heard BB let out a sound. "Lyla can't bear the fact that she might have made a mistake and is trying to pass the blame onto the woman who died. Not that there was any love lost between them."

"I thought you were all a team," I said. Tyler and BB looked at each other and choked back a laugh.

"We all believe in Jordan's message," Tyler said, "but with a little wiggle room." He held up a cookie as an example. "There are things that are important and some that seem like window dressing to me. The whole food setup is one of them. The people are sleep-deprived and probably facing some serious stuff in their lives. Forcing them to have no coffee and subsist on small amounts of bad-tasting food seems too much. But then Jordan holds himself up as an example of sticking to the plan. I guess we're just weak." He looked at BB and they both got guilty expressions.

"Do you all work together between these events?" I asked.

"No, we come from all over, well, most of us come from Southern California. We all have day jobs." He made himself a cup of the barely warm coffee. "Lyla teaches botany at a community college and she works with a yoga studio putting on detox rituals." He made a face that showed his distaste for her. "Jordan brought her on when he wanted to add some new challenges. As you can probably figure, she absolutely follows all of Jordan's rules."

"So then she does the sauna thing, too?" I asked.

"Yes. But don't let her hear you calling it a sauna. She insists on calling it a hot box and says that the heat draws out all of your negativity. I will say that she practices what she preaches. She does the whole ritual by herself before she takes the group in. She tells them they'll come out feeling cleansed and empowered," Tyler said.

"And it's not dangerous?" I said.

"Anyone can leave," BB said.

Tyler's eyes went skyward. "As long as they don't mind being shamed. She pushes them to do more than they think they can. That's the only way they're going to grow. It's the theme of the retreat. Jordan's pitch is to push through your fear and do the challenges. The empowerment you feel makes you able to deal with whatever issues you have." He looked at me. "We get it all, from fear of clowns to being part of a cult."

"Do you take part in the challenges?" I asked. They seemed fine about talking and I had a bunch of questions.

"We've done most of them countless times, now we're more facilitators," BB said.

"But you went along on the foraging?" I asked, thinking they might have seen something. He and BB looked at each other.

"We went along on the gathering part, but we knew that Lyla was going to be there and Megan, so we slipped out. It's a grueling weekend for us and we needed a little more sustenance." It was a different story than Tyler had told me before, but I was pretty sure this was the true version.

They both gave me such guilty looks, I put my hands up. "I won't tell. So, I guess that means Jordan wasn't there either."

"After his appearance at the opening talk, he has to prepare himself for the weekend. It's a big drain. The program goes from early morning until late at night and he's the main event, going out in the crowd and confronting people so they let out what brought them here. He does a solitary meditation to prepare himself for the weekend," Tyler said. It sounded like something Jordan claimed and nobody questioned.

I had a lot of questions about Jordan and how he got to where he was. Tyler gave me what sounded like a scripted description of how Jordan had been an assistant to a motivational speaker and realized his gift for reaching people. He'd studied all the greats in motivational thought and come up with his own program.

"Does Jordan have a family?" I asked. All I'd seen of him was this prowling charismatic figure and I hadn't thought about his life away from it.

BB chuckled. "He has a wife and a couple of stepkids. She's smart enough to stay away from the retreats and must turn a blind eye to whatever he has going on." After what my helper Crystal had said, I understood what BB was implying. I didn't want to push it and ask for specifics because at some point they'd figure out I was being too intrusive and clam up.

"Does Jordan have a day job?" It hadn't occurred to me before and I suddenly wondered if he went home from these weekends of wearing jeans and work shirts and put on a suit and tie.

"It's a full-time thing for him now. He puts on different levels of events and he has his subscription people," Tyler said. He explained that there were people who paid a monthly fee to have access to

Jordan.

"What about you two? What do you do when you're not working the retreats?"

"BB teaches yoga and I'm a makeover specialist, the physical kind." He leveled his gaze at me and moved his head from side to side, clearly checking me out. "You should make more of your eyes. Maybe add some eyeliner and mascara." He looked at my hair. "I'd add some highlights and a better cut." It made me feel uncomfortable and I asked about Megan to get his mind on something other than the faults in my appearance.

"She was a production assistant. She worked for Winkleman Brothers Studio." He grabbed another cookie. "I heard her saying she wanted to be a producer."

There was the sound of an alarm going off, and Tyler looked at his wrist and tapped something on his watch. "Jordan's last talk of the night is winding down." He touched BB on the shoulder. "We better go."

She had a worried expression as she put her hand in front of her mouth and blew into it. "We can't have cookie breath."

Chapter Sixteen

I went home, threw a little water on my face, gave Julius some stink fish, grabbed my shopping bag of muffin supplies and headed to the Blue Door. Lucinda was tidying up the dessert counter and Tag was readjusting the place settings on all the tables. Lucinda looked the picture of elegance in her Eileen Fisher outfit, but her expression seemed perturbed. "Sometimes his fussing just gets to me." If Tag heard her, he didn't react. All I could see was the back of his head with his unnaturally thick hair for a man of his age as he continued to move among the tables.

The chef came out of the kitchen with his backpack slung over his shoulder. As he approached the front door, we traded glances. He offered me a grunt as a greeting and then said a pleasanter goodbye to his employers.

"Does he really think I'd bother his knives?" I said, catching a last glance of the backpack.

"It's a chef thing," Tag said. "Their knives are like their artist's tools. Very personal. That's why they keep the knives with them."

The most I needed was an occasional paring knife, and I was happy to depend on whatever was at the restaurant. I went to take my bag of supplies for the muffins into the kitchen and Lucinda followed me. She was anxious for an update.

"Do you think I should wear more eye makeup?" I asked.

Lucinda laughed. "Where did that come from?"

I told her about my visitors. "One of them does physical makeovers when he isn't helping Jordan do the spiritual kind. He offered some free advice, and unasked for," I said. Then I realized the absurdity of who I was asking. Lucinda was always perfectly turned out in some designer wear and I swore she probably put on lipstick before she made coffee. My relationship with makeup was a little different. I went for the barely-there look, which actually meant that most of the time it was *barely there*.

"Your look suits who you are," Lucinda said. "Though a touch of lipstick would add a little color. I'd love to see you go brave and try something in bright red," she said.

"Never," I said, shaking my head. Just the thought of seeing blood-red lips in the mirror was shocking enough, let alone actually seeing them. Besides, Dane would probably never stop laughing. I put the muffin supplies in the corner since I'd be working on the desserts first.

"Did they have anything to say about the dead woman?" Lucinda asked.

Her question made me think over what I'd heard about Megan and put it together in a capsule. "I keep hearing over and over that she wasn't well-liked and reading between the lines the reason she continued to have a job might be because she had a relationship with Jordan or maybe knew something damning about him. The woman who handled the foraging won't talk about what happened or apparently take any responsibility for it." I stopped for a moment as something else came to mind. "It's probably just a weird coincidence, but they said that Megan's day job was working for Winkleman Brothers Studio, and one of my retreat people works there, too."

Tag called out for Lucinda, sounding impatient, and she rolled her eyes at me. "I better get him out of here."

As soon as they left, I turned on the soft jazz as I always did and tried to lose myself in baking. I was making chocolate cake and had just begun to unwrap the blocks of baking chocolate to melt when I heard a knock at the door. I was pretty sure it was Dane even before I looked through the glass of the front door. When he was working the night shift, he came by during his break, but tonight he was dressed in his civilian clothes and was carrying a cardboard holder with two cups of coffee.

"I figured you probably needed this," he said, taking one of the cups out of the holder and handing it to me.

I thanked him, and of course he was right. I'd been too busy dealing with everything else and everyone else to even think of having some of the coffee that had been left in the pot. He sniffed the air. "What's on the books for tonight? I think I smell chocolate."

"Good sniffer," I said, pointing to the brown blocks on the counter. "Chocolate layer cake with butter cream icing, and the muffins du jour are more of the biscuits in a cup, this time with raisins."

"My mouth is watering just thinking about them," he said, unabashedly looking into my eyes.

His gaze made me feel a little flustered and I pulled my gaze away. Whenever it got uncomfortably personal, my go-to was to start talking about something else. "It was a hot time at Vista Del Mar," I said. "On the beach anyway. The Jordan group walked across hot coals."

"I know," Dane said. "All done without consulting Cadbury PD. Apparently their philosophy is to not ask for permission but beg for forgiveness, or in this case it was over before anyone in the department got there." I was surprised at Dane's tone. He was usually light, but this time he really sounded like a cop.

"Have you picked up anything I can pass along to the lieutenant?" he said.

"Just gossipy stuff like the dead woman might have had something going with Jordan. The woman who handled the foraging wouldn't talk. I got the feeling she's trying to put the blame on the woman who died." I put the chocolate in to melt. "It all really comes down to whether or not she went through the woman's tote bag." I shook my head in frustration. "That really affects Cloris, too, since she was the one helping with everything." An image of the tote bag flashed in my mind as I leaned against the counter taking a sip of the coffee. "I know what to do," I said suddenly.

"Are you going to share?" Dane said, eyeing me intently.

"If I could get a look at Megan's tote bag and see if it'd been marked, then Cloris would know she hadn't messed up. It wouldn't completely get Kevin St. John off her case, but it would give her some peace of mind. And then it would all be on the woman who was in charge of the challenge."

What I hadn't said yet was that I was going to need Dane's help, which he might not be so anxious to give. I instinctively reached up and began to twirl a strand of my hair as I tilted my head and looked at Dane.

His cop persona melted into a grin. "Oh, no, you're trying to flirt." His eyes widened in amusement. "It could only mean you're up to something, that you want something from me."

I let go of the hair strand. I should have known by now that it was more comic relief than seductive. "There is something you could do."

Dane pursed his lips. "Why don't you just tell me what you have in mind."

I mentioned seeing Lieutenant Borgnine holding a tote bag. "It had to be Megan's. He rushed it out of sight before I got much of a look at it—like seeing if it had a check mark on it, meaning that Lyla Konker had okayed the contents."

"If that's all," he said with a shrug. "I'll tell the lieutenant."

"When? Tomorrow? And who knows if he'll even tell you what he finds. I want to see for myself. If there's a check mark, it'll give Cloris some peace of mind. She's always been great at helping me with everything. It's the least I can do for her."

"You know they keep stuff like that locked away," he said, seeming wary.

"I was thinking after I finish baking we could make a visit to the police station. You could say you left something in your locker and I could distract the desk officer with some treats."

"You want me to snag the keys and steal the bag?" he said, incredulous.

"Oh, no, I'd never ask you to do that. Just borrow the keys and take a picture of the bag," I said, trying to make it sound effortless.

Dane half closed his eyes and began to shake his head in dismay. "Do you know what Borgnine will do if he finds out?"

"No, but he won't find out. You're just taking a picture with your phone. And you'd be helping a good person hopefully have a reason to stop feeling so guilty," I said.

"You sound pretty sure there will be a check mark."

"If you notice, I said *hopefully*. But I know that Cloris takes whatever job she gets seriously. Whether it was working in the kitchen or helping out housekeeping, she was always super responsible. That's why it really bothers me that Kevin St. John is trying to pass the blame onto her." I realized I sounded like I was on a soapbox. To lighten it up, I grabbed the strand of hair and attempted to flutter my eyes.

"I'll do it, I'll do it, but stop with the fake flirting. It's painful to watch," he said, putting up his hands in mock horror. "But we better get going on those cakes." He went to wash his hands and grab an apron. He was a great cook, so being my sous chef was easy. He used the time to tell me about the dinner he'd planned and the romantic setup with the rose petals and candles. When I only swooned over the dinner menu, he started to tease me about only wanting him for his cooking skills.

The cakes cooled while we made the muffins. When they were frosted, we took them to the front counter and left them sitting on the pedestals under glass domes.

"Just relax and go with the flow. I don't know what you think is going to change," he said. "You can still bolt. I'm just betting you won't want to."

"Somebody has a pretty high opinion of his romance skills," I said. I almost punctuated it with some of my fake flirting, but it had become old by now. I grabbed two of the carriers and followed Dane outside.

We dropped off the muffins at the various coffee spots and went to the police station. The low building stood out from the rest of downtown Cadbury. Most of the buildings were either Victorian style, stucco with orange tiled roofs, or bland mid-century. I didn't think there was an actual style name that went with the police station other than functional. It had some red tiles stuck on the front as decoration to cover up the lack of windows. We practiced the plan as we went up the few steps to the entrance.

The lobby area was furnished with a single bench. As we walked in, the gray-haired officer looked up with a tense expression from behind a glass partition. It was the middle of the night and anyone coming in was probably trouble. When he recognized Dane, the cop's face relaxed and he nodded. I hung back while Dane gave him the story about needing something from his locker. The guy nodded and Dane went through a door into the inner area.

Presentation is everything. I'd packed the muffins in a borrowed basket lined with a checkered cloth napkin. They looked like something Red Riding Hood would have been carrying through the forest. I pulled the basket up to eye level and mentioned I'd been baking. The officer's eyes lit up and we spent a few minutes going back and forth trying to get the basket through the small open slot. I had particularly planned the basket setup because I knew it wouldn't fit through a small opening. Finally, he said he'd come around front. A moment later, he'd left his post and joined me in the sparse lobby.

"Usually when someone shows up at this hour they're bleeding," he said. "This is definitely a nice change." He reached in and grabbed one of the biscuits. I glanced up just as Dane slipped into the area the officer had just vacated. He was looking around and finally held up a set of keys with a triumphant expression.

The keys made the slightest jangle and the officer started to turn toward the noise, but I rushed to tell him that'd I brought all the biscuit muffins for him.

"Less sugar than donuts," he said with a wink as he reached for another. I let out a breath of relief as Dane disappeared from view. I wanted to make conversation to keep him occupied and was searching for a topic, when he took the lead.

"You know that Dane has it bad for you," he said. "I hope you're not just toying with him." I had managed to arrange it so that the cop had his back to the glass enclosure, but I faced it. Dane had rushed back in and seemed frustrated. He shook his head, which I took to mean he hadn't taken the right key. He was doing another search and I had to keep the officer busy. Much as I hated to do it, I was going to have to talk about Dane's and my relationship.

"I don't know what you think is going on," I said. "We're just neighbors."

The older man smiled. "Nobody believes that. And nobody wants to see Dane get his heart crushed. He's such a good guy. The way he helps keep the kids out of trouble and the way he's dealt with his family. He probably seems tough to you, but he has deep feelings."

This was my worst nightmare and why I'd tried to keep our relationship off the radar. "I couldn't agree more about not wanting to hurt him in any way," I said, hoping to convince him we were just neighbors and casual friends. "I hate to call the town gossips wrong, but we really aren't a couple." He looked disbelieving and by now had polished off all the biscuit muffins. I could tell by his body language that he was about to go back to his spot. Assuming Dane had gotten the right keys, he still had to put them back. I had to keep the officer with me. I reached out and touched his arm and looked at him with what I hoped was a believable concerned look. After being such a flop at flirting, I wasn't sure about how good I was at any sort of pretended emotion.

"I just don't know what to do," I began. I wasn't sure what I was going to say after that and so I sniffled a few times as if I was holding back tears. "You have it all wrong. I'm the one who had it bad for Dane, but he thinks I'm just a neighbor."

The officer made some movements with his head that seemed a little disbelieving, so I gripped his wrist this time. "Dane's a wonderful person, but you know he just can't commit."

"Really?" the officer said. He made a *tsk* sound and shook his head. "I ought to have a talk with him. I've been married for thirty years. The young guys today are all about being free. Funny though, I thought Dane was different. Don't you worry, honey. I'll do what I can to talk some sense into him. You're baking alone should be enough to seal the deal."

Dane rushed into the enclosure and gave me a thumbs-up as he leaned down to put something in a drawer before sprinting away. The station phone started to ring and the officer gave my hand a squeeze before he rushed to the back to answer it.

Dane came out a moment later with a hoodie on his arm and waved a thanks to the man. He pointed at the sweatshirt jacket. "I wanted to be authentic," he said with a smile. "Good work at keeping him occupied."

"About that. I might have cried on his shoulder a little about how you just wanted to be free."

Dane put his hands over his eyes. "Here comes a lecture."

Once we got outside, he looked at me. "The things I do for you."

"So?" I said, when we were a distance away.

"I think I need some kind of thank-you before I give you the results," he said. He sounded all serious cop, but I knew he was being smart-alecky. We got to his truck and climbed in.

I gave him a hug as I said thank you, but he gave me a disparaging look in return. "That's all I get for sneaking around and borrowing the keys to the evidence closet?"

"Okay, you get a kiss for your efforts," I said with a smile. I leaned over and gave him a kiss on the cheek.

"Really?" Dane said. "That's it?" He sounded devastated, but I knew he was joking. He puckered up and used two fingers to point out his lips. Laughing, I leaned in and attempted to give him a light kiss, but, well, let's just say nature took over and it turned into something hot and long. We were both a little breathless when a car driving by brought us back to the reality of where we were.

"Now, how about you give me the goods," I said, pulling myself together.

"I don't know. Maybe I need more signs of your gratitude," he said with a hopeful lift of his eyebrows.

"I'll pay up tomorrow night," I said and gestured with my hand for him to show me what he had. He pulled out his phone and showed me the photo. There was no mistaking the check mark next to the name. I couldn't wait to tell Cloris that she hadn't screwed up.

Chapter Seventeen

But of course, I had to wait. It was the wee hours of the morning when I finally got home. Sammy's BMW was parked on the street, reminding me he was in the guesthouse. It was dark and quiet, which probably meant he was in the depths of sleep. Julius got up from his sleep to remind me I owed him a stink fish treat. And then I fell into bed, falling asleep in my clothes. There was no question that I burned the candle at both ends when I put on a retreat.

I was lost in a dream about tote bags and giant mushrooms until an insistent sound cut into my sleep. When I opened my eyes, I realized it was my landline. I glanced around the room and saw that it was light outside as I reached for the cordless phone.

I mumbled a sleepy hello. "Feldstein, don't tell me I woke you up," Frank said. "I thought when you had a retreat going you got up with the sun."

"More like I went to sleep just before it came up," I said. I thought he'd sign off after that, but instead he continued.

"As long as you're awake," he said. I heard him take a drink of something, which I imagined was probably coffee with a lot of additions. "I just wondered how things were going with the Jordan retreat. Did you find anything out about him? Something bad?"

It took a moment for my brain to kick in and I asked Frank why he cared. "It's that client I did the investigating for. She was so upset about what happened."

I was sitting up now. "I get it, Frank, you cared about her."

"Did not," he said defiantly. "The refund didn't undo the damage. I just thought if you got some dirt on him I could get it out in the world."

"I don't know if you consider it dirt, but it seems like he probably has his special friends and the woman who died might have been one of them. I gather his wife knows and looks the other way. His taste in groupies seems a little off since it seems unanimous that Megan was inept and irresponsible."

Frank let out a disappointed groan. "Nothing very interesting there. Did you find anything else out?"

I told him about my escapade with Dane and he laughed. "Good work, Feldstein, that sounds like real PI stuff, getting cops to sneak around the evidence locker. What was the point?"

I explained the issue with whether the bag had been looked at by the foraging expert. "At least seeing that it was checked by her helps my friend know it wasn't her fault," I said. "But the woman who did the checking is insisting she never makes mistakes."

"Just a thought, Feldstein, and then I have to go. You said the dead woman wasn't well-liked. Have you considered that it wasn't a mistake or an accident? What about the woman who checked the bags? How did she feel about the victim?"

"She didn't like her," I said. "I see what you're getting at. She could have added the mushrooms when she went through the bag." I remembered now how Diana, the woman who'd foraged with Megan, had made a point that they deliberately didn't gather any mushrooms. "I even know where she could have gotten them." I told him about Lyla's display of things they shouldn't gather.

"Now that you think you have your friend off the hook though, is there any reason to pursue it?" Frank leaned back in his chair and I heard it squawk in protest. "Unless you want to show up that cop again. But weren't you supposed to be feeding him information?"

"Yes," I said, "but wouldn't it be better if I handed him the whole thing all wrapped up?"

"I think you know the answer to that. He's not going to like it." Frank had run out of bandwidth to talk, and after a hasty goodbye, hung up.

He'd left me with a lot to consider. I had bought into the idea that Megan eating the mushrooms was an accident from a mistake somewhere along the line. But what if Lyla had added the mushrooms? She seemed to dislike Megan more than the others did. Hadn't she said something about her pulling down the whole retreat? I'd heard them complain about Jordan keeping Megan around. Maybe Lyla decided to take matters into her own hands and do something that Jordan wouldn't.

I showered and got dressed, thinking about the situation. I could just pass on my thoughts to the lieutenant through Dane, but I realized what I really wanted to do was what I told Frank. I wanted to put all the pieces together and then hand it over to Lieutenant Borgnine. I wasn't sure how to go about it. The place to start was with Lyla Konker. I'd have to find a way to get on her good side so she'd talk to me and maybe let something slip about the mushrooms. How likely was that?

I went directly to the Lodge and found Cloris and told her the good news without giving the details how I got it. I didn't think she'd approve. She showered me with hugs and thank-yous. I was amazed at how it transformed her. Her brows unfurrowed and the pinched look left her face. She even managed a smile. "Well, then somehow Lyla Konker missed it," she said. Her smile faded. "It's still sad what happened, but such a relief that it wasn't my fault."

With that taken care of, I moved on to the breakfast setup for my group. Cloris had arranged for us to use the Cora and Madeline Delacorte Café. I'd brought some of the biscuits in a cup and a breakfast casserole had been dropped off the day before and just needed heating. The café would provide the drinks.

When I went into the café to set up, several of the Jordan people were at the counter arguing with the barista.

"I can't serve you," the guy said. "Jordan gave strict orders that we can't sell you coffee or food. The best I can do is offer you some water, though he stipulated no ice."

The three Jordan people continued to grumble and were joined by Diana, the retreat repeater who I'd spoken to before.

She pulled the small group off to the side and I took the

opportunity to talk to the man behind the counter. He was new and the first thing I had to do was convince him that I wasn't with the Jordan people. He was clueless about the casserole and I figured that it must have been left in the kitchen refrigerator. I went through the door that led directly outside. A moment later I was surrounded by the Jordan group.

"We were wondering if you could do us a favor," Diana said. She had a handful of money. "I feel like we're a bunch of teenagers trying to get someone to buy us beer, but could you get us some coffee and snacks?"

I felt for them since I was definitely in need of a jolt of java myself and agreed before going back inside. The barista gave me an uncomfortable look as I presented their order. "I know what you're doing." Then he shrugged. "But it's not my business if you're some kind of coffee hound with a hunger for a bunch of trail mix." He made up the order and put it into a cardboard carrier. The snacks they asked for were in a bag. They were huddled waiting in the shadows when I came back out. I handed over the carrier and bag. They showed a lot of gratitude, and the three people slipped off into the wild area next to the Lodge, while Diana stayed with me.

I listened when she told me how pumped she was from doing the fire walking, but I was thinking back to what she'd said about Megan and her avoiding mushrooms. She made it easy to segue when she moved on to talking about Lyla and how she was such a fanatic.

"Everything has changed since Lyla became second in command," she said. "They never served coffee and the food has always been sparse to say the least, but nobody stopped you from getting coffee or snacks on your own as long as you didn't flaunt it."

"You don't sound like you're a fan," I said.

"She's just so fanatical about everything. It's lucky the whole retreat is vegetarian. When she did the program before we left to go foraging, she brought up insects and what a good source of protein they were." Diana made a face at the thought then washed it away with a slug of coffee.

"As I recall, you felt the same about mushrooms," I said.

"Even though we knew the contents of our bags would be examined, Megan and I were turned off to the whole idea of having mushrooms in a smoothie. We'd decided before we went out that's what we were going to do with our find."

"And you saw Megan make her blender drink?" I asked.

The plain-looking woman shrugged. "She dumped in the stuff from her bag."

"But did you see what it was?"

Diana thought for a moment. "Not really. She held the bag over the blender carafe and shook it in." She turned to me. "Why are you so interested?"

I decided to tell her the truth and explained that it was pretty certain that Megan had died from eating poison mushrooms and Diana gasped. "But how is that possible. We didn't gather any."

I glanced up and saw Fern, Daisy and Hanna approaching us, making me drop the line of conversation.

"I was just working on your breakfast," I said to the women. That sounded better than that I was trying to locate their breakfast. I wondered if I should introduce everybody around, but Jordan had made such a point that our groups not mix that even though it seemed rather rude, I decided not to. It didn't matter anyway. Diana saw Lyla marching toward us and pushed her coffee cup on me before she rushed off.

I was surprised when the white-haired woman stopped next to us. Silly me thought she was going to say good morning or something along those lines, but instead she shook her head with disgust. "I know what you did and I'm going to tell." Then she moved on and joined the group going to the dining hall just as the bell began to ring announcing their breakfast was served.

"Isn't she Miss Sunshine," Fern said sarcastically. When I told them that my big crime was that I'd gotten coffee for some of the Jordan people when the barista had been instructed not to serve them, they shook their heads with disbelief.

I sent them back to the café and told them to get coffee and have it put on my tab, while I went on in search of the breakfast casserole.

I went around the back entrance to the dining hall that led directly into the kitchen. The people on KP duty were too busy doling out watery-looking oatmeal from a big pot to notice me as I checked the refrigerator and found nothing but a pitcher of grapefruit juice.

Had someone gotten wind of what their breakfast was and absconded with the casserole? I had no choice but to call Lucinda at home and see about getting a replacement.

I staved off my group's hunger with juice and the biscuits in a cup until Lucinda arrived with a replacement breakfast. The only mishap was when Fern spilled some cranberry juice on Hanna's patterned peasant blouse. "It's red on red, or almost," Hanna said, seeming unconcerned by the blotch on the tiny yellow flower on her sleeve.

"I brought some extras," Lucinda said, showing off a bowl of fruit salad and some breakfast sausage patties. "I hope no one objects to you having the meal here," she said, remembering the previous breakfast. She glanced around the café as if Jordan would suddenly appear.

I gave her a weary shrug as my people dove into the mini buffet. "I'm tired of having to walk on eggshells because of that group," I said. "They aren't even nice." I told her about my encounter with Lyla Konker.

"You're earning points in heaven," Lucinda said. "Just like I am for putting up with Tag. He was beside himself when I told him the casserole had disappeared. Can you believe he wanted to call the Cadbury PD?" We both laughed at the image of Tag with his fussiness dealing with the rumpled Lieutenant Borgnine.

"At least I gave Cloris some peace of mind," I said, explaining what I'd found out. I told her how I'd done it as well and she got a good laugh.

I thanked Lucinda for all her help with the meals. "They'd thank you too if they'd seen what I'd seen." I brought up the thinned-out oatmeal. "All I could think of was gruel and Oliver Twist in a workhouse."

My group went off to free time and I stayed with Lucinda to clear everything up. I finally helped her carry everything she'd brought back to her car. As she drove away, I saw Sammy coming down the driveway. Even with his tall bearlike build, he had a spring in his step. His face lit up when he saw me and I felt uncomfortable all over again about my night's plans with Dane. It didn't matter that I'd told Sammy countless times since he'd arrived that we weren't going to get back together, I felt pretty sure he thought there was still hope.

His smile broadened as he reached me. A moment later he was magically extracting a plastic monarch butterfly from my ear. "I just added it to my act. What do you think?"

"It's certainly relevant to the area," I said.

"But what do you think since you're part of the act?" he said. Yes, on top of everything else, I was his assistant in his magic act. I'd thought it was just temporary, but what had started out as a mistake had turned into a comedy magic show and Sammy insisted he couldn't replace me.

"I think it's good," I said with a shrug. I looked at the plastic grocery bag he was carrying. "What's going on?"

He reminded me that he'd been hired by Jordan to help set up the grand finale of the weekend. "Their final challenge is to pass through a bunch of escape rooms. It's really cool," he said. "I'm still working on the illusion at the end. Want to have a look?"

I started to say no. "I've kind of had it with Jordan. He may be helping all the people that came to his retreat, but he's a real pain in the you-know-what to me. I had to make all new arrangements for meals, his staff seems hostile to me and I have to try to keep my people out of sight of his people." I thought over the last thing. "That's ridiculous—I don't think his people would even realize it if some of my people crossed their path."

"Sorry it's such a pain," Sammy said. "Maybe I could say something to Jordan."

It made it so much harder that Sammy was such an all-around nice guy. How could I not care about him? "Thanks, but it's better if you don't," I said.

"Okay then—if you don't want to see what I'm working on . . ." He gave me a look with his mournful puppy-dog eyes and I relented. It wasn't like Jordan was hanging around anyway. Sammy lost the dejected look as soon as I agreed and I let him lead the way.

"This way," Sammy said when we neared Hummingbird Hall and he took me around the side. The building appeared to be a single story, all of which was taken up by the auditorium, but when approached from the other side, it became visible that it was built into a slope and had a lower floor. "Open Sesame," Sammy said in his magician voice, and then when nothing happened, he pushed open the door.

The lower floor was really a big storage space and had pipes for the upper floor running along the ceiling. When I'd seen it before it was empty, but now it was filled with a structure.

"This is it," he said, opening the entrance. "It's kind of like a maze or maybe you could call it a network of rooms." He went inside and waved for me to follow. The room we entered was narrow and the door shut behind us. "When it's functioning, the door will lock as it snaps shut. No chance for second thoughts and backing out. The only way to go is forward. This is the welcome room." He adjusted something on the wall and Jordan's voice offered the beginning of a pep talk, and then it cut off. Sammy said it explained how the setup worked, but he'd just show me. He pointed to the keypad on the door at the end of the room. "The code is hidden somewhere in each of the rooms. You find it and unlock the door and move on. Each of the rooms spotlights a different fear." He led the way into the second room. A crowd of clowns was projected on both sides of the walls. Sammy showed how we had to watch the clowns coming toward us until one of them had four numbers written on his hand.

The next room seemed to have black walls, but when the door shut the walls seemed to come alive and appeared to be covered in big water bugs. Sammy touched the wall and showed me how it was just another projection, and the spiders that brushed my face were all fake and hanging from a lattice of wood that formed the ceiling. The exit code was on the leg of a hairy fake tarantula.

"You've got to see this room." As we walked in the floor seemed to slant down and it felt soft and uneven. I looked to see what I'd stepped on and squealed when I saw that the floor was littered with snakes that began to writhe. I brushed against something hanging from one of the wood slats that ran along the top and recoiled in horror as I saw that it was a python.

Sammy grabbed my hand. "It's okay, they're all plastic," he said in a reassuring voice. The code was on one of the fake reptiles hanging next to the door. I don't have a reptile phobia, but I'm also not a snake fan, even plastic ones, so it was with trepidation that I grabbed the slithering plastic to get the code.

"This is the claustrophobia room," Sammy said. As soon as the door closed behind us the ceiling began to lower. It seemed like it would keep going, but he did something and abruptly the ceiling stopped moving. Even so, we had to squeeze through a small space to climb up on a step in front of a half-size door. I'm not particularly claustrophobic, but my breath got a little ragged when I had to squeeze through the small opening.

We landed on a step up from the floor in the next room, which was longer than the others. "And now for the grand finale," Sammy said. There was a bit of everything. Marching clowns were projected on the walls. A cardboard cutout of a rather threatening looking clown hung from the wood slats along the top. Beyond the projection changed to squirming water bugs. The way forward was blocked by a wall that went up about two-thirds of the way. The only way to go forward was by crawling through a short tunnel. Sammy urged me on, and as I started through it, I saw the bottom was covered in the plastic snakes. My breath got ragged again and I tried to move through as quickly as possible, and I jumped to a standing when I got to the end. I had to face a curtain of dangling snakes hanging from wood slats across the open top. When I pushed through the curtain of reptiles, the exit finally came into sight. There were two glass enclosures on either side of the door. I peered inside but they were empty.

"That's Jordan's big finish. There will be a rattlesnake in each one. Live ones, though it's just for show. There's no real danger since they'll be safely shut in their enclosures. And then comes the payoff," Sammy said. "But it's also what I came to work on. When the last door opens, there's supposed to be cheers, applause and a puff of glitter as a sign drops that says congratulations." He went to punch in the final code, and as I went through the door, everything went off at once and the congratulations sign would have hit me on the head if Sammy hadn't grabbed me. "I have to fix the timing or move the sign."

"What about a banner rather than a wooden sign," I said, thinking how much that would have hurt.

"I can't really make any changes," Sammy said. "Jordan insists on everything being his way." Sammy shrugged it off. "But what do you think of the setup?"

"It's really something," I said. "But then these people already walked over hot coals, so I guess they're ready to do anything."

Chapter Eighteen

I left Sammy to work on Jordan's final challenge for his people. It certainly wasn't my idea of a good time, but then the whole Jordan retreat was about doing things that made you uncomfortable. It felt good to get outside. The area around Hummingbird Hall had more open wild space than the rest of the grounds. It also felt more secluded because the brush and trees blotted out the view of the other communal buildings. I was going to turn back but I noticed an unfamiliar structure. It almost blended in with the surroundings, but as I got closer, I got a better view of the wooden building. It had to be the sauna I'd heard about, or what Lyla Konker called the hot box. There was no one around so I went for a closer look. The door was glass and inside there were benches around a center pit of rocks. I heard voices in the distance and rushed back to the path that led back to the center of the grounds.

When I neared the dining hall, I saw Tyler coming toward me leading a group of people. I tried to catch his eye and offer a greeting, but he turned away without even a flicker of recognition, and the whole party passed me as if I wasn't there. It was a weird feeling after the conversation we'd had and how I'd provided him and his other staff people with coffee and cookies.

Apparently, whatever the Jordan people were doing had to do with small groups because I saw other staff people with similar size groups. It got quieter once I passed the Lodge and the driveway that served as the main entrance to the grounds. I was glad to see that our meeting room was all set up this time. The fire was going and the counter held hot drinks. The cookie tin was getting low, but there were enough to get through the morning.

I did a quick check of the meeting room in the other part of the building. The door was open, but the room was empty.

Crystal arrived just as my people started coming in. She looked so colorful with her purple fleece jacket, overlapping shirts of pink and yellow, and Kelly-green leggings. I bet Tyler would have approved of her heavy eye makeup. I was too timid to try all the colors of her clothing. Most of what I owned was like the black jeans and black sweater I was wearing. I did always try to add some color with something from my aunt's stash of knitted and crocheted accessories. I'd gone a little bolder than usual today and pinned a grouping of bright-colored crocheted flowers on the sweater. Crystal glanced at them and gave me a nod of approval.

When they were situated, Crystal put a bunch of small plastic bags in the middle of the table as I spoke to the group. "We figured by now you might want a break from working on the switched projects." Then I turned it over to Crystal.

"I brought kits with assorted projects," she said, picking up a handful. "They're mostly crochet and for quick items." They came with everything needed to make a small project, with a sheet inside the clear bag that had a photo of the finished item and instructions. They all began to shuffle through them.

"These will be perfect for me," Suzy! said, showing a photo of a pair of hand warmers. "It leaves my fingers free to text." She caught herself. "Not that I'm thinking about using my phone. I really don't have a problem. My son was making a problem out of nothing." She had finally followed Hanna's advice and kept the phone out of sight during the workshop.

Crystal held up two kits for John. "These are the most unisex." One was for a washcloth and one for a brown-toned cup huggie. He half-heartedly took the huggie kit.

"I'll keep it in my office to remind me of this," he said with a sigh. By now I'd seen him knitting enough to make it clear he knew how, but there was no passion in how he worked his needles.

She told him it was made with crochet and started to give him a lesson.

Vonda went to take two of the same kits for scrunchies, but Yolanda objected and said she wanted to pick her own. The funny thing was she picked a scrunchie kit, but a different one than her sister had chosen.

Fern grabbed a summer-weight beanie kit.

"This would be perfect for my niece," Hanna said, showing the bag holding a kit for a different style of scrunchie in sparkly silver. "My sister would have loved these." She picked up a sample that Crystal had brought and put it on her wrist like a bracelet. "She used to always have one ready for Tracey."

"I bet your sister wouldn't have minded if you'd picked out kits for both of you," Vonda said, giving her sister an annoyed stare.

Hanna's face grew sad. "Actually, she would have been just like Yolanda. She went her own way, no matter what I said."

"I'm so sorry," Yolanda said, realizing from the past tense that Hanna's sister must have died.

Hanna took a breath and forced her mouth into a wan smile. "I didn't mean to bring down the group. These look like fun to make." She pulled out a piece of gum and began looking through the supplies in the bag.

Daisy was hesitating over two kits in her hand. "I think I'll go for the silver scrunchies, too. I use them a lot," she said, giving her long honey blond hair a shake.

Crystal took a few minutes to demonstrate how to start the scrunchies and went back to helping John.

Fern was able to work on the beanie on her own. I grabbed one of the scrunchie kits. I used them all the time and thought it would be neat to have one that I made. Once everyone was working, Daisy brought up the Jordan group and the comment Lyla had made to me.

"It seemed a little extreme," I said, then realized the others didn't know what we were talking about, so I explained that the Jordan people had been barred from getting drinks or snacks from the café and I'd helped them get around it by buying the stuff for them. "I think she was out of place with her comment. I've been going along with letting them run things, but that was really pushing it. I should have said something then." I thought of how she'd glared at me in front of some of my people. "I'm going to have a conversation with her," I said.

"That woman better look out—she'll pin her to the wall," Crystal said. "Not only did Casey work for a PI, but she's like our local Miss Marple—only with more pizzazz."

"I don't know about that," I said, blushing.

"You go, girl," Fern said. "But I have to say that Jordan really knows how to work the crowd.

We all turned to her in interest as she admitted slipping into the back to hear his morning pitch. "I didn't stay very long. I was afraid his security people would out me."

As long as they were talking about his program, I told them about what Sammy had taken me through. "It's like their graduation, I guess."

"Did you say there are actually live snakes?" Daisy asked, incredulous.

"That's what I heard. I guess Jordan wants something real with all the fake things and projections. Though there's really no danger since they will be in enclosed cases."

"Do you think programs like that really work?" Hanna asked.

I told them about Diana and how she kept coming back. "She said she always leaves feeling empowered, but that it fades," I said.

Crystal added her take as she got up to leave. "The one sure winner in all of this is Jordan. He gets to feed off the crowd and go home with a nice payday." The workshop time was officially up, but no one else seemed in a hurry to leave.

"And what about that woman who isn't going home?" Daisy said. "It makes you realize those challenges of his have risk."

"But isn't that what makes accomplishing them meaningful?" John asked.

"I thought the point was that you were supposed to overcome your fear in a safe environment. That the risk was in your mind," Hanna said.

"All I know is that I like our weekend a lot better," Fern said and they all agreed, particularly when I reminded them of our upcoming activities—lunch at the Blue Door followed by the yarn tasting at Cadbury Yarn.

"I don't know about the rest of you, but I want to change before our outing," Hanna said, getting up to go. Crystal followed her out. It took the rest of them a little longer to pack up their stuff and then we all agreed to meet outside the Lodge in an hour.

I rushed home and made a batch of cookies and gave Julius his treat.

The large metal bell near the dining hall was ringing, announcing lunch for the Jordan group as I came back down the driveway. The van was already waiting, and I went to reconfirm the timing of everything when I sensed someone next to me.

"I don't even want to know where your people are having lunch or what they're eating," Diana said with a wistful smile. "I'm just finding it so much harder this time." She showed me her schedule, which had the menu for lunch. "They didn't even try to make it sound appealing." I read it over and saw her point. All it said was *Bean soup and slice of wheat bread*. "No reason to rush for that," she said. She seemed particularly perturbed. "I can't even depend on the snacks I brought with me. Lyla saw me eating a bag of nuts and confiscated it."

"I can't say I'm a fan of the woman," I said. "In fact, I plan to have a little talk with her when we come back." I asked Diana about the afternoon schedule. "Do you know where I'll be able to find her?"

"Probably nowhere until this evening. She's the one who handles the hot box challenge and I heard she does some kind of mental preparation first." She took a deep breath. "I shouldn't be complaining about the food. It's all about the challenges and this time I'm doing them instead of watching someone else do them." She put up her hands in a triumphant mode. "This time it's going to stick."

. . .

Lucinda greeted each member of my group by name as she took them to the sunporch. I looked them over to check their mood. John seemed in better spirits. Vonda and Yolanda had brought their scrunchie projects and had their heads together over them. Daisy was writing something down. Fern was talking to Hanna, more like talking at Hanna, who seemed distracted. Suzy! had made a big point of not having her phone in her hand as she walked in the restaurant and now seemed to be reading a paperback. It seemed a little odd and when I walked around the table I saw she had her phone between the pages.

I hung with Lucinda while they ate. "I don't know why you don't sit down with them," my friend said, and then she got a knowing smile. "I get it. You're supposed to be in charge, not *in* the group." Then she insisted on setting me up with a table outside and bringing me lunch.

I'd brought her one of Crystal's kits so she could feel part of the retreat. The cup huggie seemed appropriate since she had the restaurant and dealt with a lot of cups. I thought when the retreat was over, we could work on the projects together. Wasn't that what best friends did?

And having a best friend meant that I'd put down some roots. Much as I liked to think I could change my mind and leave Cadbury without a backward glance, I suspected that it wasn't true. All my excuses to Dane about keeping a distance in our relationship because I might take up my mother on her offer for cooking school in Paris or detective school seemed pretty weak. As he'd pointed out I had a house, a business, and friends. Whether I acknowledged it or not, I'd become a Cadburian. If I left, I might be the one with the broken heart.

A yarn tasting had become a regular part of the retreats I put on. As much as the retreats were getaways, everyone seemed to enjoy being back in the outside world for a while. This group had already spent a lot of time off the grounds and out of Jordan's sight. I was glad that they seemed enthused about going to the yarn store.

When lunch was done, we walked over to Cadbury Yarn. It was on a side street and housed in an appealing bungalow. A brightly colored windsock flapped in the breeze on the front porch as I held the door open for them to file in. Crystal was waiting inside and took them through to a room in the back that once had been used for dining. It still had an oval wood table, but it was set up with a selection of yarns to try and an assortment of needles and hooks.

Once they were all situated around the table, Gwen came in and greeted them. Even after all this time, the difference between Gwen and Crystal was astounding. I doubt anyone in the group realized they were mother and daughter. Crystal was all colors and earrings that didn't match, while her mother was dressed in neutral tones and a utilitarian style. Gwen was describing the yarns set out on the table while Crystal and I hung back.

"What a wonderful idea," Fern said. "I have all kinds of yarn I've bought because I liked the way it looked, but when I tried using it, it was a nightmare." She smiled at the group. "And it's still sitting in my stash."

Once she broke the ice with her comment, I saw they were all nodding—except John, who seemed unconcerned. I wondered if he'd been so lucky as to never encounter yarn that looked pretty but had a texture that made getting needles through it difficult, or if he didn't want to admit it. Maybe he had a whole closet of yarn skeletons, with half-finished projects that had gone wrong and he'd tossed aside. It was hard to tell with him. He definitely knew how to knit and Crystal had showed him how to crochet, but he seemed half-hearted about the whole yarn craft thing. I had to find a way to bring up that Megan had worked for Winkleman Brothers Studio and see his reaction.

There was no reason to hover over them, so once they started grabbing for the yarn and tools, Crystal and I left them to it. We went to a table in another part of the shop. She had laid out some books with paracord patterns and some rolls of the colorful nylon cord along with a couple of lighters.

"I thought we could make a few, so we'd have it down when we have to teach his people to make them. I found an easy pattern that doesn't need clasps and it's adjustable, so one size fits all. I thought we'd go with type two paracord—it holds up to four hundred pounds."

"That should cover it," I said.

We both took lengths of the cord and she showed me how to begin. She went on to explain that she'd figured a basic size to make them and that it took about a foot of the cord to make an inch of the bracelet. She and Cory would cut the lengths of cord later and print up the basic instructions. At the mention of Cory's name, her expression darkened.

"Those Jordan people are a real problem," she said. "A woman was struggling with her suitcase when one of the wheels fell off and Cory went to help her. That woman with the white hair swooped in and told him to stay out of it." She looked at me. "He's such a good kid. All he wanted to do was help and she gave him a lecture that their people were supposed to be self-sufficient and solve their own problems."

"I'm not a fan of hers either," I said. I told her about my last encounter with her.

"I know that I've stayed out of the running of Vista Del Mar, but when the Delacorte sisters get back, I'm going to have a talk with them. Kevin St. John outdid himself this time. I know he was desperate to get a big-name guru type to use the hotel and conference center, but he never should have given Jordan carte blanche to take over the whole place. There was no reason for that woman to be so nasty to my son."

"The only explanation I can offer is that everything I've heard or seen about her is that she is an absolute fanatic. The kind who would snap in half if she had to bend." I considered if I should share my other thoughts about her and figured why not. "She really didn't like the woman who died. I don't know if it was personal as much as she thought she didn't belong working for Jordan."

"I bet that woman views herself as his work-wife. Rixx didn't have a work-wife—he had a road manager. Work-wife, road manager," she said with a shrug. "Their work is the same. Take care of the dirty work. That's who took care of firing band members and unloading clinging groupies. The road manager might have been the one to do the dirty work, but Rixx was always behind it."

"I get it. You're saying that Jordan might have told Lyla to get rid of Megan. Do you think he would have specified killing her?" I asked.

"Probably not. They could have thought the mushrooms would just make her sick enough to leave."

I was struggling with the bracelet until I got the pattern down, then it was just repetitious. "That's possible. Fern said something about people getting sick who ate poison mushrooms, but then recovering. The other staff people seemed to regard Megan as a bubblehead who wasn't really paying attention to anything, so the idea of her picking up bad mushrooms would seem possible. The only thing is Lyla Konker keeps insisting she never makes mistakes and I know the bag was examined by her."

Crystal smiled. "It could be a cover-up and she could simply be telling the truth. She didn't make a mistake because the mushrooms in the bag were deliberate."

"Interesting thought," I said. I finished with the bracelet and Crystal had me do another. She showed me how to use the lighter to melt the ends together. I was impressed with my achievement and slid them on my wrist.

I'd known Crystal for a while, but it was only recently that we'd started hanging out more. I'd attributed it to the fact that I was an outsider and she was a native Cadburian and that we didn't really have much in common other than we were both about the same age. She was divorced with two teenage kids, and I just had me to worry about.

She knew all about the situation with Dane. "This is it—you're going to seal the deal with your hot cop neighbor," she said with a grin.

My expression flattened and I let out a sigh. "I just want to be done with it," I said.

She laughed and started singing the Rod Steward song "Tonight's the Night." I threw up my hands. Of course, I was being ridiculous.

Chapter Nineteen

Everyone was in good spirits when the yarn tasting ended. My group had thoroughly enjoyed it and Gwen was pleased to ring up their purchases. Crystal and I had finalized the details for the next day when we had to help the Jordan people make their bracelets. I was actually glad it was just the Elite group of thirty or so people instead of the hoard. I looked down at my two bracelets with pride.

Since I had planned for my group to have free time until our late afternoon workshop, I asked them if they'd like to spend some time looking around the downtown area of Cadbury. It seemed like a good way to keep them out of the way of the Jordan group, too. No surprise they all agreed, and we set up a time to meet.

Crystal's teasing snapped me out of how whiny I sounded and I realized Dane was the one putting in all the effort with candles and rose petals. The least I could do was add something to the evening. He had an aversion to alcohol because of his mother's problem, so wine was out. I considered some lingerie, but all that barely-there stuff wasn't me and I was afraid Dane would respond the same way he did to my attempts at flirting and end up laughing. What about chocolate? It was supposed to be an aphrodisiac, right? Then I came up with one better—chocolate fondue. I picked up a set and the right kind of chocolate along with sweet treats to dip in it. I still had time to spare and went to Maggie's coffee place.

The air seemed permeated with the pungent scent of coffee both from the brewing of it and from the burlap bags that had held the roasted beans and now decorated the dark red walls.

I did a quick check of the counter and saw that the basket she used to display my muffins, or this time biscuits in a cup, was empty, which meant that they were a hit. Maggie waved at me and started to make me a double cappuccino without me even having to ask. As always, she was wearing a bit of red. It was her way to counteract all the sadness of losing family members she'd endured. She pointed to an empty table, meaning that she'd bring it over when it was ready.

With all that had gone on with this retreat, it was nice to have a few minutes to myself.

Maggie brought the coffee drink over and I thought she was going to join me, but some people came through the door and she went back to the counter to deal with them.

I was admiring the heart Maggie had swirled in the milk foam when I sensed someone nearing the table. I looked up, and even with the baseball cap and the man next to him partially obscuring my view, there was no mistaking it was Jordan. "Are you following me?" he snapped.

"More likely you're following me," I countered. "Since I was here first." I'd put up with enough deferring to him at Vista Del Mar. As far as I was concerned, we were on equal footing here. I even dared to offer joining me at my table.

"No," he snapped when the words were barely out of my mouth. "You don't know who is watching and who will make it seem it's something that it's not." His muscly assistant escorted him to a table in the corner, which because the place was so small wasn't far from mine. The assistant waited until Jordan sat and then gave me a warning look before he went back to the counter to order their drinks.

"Wow, you sound a little paranoid," I said. The assistant set a cup of something in front of Jordan and then took his own drink to a nearby table where he could keep a watch on things. Probably keep a watch on me, I thought, forcing my eyes not to roll at the absurdity of thinking I might be some kind of threat.

"What I do comes with a price. People always want something from me, or at the very least to get close to me."

I nodded with understanding. "So that's why you're here. To get away from your people."

There was a shadow over his face, but I could just make out the slightly annoyed twist of his mouth. I got a look at his outfit, which was meant as a disguise. No tight jeans and work shirt this time. He was wearing old jeans and a graphic T-shirt. Between that and the baseball cap he blended in with the crowd.

"I give them one hundred percent when I'm with them, but I need to get away, to refresh, regroup."

"And have some coffee," I said, eyeing his cup. The assistant dropped off a piece of cake with a fork stuck in it. "I heard you were on a juice fast for the whole weekend."

He started defending himself, saying that they were there on a mission that required them to adjust their relationship with food and things like sugar and caffeine, but he was past all that and had to replenish his core energy before the Saturday evening event.

"You've certainly kept it quiet about your staff member who died," I said. "It's amazing how you managed to keep on going as if nothing had happened."

He started rubbing his forehead and the assistant jumped up and went to stand between the tables to protect him, but Jordan waved him away.

"What exactly did you hear?" he said, leaning toward me, which implied a sense of urgency.

"That she ate a poison mushroom," I said.

He let out a frustrated grunt. "What we said was that it was food poisoning."

"I suppose technically that's correct. She was poisoned by some food she ate." I took a sip of my cappuccino and looked directly at him. "But how could that have happened since I understand the woman on your staff who checked the bags is an expert?"

"It happened," he snapped. "Leave it at that." He grew wary. "I've seen you nosing around my people, asking questions. The manager said you fancied yourself some kind of PI."

"I'll have you know that I worked for a top-flight private investigator in Chicago. And we still talk to brainstorm." It was a stretch. I'm not sure what the definition of top-flight private investigator was, but I doubted that it meant Frank. And I'd only worked for him for two weeks. I also didn't mention that the brainstorming was usually about help I needed.

I thought he was going to drop it, but he went on. "I can tell you there is nothing to investigate about what happened to Megan. It was just a mistake. You didn't know her, but she was quite capable of making mistakes."

"Then why did you keep her on your staff?" I asked.

"I don't have to explain that to you. I believe in what I do. I help a lot of people. That's what's important." The assistant got up and stood over me.

"It looks like you finished your drink," the man said, looking toward the door.

"I must have hit a sensitive spot," I said, shooting a look back at Jordan. It seemed like a good exit line, so as much as I wanted to defy his bodyguard, I gathered up my packages and went toward the front.

As I went to wave goodbye to Maggie, I noticed Daisy lurking in the shadow by the entrance. "Were you looking for me?" I said. The tall woman seemed a little disconcerted but joined me as I went out the door.

There was still some time before the group was to meet and Daisy seemed at loose ends, so I took her to a cat rescue place that had an area where you could play with the cats. It was hard to pull ourselves away when it was time to go.

The rest of them were already at our meeting spot when we arrived. John had a bag from the yarn store, but I had the feeling he'd bought something more out of a sense of obligation than real desire. He looked tense and I thought back to his admission of overusing marijuana as a stress reliever. But what could be causing him stress here? Maybe it had something to do with Megan?

Yolanda and Vonda seemed to be fussing about something. Yolanda held up a T-shirt with *Cadbury by the Sea* with a sun setting in the water and tried to push it on her sister, who resisted, saying it wasn't her style. I was so worried that Suzy! was going to be trouble, but she was really one-dimensional—all about her relationship with her phone. I recognized the brochure Hanna was looking at from the local natural history museum by the profusion of monarch butterflies on the cover. Fern had found a ledge to sit on and had opened the kit she'd bought at Cadbury Yarn and her needles. We did a scenic loop through town, passing the statue of the monarch butterfly again and made a brief stop at the lighthouse.

The glow of the pleasant afternoon came to an abrupt halt as the van pulled into the Vista Del Mar driveway. The lights were flashing on an ambulance next to the Lodge and there seemed to be police cruisers everywhere.

Chapter Twenty

"Maybe we shouldn't go in," Suzy! yelped. "Who knows what's going on." By now the van had maneuvered around the police cruisers and stopped in a small parking lot away from the trouble. No one made a move to get up.

"It has nothing to do with us," Hanna said. "It's that other retreat. No surprise there's another problem. They're just so irresponsible." She stood up and announced she was getting off. John echoed her sentiment and made a move to exit as well. The rest of them followed, with Daisy taking up the rear. She seemed to be grabbing some photos of all the vehicles outside.

"I'll take everybody back to the Sand and Sea building while you find out what's going on," John said. I was glad to let him take charge and the group followed behind him.

I went inside the Lodge and found a chaotic scene. Lieutenant Borgnine was huddled with Kevin St. John and Cloris in front of the registration counter. Tyler and BB were holding the door open on the opposite side of the building, telling their people there was a gathering on the beach and that Jordan was breaking from his meditation time and would speak to them.

I slipped back outside unnoticed, hoping to find out what had happened. I followed the paved pathway to the dining hall. It seemed desolate and I continued on the path to Hummingbird Hall. It was empty as well, but I heard voices coming from the wooded area beyond it. As I got closer, I saw that several cops were hanging around the wooden building I'd peeked in earlier.

I recognized one of the cops who had teased Dane and me when he'd caught us on our first date. I thought that qualified us as acquaintances. "Hey, how's it going?" I said with a greeting nod. I turned toward the small structure. "Did something happen?"

"Those Jordan people," the cop said, shaking his head. "First it was that woman who ate the poisoned mushroom and now somebody got cooked."

"Cooked?" I said, incredulous.

He pointed at the portable building. "One of their staff stayed in there too long," he said, shaking his head. "Way too long."

I remembered that the hot box was Lyla's thing and I asked him if he'd seen the person.

He shook his head again and let out his breath. "You see a lot as a cop, but I didn't expect to see her. She was all red like a boiled lobster except for the white hair."

I was stunned to realize it was Lyla. What could have happened? I made a move to get a closer look and the cop pointed out the yellow tape before suggesting that I move along.

Apparently Tyler, BB and Jordan were successful at rounding up their people and herding them out of the way, because the Lodge was deserted when I went back inside. Even the group at the front were gone, for the moment. As I walked across the large open space cutting through to the door by the driveway, Lieutenant Borgnine came through the door to the business area. It seemed like he made a grumbling sound as he called my name.

"I had nothing to do with what happened," I said, putting my hands up in a posture of innocence. It was kind of a lame joke and fell flat.

"Whatever," he said impatiently. "I'd like to talk to you."

The feeling was actually mutual because I wanted to find out what he knew. I suggested we sit in the seating area, but I suppose that seemed too friendly and he insisted we could stand. He looked at his notes. "I understand you had a confrontation with Lyla Konker," he said. "What was it about?"

"You're just trying to get some background on her, right?" I said. He made no response to my question. I told him about the coffee business and that she'd been upset about it. I repeated that she said she was going to tell on me. I thought he would understand how absurd her comment was, but instead he furrowed his brow and looked at me intently.

"That sounds like it could have been a threat," he said.

I ignored his comment and instead tried pumping him for information. "I know she's dead," I said. "Your cops made it sound like she stayed too long in the sauna." I figured that if I seemed to know what happened already, he might be more likely to give away some details.

I noticed he was massaging his temple. He was going to blame his headache on me. "Do you want some aspirin?" I asked, hoping to smooth things over.

"I have my own," he said. "Just tell me what you know about the victim. Did she tell you anything about going into the sauna?"

"The Jordan people probably know a lot more than I do," I said.

"Maybe, but they're not talking," he grumbled, then realized he'd made a mistake in admitting that. "I know how you are." He paused and I figured he was going to say something negative, like that I fancied myself as a PI, but he seemed to come to an agreement with himself. "You notice a lot of things other people might miss."

What? Had he almost given me a compliment, or at least recognized my skill?

That was all it took and I let loose on everything I knew about Lyla. She seemed to be at a higher level than the rest of the staff and I threw in the work-wife thing. "She had taken it upon herself to be responsible for the integrity of the retreats. Did I mention that she was fanatical?" Borgnine nodded. "I heard she was doing some preparation for the hot box challenge that was supposed to take place today." Now that I'd offered him what I knew, I hoped he'd answer some questions. "Who found her?"

He hesitated for a moment and then surprised me by starting to talk. "There was supposed to be an event in the sauna. The group went there this afternoon and found the victim in a fetal position on the floor. The paramedics didn't even attempt to revive her. It was clearly too late for that."

"It sounds like she stayed in there too long. You'd think she would have known better though," I said.

"People do crazy stuff," he said. "She was known for pushing things to extremes." I started to ask him how he knew that since he'd said that the Jordan people weren't talking.

"Jordan wasn't on the grounds when we got here. We got in touch with Bethany Lowe, Jordan's wife. She handles the business end of the retreats. She's the one who said that the victim went to extremes."

I asked about Jordan's wife, but all I got out of the lieutenant was that she didn't attend the retreats.

• • •

"Well?" Suzy! said anxiously as I walked into the lobby of the Sand and Sea building. "I think we should pack up our things and get out of here." She glanced around at the group. They had pulled the chairs together and were huddled in front of the fire.

"Why don't we give Casey a chance to explain," Daisy said, turning to me expectantly.

"There's no need to panic," I began. "What happened has nothing to do with Vista Del Mar. It actually occurred in a piece of equipment that the Jordan people brought in." I was going to leave it at that, but it didn't cut it and they demanded more details.

Before I'd parted company with the lieutenant, he'd said that most likely Lyla's death would be chalked up as an accident, as it seemed the mushroom poisoning would be. We both agreed that the Jordan people were certainly guilty of bad judgment. I had considered telling Borgnine about my thoughts that Lyla might have planted the poison mushrooms in Megan's bag, but it seemed a moot point now so I said nothing.

I explained the concept of the hot box challenge to my group and that it was assumed that Lyla had gone in for her own personal session and stayed in too long.

"A sauna," Suzy! said with disgust. "I don't understand why anyone would go in one of those. Isn't it just inviting yourself to be cooked?"

"A lot of people find them therapeutic," Fern said.

I suggested we move to our meeting room, thinking it would get their minds off of what had happened. I was relieved that it was all set up, and as they helped themselves to drinks and the cookies I'd made earlier, the conversation continued.

"I like a good steam," John said.

"All of it sounds bad to me," Yolanda said, her mouth curled in distaste.

"Dry heat is easier to tolerate," Hanna said. "Remember, I'm a science teacher. Personally, I'm with Yolanda and neither one appeals to me." She had a teacherly way of explaining something about how dry heat didn't easily transfer to the body. She brought up weather and how it was the humidity that made heat so unbearable. I was hoping someone would come to the meeting room next door so I could find out if there'd been any changes to the Jordan seminar.

They had all taken out projects to work on and seemed to be happy to be in the cocoon of our room. It had become a real hodgepodge. Some of them had finished with the switched projects and laid out the completed items on the table to be admired. Some were still working on them, and a couple had moved on to work on the kits they'd gotten from Crystal.

I heard someone come into the room next door, and while they were all busy, slipped in there. Tyler was sprawled in a chair staring at the ceiling. He looked in my direction as I came in the room. "Can I hit on you for a cup of coffee?" he said. "I really need it after this afternoon."

I almost said something about at least this time there wouldn't be a scolding from Lyla, but I caught myself and just nodded as an answer.

My group was so busy with their yarn work that they didn't even notice when I grabbed the coffee doctored with cream and sugar along with a few of the cookies.

Tyler took a generous sip of the coffee and let out an instant groan of pleasure. He leaned back in the chair and put his feet back up.

"Where is everybody?" I asked.

"Jordan is doing a session with them at the beach. Everything got thrown to the wind after what happened," he said.

"Did something happen? My group was gone all afternoon," I said. I might not be good at flirting, but I was good at feigning a dumb expression. Tyler instantly sat forward, seeming anxious to share.

"You remember the woman with that fabulous white hair," he began. "She's dead." He stopped and checked the area. "We're not supposed to talk about it. But how can you keep it in?" He shrugged. "All I can figure is that Lyla must have overdone it. I would have thought she would know her limits, but she was always pushing the envelope. The rest of us just help with the challenges, but she insisted on doing the time in the sauna with the group and doing a meditation cleanse in there preparing for it. No one could say that she didn't practice what she preached," he said.

"I had no idea there was anything wrong when I took the Elite Jordanaires to the wood building," he went on. "At first I thought it was empty. I just saw the benches around the hot rock pit." He stopped and fanned his face with his hand. "I hope I never see anything like it again." He covered his emotion by drinking more of the coffee.

"What happens now?" I asked, realizing he couldn't handle saying anything more about his experience. My question seemed to offer him the out he needed and he heaved a sigh.

"Needless to say, the Hot Box Detox is out for this retreat," he said. "But Jordan isn't missing a beat. The show must go on. Right now, he's doing a pitch for the groups dealing with vagaries of life and going on despite setbacks. We tried to get Jordan to change the dinner from bean stew to ordered-in pizzas, but he wouldn't go for it. He said Lyla would want things to go on as planned. He's right about that. If something had happened to Jordan, she would have stepped in his place and gone on with the program. So it's on with the spirit dancing."

"What's that?" I asked.

"Jordan made it up and calls it Dance Out Your Demons. Spirit dancing is my name for it. Basically, loud music, low lights and an order to dance out your emotions. It'll end with a bonfire and cups of herbal tea. Then tomorrow the Elite group will go through the grand finale." He started to explain what it was and I told him I had seen it courtesy of Sammy.

"The magician," Tyler said with a smile. "He's a good guy and taught me a card trick. But Jordan leaves the final arrangement up to his assistants." I heard noise coming from my room and excused myself.

Kevin St. John was standing in the room with Cloris right behind. Crystal had come in while I was gone and was by the table. The manager looked as out of place as always in his dark suit. His moon-shaped face was contorted and I tensed, expecting that he was there to talk to me, but he totally bypassed me and went up to Crystal, pulling her aside.

Whatever was going on belonged out of the earshot of my group, and though I tried to move them outside, Kevin St. John wouldn't move. After everything that had happened, was there any point to keeping anything from them?

"I talked to the Delacorte sisters on their cruise," he said, seeming very agitated. "They wanted me to talk to you."

Crystal seemed stunned. It seemed as if Kevin St. John had chosen to ignore that she was part of the Delacorte family. This was the first time he was acknowledging it.

I was surprised too, but figured he had a motive. He quickly filled in Crystal about Lyla and she shuddered.

"I wanted to let you know that the sauna has been shut down and I tried to get Jordan to shut down the last challenge he has for tomorrow." He took an exasperated breath. "The problem is that he has it in writing that his retreat can set up their challenges without any approval from us," he said. "After what happened with the sauna, I thought he would agree, but he's adamant that he has the right to do it and he mentioned lawsuits." He shook his head in disbelief. "The foraging went wrong, the sauna malfunctioned, you'd think he wouldn't want to take any more chances. He said the two victims were staff people and what happened to them was their own fault." He looked to Crystal as if expecting an answer.

Crystal didn't seem to know what to do with the information and she turned to me. "What do you think?"

I couldn't believe that I was going to stand up for Jordan, but it seemed to be the only way to keep the peace. "The retreat is almost over and it's probably not realistic to shut it down. I've seen the challenge for tomorrow." I explained to all that my friend Sammy had helped putting it together and that it was located on the ground floor of Hummingbird Hall. "It might be upsetting if you have certain phobias, but there's no real danger. Everything is fake, you know, like rubber spiders and such." I wondered if I should leave it at that but felt like I had to offer all the information. "Apparently, Jordan wanted it to have some sense of a threat, so there will be a couple of rattlesnakes along with the rubber ones, but the real ones will be sealed in a glass enclosure."

At the word *rattlesnake*, Kevin St. John's eyes shot open even wider. "Rattlesnakes," he repeated. "Where are they now?"

I shrugged. "Sammy didn't say, but I'm guessing somewhere Jordan can keep an eye on them."

"If Casey says it's safe, I'm sure it is. Snakes in a glass case can't hurt anybody," Crystal said.

"Okay, if it ever comes up, I have your okay," Kevin St. John said to Crystal, and she nodded her agreement. He glared at Cloris.

"You heard her say it's okay, so if anything goes wrong, I tried to stop it," he said.

Then he waved for Cloris to follow him and they left the room.

"What was that about?" John asked, looking at Crystal with new interest. She tried to brush it off and put it on me.

I realized that my group didn't know the Delacorte sisters or that they were like the local royalty, owning lots and lots of property, including Vista Del Mar. I hated those stories where someone started telling convoluted details about people that you didn't know. I was sure their eyes would glaze over if I began telling them about the sisters and their late brother, his women and his will. So I just said that Crystal was part of the family that owned the hotel and conference center.

"A silent member," she said. It took a few minutes for the mood to be restored, but finally the group went back to working. I think Crystal was glad when the time was up and she could leave.

The group hung around for a little while after Crystal left. I apologized for the intrusion the Jordan retreat had turned out to be.

"Don't feel bad," Fern said. "It's added a lot of drama. Something is always happening with those people."

"That's the truth," Daisy said. "There's a lot more going on than their website promises."

Vonda seemed troubled. "Two people died and nobody seems to care. It's just go on with the show."

"It makes you wonder how many other accidents have gotten swept under the rug," Hanna said. "I can't believe they will be able to keep putting on these retreats."

"There's nobody to really stop them," I said and told them what Frank had said. "It's a billion-dollar industry with no oversight."

"Somebody should do something to change that," Suzy! said. She looked at John. "You seem to be somebody important. Maybe you can do something."

John let out a tired sigh. "I didn't come here to take up a crusade.

I'm sorry about what happened, but Jordan and all of it is really not my business."

Was this the moment to mention that Megan had worked at Winkleman Brothers Studio? It did seem like a non sequitur, but I went ahead with it anyway. "Did you know that the woman who ate the mushrooms worked at Winkleman Brothers?" I said, looking directly at John. I was curious about his reaction as well as his answer.

His expression froze for a moment, then it was as if he was considering his answer. Finally, he got a kind of shrugging-it-off look. "Winkleman Brothers is a big place. I don't know everybody who works there." Then he turned the tables on me. "Do you know what she did?" he asked.

"I heard she wanted to be a producer," I said.

"She was probably a production assistant then," he said. "It's doubtful our paths would have crossed." I thought about his answer, which was really a nonanswer. He never said if he knew her or not. Was that just the way executives handled things or was he hiding something?

"Haven't we heard enough about those Jordan people?" Yolanda said. "I'm sorry for what happened and all, but . . ."

"She's right," Daisy said. "How about we get some wine—my treat." They all nodded their assent and filed out, heading for the café. Nobody even gave John a dirty look.

I started to do my usual straightening. They'd all left their tote bags, so I had to work around them gathering up bits of yarn and the stray paper cup.

"I heard this is the place to snag a cup of coffee," Diana said, stopping in the doorway. I was no longer worried about Jordan finding out that his people were cheating with my help, since I'd caught him with coffee and a piece of cake.

I shook the pot. "There's a little left," I said. "Help yourself."

She had become my eyes and ears into the Jordan retreat and I was curious what she would say about the latest happening.

"I can't say I was exactly looking forward to spending an hour in the hot box. It's that way with all the challenges. You worry about them, but then the euphoria when you've accomplished them makes it all worthwhile," she said.

"What did Jordan say about what happened?" I asked.

"He did a whole speech about Lyla and her passion. Then he said it must have been her time to join the angels and that we should all wish her well."

"So, he was saying that she died of natural causes?" I said.

"He didn't exactly explain or go into detail about what happened." Diana had made herself a cup of coffee, and like the others added copious amounts of cream and sugar. "I went by the little building around lunchtime just to get an idea what it looked like and all." She stirred the coffee and took a long sip. "But when I tried to look in the window on the door, I saw she was in there with her back to the door. We'd been told that she was doing a meditation preparation for our challenge so I didn't want to disturb her." She drank some more coffee. "You'd think she would have known when to leave."

I asked her how the people felt about Lyla. "She didn't have Jordan's magic. He talks to you and you get pumped up. Her spiel seemed to be all about needing to overcome your weakness. It always felt like scolding."

"Are you worried about the final challenge?" I asked.

"You mean the escape room thing," she said and shrugged. "I watched others go through it at the past retreats. I'm a little nervous about going through the room with the collapsing walls, but when I pop out at the end and get all the applause it will make up for it." The bell was ringing outside the dining hall, which I now realized they used for more than announcing meals. "Time for another Jordan talk," she said, getting up.

I urged her to take a couple of cookies and she gratefully accepted. "May she rest in peace, but I'm glad there's no chance Lyla is going to pop up and scold me."

Chapter Twenty-one

When I went outside, the cloud layer was thin enough to have a golden hue as the afternoon faded. The ambulance was long gone and any police cars still there were hidden. It was a little unsettling how quickly everything had returned to normal. But what happened was not my business. I was more concerned about the guilt I felt for ducking out on my group for my date with Dane.

Since the café was off-limits to the Jordan people, I didn't see how he'd fuss about my group having their meals in there for the rest of the retreat. Tag was delivering dinner, so I knew it wouldn't matter if he got there before I did. He would probably be glad to be able to do things his way without my interference.

I could tell that Sammy was in the guesthouse. The window was open and he was practicing the patter he did with his illusions. Julius was sitting in the kitchen window giving me a stare. I was sure he was probably thinking how could I have left him all day without any stink fish snacks.

He was swirling between my legs a moment after I opened the door. Then came the complaining meows as he went directly to the refrigerator. He looked up at me and gave a long stare and I wondered if he'd picked up the scent of the cats I'd played with at the rescue place.

I barely had a chance to set the tin down before he let out another meow. This one sounded scolding. My landline rang in the midst of all this.

I saw that it was Frank and jammed the phone between my ear and shoulder so I could multitask.

"You're not going to believe it," I said to Frank after we got out our hellos. "Someone else at the Jordan retreat died." While I was speaking, I was dealing with the odorous food the cat adored. The only way I could stand the stench was by holding my nose.

"You sound funny," Frank said.

"I was hoping you wouldn't notice."

He let out a chortle. "I'm a detective. It's my job to notice." I detoured from talking about Lyla and explained the cat food situation.

"You're a softie," Frank said. "My cat eats what I give him."

"You have a cat?" I said, surprised. "You never mentioned it." I started asking what it looked like and how long he'd had it. I had a vision of him pulling off a piece of sub sandwich and offering it to the cat. Did he try to share his doughnuts with the cat, too? I'd done a bunch of research on cats' dietary needs and I prepared to give him a lecture on their need for tasty protein.

"It didn't come up in conversation," he said.

I suddenly wondered what else he had that he hadn't mentioned, like a wife, or maybe an ex. What about kids? Was there a Frank, Jr. somewhere? "What's the cat's name?" I asked, expecting something like Rocky or Magnum. I heard his chair making noise and the way he was breathing I sensed he was stalling. "I found him when I was on a surveillance. He was a kitten and all alone on a cold night. What kind of person could ignore that? I brought him into the van. I'm sure it was just because he was so cold, but he climbed into my lap. I pulled off some meat from my sub and he chowed it right down and then he went to sleep."

"I knew you're feeding him sub sandwiches and doughnuts."

Frank let out a laugh. "What kind of pet owner do you think I am? One time I gave him part of my sandwich. C'mon, I wasn't expecting a cat to show up. I said you were a softie because you feed that animal of yours something that stinks. Mine gets that stuff that smells like prime rib, which he loves. You were saying something about another death," he said.

He'd done what I often did. When something got too uncomfortable, I changed the subject. My time was limited with him anyway, even if he'd been the one to make the call, so I told him about Lyla.

"Not a good way to go," he said with an ugh. "What happened?"

"I don't know all the details. Just that the sauna thing was her idea. They called it the hot box and it was supposed to inspire some sort of catharsis. It seems like she was having her own time in it from what I understand. One way or another she stayed in too long."

"Then it was another accident?" Frank said. "Wasn't she connected to the first one?"

"Yes, and I'd had a thought. I know she didn't like the victim and she was the one who checked the bags. She also had access to death cap mushrooms."

"I get it, you think she could have planted them and now she's dead. Feldstein, you should really leave this one alone. It doesn't affect your group."

"I suppose you're right. I did get the heat off Cloris. I can't imagine anyone is going to blame her for what happened to Lyla," I said.

"There's something else," he began hesitantly.

"I know," I said in a singsong voice. "The rule of threes."

"Feldstein, you know I'm not into that airy fairy stuff, but things do seem to happen in threes."

"Frank, you surprise me," I said with a shrug. "Fine, I'll let it go." I paused as I finally dabbed the spoon of pink fish bits into Julius's bowl. "And what did you say your cat's name was?"

"I didn't. And I could lie and tell you his name was Mugger or Sherlock Holmes, but it's Mittens. There, are you satisfied?"

I considered asking him about what else he might have not told me, but decided that any news about Mrs. Frank or Frank, Jr. would have to wait for another time.

● ● ●

I'd promised Yolanda peach cobbler for dessert. I was on automatic pilot as I put it together and slid it in the oven before slicing up more of the cookie dough. I was grateful for the second oven and put a batch of cookies in to bake. My thoughts were going back and forth between getting my group situated and my own event after. Something had clicked and all my second thoughts had melted and I felt a buzz of anticipation. The fondue set was on the kitchen table and I set up a tray of the fruit I'd gotten for dipping. I'd add some of the cookies. I imagined Dane's surprise that I'd finally pulled off a romantic touch as I offered him a strawberry covered in molten chocolate.

I did a little refresh on my appearance, and as soon as the cobbler and cookies were cool enough to handle, packed everything up for their different destinations. I left the platter and fondue set ready to grab when I went to Dane's.

I decided to leave the peach cobbler in the meeting room so there would be no chance that it would disappear like the breakfast casserole. The grounds were quiet, and even after what Frank had said, I decided to have another look around.

I went up the slope toward Hummingbird Hall and the open area where the sauna had been set up. The door to the auditorium was open and the rows of chairs were being moved out for their dance event. I kept going until I got to the wild area beyond. Because of all the trees most of the area was in shadow. The small wood building almost disappeared into the background. As I made a move toward it, someone grabbed my arm.

My heartbeat went through the roof as I tried to pull free, swinging my fist back to sock my grabber.

"Not bad," Dane said. "You almost made contact. You really should come to more of my karate lessons."

"And be teased by all those teenagers," I said, pulling loose.

"They'd probably only do it once. Then they'd get used to the idea we were together and drop it," he said.

"About that," I said. "You've been the one getting the rose petals and candles. I thought I ought to add something." I told him about the fondue set and all the things to dip in the chocolate.

"I like it," he said with a smile. "Feeding each other strawberries dipped in dripping chocolate sounds super hot. Maybe you finally figured out the romantic gesture." Then his smile faded. "About that— I have some bad news." He gestured toward his outfit and I saw that he was in uniform. "We're off for tonight," he said, touching my cheek. "I had the rose petals ready to sprinkle and a bunch of flameless candles. Dinner was all planned." His shoulders dropped in disappointment. "Lieutenant Borgnine called me on duty for an all-nighter to make sure nothing else happens."

"Then that was an official grab," I said as a joke.

He nodded. "You were getting too close to the crime scene." He pointed out the yellow tape across the door of the small building. He put his hands up. "I have to do my duty. Protect the crime scene, even from you."

He looked me in the eye. "So what is it? Are you disappointed or relieved?"

"Disappointed, of course," I said. "Remember, I got the fondue stuff."

"Really?" he said, and I felt my shoulders drop.

"Okay, maybe a little relieved."

He shook his head and rolled his eyes. "You're nuts. Just because we spend a night together doesn't mean anything has to change."

Maybe not for him, but the truth was it was all about me. It was my last stand not to get sucked into something that was scary. I didn't want to think about it or talk about it, so I changed the subject.

"What does Lieutenant Borgnine think happened?" I pointed to the small building and took a step closer.

Dane looked at me and just kept shaking his head. "I know what you're doing and I think I know what's really going on. It isn't about me at all, is it? You're afraid of going all in." He cocked his head, waiting for my response.

"I can't deal with that now," I said. "I have to think about my retreat people and the rest of the weekend. We can talk about that when it's all over."

Dane put up his hands. "Fine, we'll talk about police business. But when your retreaters leave, we'll discuss a rain check."

It was fine with me as long as it let me off the hook for now. "You were going to tell me what Lieutenant Borgnine has found out."

"Most likely, the timer on the sauna malfunctioned and stayed on too long. It's on the outside of the building. The victim was accustomed to putting up with discomfort and forced herself to stay until the timer went off. At some point, the heat must have gotten to be too much and she passed out. " I listened, and from everything I'd heard about Lyla, it sounded right.

"She was pretty rigid and definitely went along with the idea there was no gain without some pain, but still, it's surprising she wouldn't have recognized that she was overheating."

"We'll never know," he said. He noticed that I was still staring at the building. "You know I can't let you check it out," he said.

I nodded in agreement. "But I can go a little closer, can't I?"

He looked at the yellow tape across the doorway. "Okay, but just a few steps."

I crunched through the undergrowth to see if I could get a view through the doorway. Even with all the shadows, I could make out the pit of rocks and a bench. It was as close as Dane was going to let me get and I went to take a step back and caught my foot on something in the dry tall grass. I reached down to release my foot and felt something hard next to my shoe. I instinctively went to see what it was and picked up a small wedge of wood. I was going to drop it back on the ground when I had a thought. I looked at the door of the sauna again. There was a space between the bottom of the door and the frame around it.

"Somebody could have used this to jam the door shut from the outside," I said. "That would change everything."

Chapter Twenty-two

Dane and I had debated what to do with the wedge of wood. I finally got him to promise to let me tell Lieutenant Borgnine about it even if it got me in trouble for touching it. We tried to put it back where I'd found it and I marked the spot with a strand of yarn I had in my pocket.

"Well," Dane said, looking at me. "You have your retreaters to deal with." He sounded resigned that duty called for both of us. I gave him a hug before I went back to deal with my group. They were already waiting outside the café when I came into the Lodge.

"Good, you're here," Suzy! said. "We tried to go inside, but that man with all the hair insisted we stay out here." Of course, she meant Tag. It was funny coming from her since she also had unnaturally thick hair.

With Tag's need for perfection, I had thought I didn't have to worry about anything going wrong. I knew he'd take care of all the details, but it hadn't occurred to me that he wouldn't let them in.

Tag was rearranging the buffet of food and was adjusting a serving spoon. As soon as I stepped into the café, he looked up with his hands positioned to shoo me away.

"Oh, it's you," he said, letting his hands drop. Without me saying anything he started to explain why he hadn't let my people in. "I couldn't have people milling around and checking out what's on the buffet while I was still setting it up." He sounded a little defensive, which I took to be a good sign. At least he had some awareness that he was being extreme. But I also understood his point. It made me think back to what Cloris had said about the foraged meal the Jordan group had had. Hadn't she said it was just supposed to be Lyla checking the bags while she and another of the Jordan staff people brought the bags back and forth? But somehow people had wandered in. And look how that had turned out.

"They can begin," he said, backing away. He certainly got an A for presentation. He'd pushed two of the square tables together and covered them with a snowy white cloth. Instead of the usual covered serving containers, the food was arranged on platters and in colorful bowls. The one hot dish was in a covered china dish on a heated tray. Another table was set up with plates and cloth napkins wrapped around silverware settings. I brought my group in and left to get the cobbler.

They were already eating when I returned. I showed off the dessert before setting it on the end of the array of food. It sent Tag into a frenzy of repositioning the long pan. I was still adjusting to the fact that my plans had changed and my feelings were all over the place. I was relieved and at the same time let down. It did leave me free to spend more time with my people, but no dinner. I decided to break my rule of keeping separate from the group and would eat with them. Tag would have brought an exact amount of food, but I knew that Lucinda planned for contingencies and would have put in extra food. While I went to help myself to the buffet, he was already setting up plates and cutting the cobbler into portions.

It was the first meal I'd actually eaten with my people and they seemed pleased that I'd joined them. I was hoping to keep the conversation about yarn and asked them about what different types they'd tried. They all gave brief answers and then, despite what Yolanda had said before, they went back to talking about the Jordan retreat.

"It seems kind of creepy how the Jordan people seem to be going on like nothing happened, even though two people are dead," Daisy said. "Doesn't that seem strange to you?"

"Jordan is probably thinking about the rest of them. And his bottom line if he were to end things early and have to hand out refunds," John said.

"But they were both accidents, weren't they?" Hanna said.

"You probably know the most about what's going on with that group since Crystal said you were kind of an investigator," Fern said to me. I blushed a little and said it was true that I'd worked for a PI in Chicago.

"It must have been interesting working for a detective. What did you do?" Hanna asked.

"Mostly phone work. Talking to people and getting information out of them they didn't realize they were giving."

"Really?" Daisy said. "How'd you do it?"

There seemed to be no reason to keep it a secret. "I made friends with them and acted like I knew more than I did. I made it seem kind of like gossiping and they let their guard down."

"Isn't that cheating?" Vonda said.

Yolanda turned to her sister and blew out her breath. "According to who, the World Organization of Catching the Criminal? There aren't rules in that sort of business. Casey could use any means she wanted to."

"So what do you think about what happened here?" Vonda asked.

I probably should have tried to change the subject to something more cheerful, but I couldn't help myself and told them about finding the wedge of wood. "It could mean that it wasn't an accident. That someone made it so the door wouldn't open. The controls were on the outside, so they could have extended the time and turned up the heat. Then later pulled out the wedge and tossed it in the brush thinking no one would find it."

Suzy! looked up from her phone, which she had sitting in her lap, and suddenly rejoined the conversation. "Two people died? You know how they say things go in threes," she said, glancing over the group. "I wonder if something else is going to happen. If somebody else is going to die?"

"I hate to seem self-serving, but if that three thing is true, it wouldn't include us," Fern said. They all looked at her and shook their heads. She turned to me. "What are you going to do with the story about the piece of wood?"

I put up my hands in a gesture of uncertainly. "That's a good question. I have been involved with solving some crimes here in Cadbury and it hasn't made me very popular with that cop you saw in the rumpled jacket. His name is Theodore Borgnine and this time he actually asked if I knew anything because the Jordan people were being so closemouthed. I have had some thoughts about what happened, like I'm not so sure the first death was an accident. I think the poison mushrooms might have been planted." They were all listening intently to me now. Tag was taking the opportunity to clear the plates and I heard someone yelp followed by Tag apologizing. The attention swung to Hanna trying to tell Tag it was okay. She held up her sleeve and said something about two spots on her peasant blouse now, but due to the pattern they barely showed, and he finally calmed down.

"You were saying," John said.

"I wanted to have the whole picture of what happened before I gave the lieutenant the goods. I plan to hand over everything I know the next time I see him." Now it was time to lighten the mood. "Dessert anyone?" I said with a smile.

As they finished eating, I floated a plan for the rest of the evening. I suggested we meet up in an hour in the Lodge. The Jordan people were occupied so we'd have the whole space to ourselves. I offered to bring over the fondue stuff and they could have another game night and social yarn craft.

After they all scattered, I stopped to talk to Cloris. She was almost back to her usual calm confidence now that she knew she hadn't screwed up with the bags.

"I can't wait for this weekend to be over," she said, letting down her guard for a moment. "It's not your retreat. Your people are easy. It's the Jordan group." She glanced toward the direction of Hummingbird Hall. "Everything they do is weird. They can't even seem to have a normal dance. You should look at it." She rolled her eyes.

Now she had me curious, so when I went out of the Lodge, I

followed the throbbing sound to Hummingbird Hall. As I got closer the throbbing turned into music. The door was open and no one was blocking it, so I stepped inside. The dancers were all gyrating in place, like they were trying to shake off something. The music stopped and they all froze, and I saw that Jordan was on the stage. He did a spiel how this dance challenge was his original idea. The shaking would loosen the negative energy and then when they stopped, it would fall away. Each time they did it, more would be released, and by the end, they would have let it all go. Of course, when he said it, it sounded very convincing and all his minions were nodding their heads in agreement. I was looking over the crowd when I saw something that made me stop in my tracks.

John was talking to a woman who did not resemble anyone in my group. Maybe talking was the wrong word. It looked like arguing and she seemed to be pushing him away. I moved closer to get a better look, but one of Jordan's assistants had spotted me and was closing in. I had no choice but to make a fast exit.

Chapter Twenty-three

When I returned with the fondue fixings, I could still feel the throb of the music from the Jordan's people dance party, if you wanted to call it that. It seemed more like shake till you ache to me, but what did I know about how his methods worked. I did glance around with a little apprehension, afraid a straggler might smell the chocolate even though I had everything packed in a bin. By this part of the weekend with little sleep and little food, who knew what they'd do if they got a whiff of something sweet and decadent. I felt a little guilty bringing it to my group since Dane had been so excited about it. The chocolate certainly would have kept, but not the strawberries, pineapple pieces, apple slices and marshmallows. Better to have somebody enjoy it instead of going to waste.

I hoped it would make hanging out in the Lodge a little more exciting. You know that saying about not appreciating things until they were gone—well, it was certainly true about the Saturday night events Vista Del Mar put on. Yes, I'd chuckled at the talent shows and been a reluctant participant in the old-fashioned dances, but I sure would have appreciated one of those now. I'm sure my group would have as well. They were being good sports about all the logistical challenges thanks to Jordan. Meals had been all over the place and we'd had to make ourselves scarce when the Jordan people were all over the grounds. This was not the retreat I had intended to put on for them.

My group was waiting in the Lodge. The big room seemed extra empty with just the seven of them in the seating area in front of the massive stone fireplace.

If they were having game night fatigue, it ended when I started setting up the fondue pot, which was already loaded with warm chocolate. I lit the candle below it so it could reach full molten while I set up the platter of sweet things to dip. They were already looking over everything and talking about what they wanted to try first and I realized how much fondue invited socializing. I was going to remember that for the future.

To say it was a big success was an understatement, which made me feel a twinge of regret since all that socializing was supposed to have been between Dane and me. When the last of the chocolate had graced a strawberry, they decided to sit around and work on their projects instead of taking out any of the games.

The conversation stayed on knitting and helping Yolanda deal with a dropped stitch. John had the scarf out he'd gotten in the switch, but he seemed rather lackluster about working on it. I moved in next to him, curious about what I'd seen.

"That dance thing is something else," I said to ease into talking about it. He remained noncommittal as he moved his needles through the yarn.

I pushed a little more. "It looked like you were really into it. Was that woman shooing you away because you weren't in their group?"

"What?" John said, stopping in mid-stitch and looking at me.

"You were at the Jordan dance thing earlier. I saw you talking to a woman," I said.

His face relaxed into a smile. "I'm sure you mixed me up with someone else. I get it all the time. I guess I look like a lot of people. I wasn't anywhere near that . . . that, whatever it's supposed to be called."

I was stunned and confused. I didn't think I'd been mistaken. My expression must have given me away and he continued. "I was nowhere near Hummingbird Hall," he said. "With all that's gone on this weekend, it's easy to mistake one tall dark handsome man for another," he said in a joking tone. He was so convincing that I began to question what I saw. Had I just seen a man with dark hair and similar colored clothes and jumped to the conclusion that it was him?

He was probably right—the weekend had scrambled my brain.

When I finally left for home Vonda and Yolanda were the only ones still sitting there. I was so ready to call it a night.

As the Lodge door closed behind me, it felt cold and dark after the warm brightness of the inside. The throbbing music had stopped and the grounds seemed deserted. My bin made an echoing sound as I pulled it toward the driveway. A sharp wolf whistle pierced the silence and I turned to find its source. The cruiser was almost completely hidden in the corner of the small parking lot just off the driveway in a position where Dane could view what was going on, but not really be seen.

"Hey," I said, approaching the car.

"You do know this is just a delay, not a cancellation," he said, sticking his head out the window. He appeared seriously concerned and I felt bad, particularly since I'd given away the fondue. I didn't even have any peach cobbler to offer him. My people had taken care of most of it and I'd offered the rest for Tag to take for him and Lucinda. It was the most enthused I'd seen him about anything. He was already planning to warm it up and serve it to her when the Blue Door closed. They'd have the place to themselves since I never baked on Saturday nights. At least somebody would have a romantic evening.

Dane had a long shift ahead of him with only a tall cup of coffee to keep him company. It was hardly how he'd expected to spend the night and I felt bad for him.

"Oh, really," I said, trying to bat my eyelashes in one of my lame flirting moves. "Well, here's something on account." There was no one around so I leaned in and kissed him. He had a surprised smile like I'd just handed him a wonderful present, for a moment anyway, then he got playful.

"I knew you were teasing with all that playing hard to get. You want me, you really do," he said, doing his version of the Sally Field Academy Award acceptance speech.

"Don't let it go to your head," I said with a roll of my eyes. "I just felt bad for you sitting out her all night alone."

"That's what you say, but that kiss told a different story," he said.

"It just showed—"

"I know, I know. You're going to repeat that 'I want you' speech, aren't you?"

"You know it's true," he called after me.

Well, maybe he was right.

Chapter- Twenty-four

It wasn't how I'd expected to spend my Saturday night either, I thought as I trudged up my driveway. Sammy was either asleep or out somewhere. He'd been right that I'd barely know he was there. Julius was my greeting committee. It was a combination of happy to see me and a chance for some stink fish.

I went through the motions of serving him as soon as I walked in. Then I could finally let go and relax. Most of the retreat was behind me. Sunday was just tying up loose ends and everyone saying they wanted to be friends forever. They would all trade contact information, but who knew if any of them would actually ever get in touch.

Every group I'd had was different and some of them had bonded more than others. It had taken this group longer, but then they seemed such a disparate bunch to start with and there was the additional situation that some of them were in the throes of getting over habits—which were really addictions.

I laughed at myself for the way I'd made it sound like I was such a hot-shot detective and that I was going to lay out all kinds of evidence to Lieutenant Borgnine. Even though he'd seemed interested in hearing information from me, he'd probably dismiss my thoughts that the two deaths might not have been accidents. The only reason he'd asked me what I knew was because the Jordan people were being so closemouthed.

I didn't want to think about it anymore and went to bed hoping to dream of sugar plums, but of course dreamt of giant mushrooms shriveling in a sauna instead.

Julius was my alarm clock. If I didn't stir early enough, he'd start nudging me. If that didn't work, he'd run his sandpaper tongue over my check. It took two licks to wake me up on Sunday morning. As usual, the light coming in the window was flat due to the cloud cover. It wasn't dim and gloomy, more of a bright white, but not the same as having sun streaming in. It was not quite cold enough to turn on the heat, but chilly enough that I wanted to stay buried in the covers. Julius was standing guard next to me, ready to offer more prodding to get up, so I pulled back the covers. I was used to the chill now and had positioned a rug right where my feet landed and slid into my slippers.

Normally, I took my time on the Sunday morning of a retreat, and unless I wanted some of the breakfast Vista Del Mar offered, I'd join them after it. But this time I had to make sure there was breakfast for them. I dressed quickly and rushed out.

The bell was ringing announcing breakfast for the Jordan group. I usually picked up a whiff of the pancakes and sausages and other goodies the kitchen prepared on Sunday morning. This time there was nothing in the air. I passed a few people on their way to the dining hall. They seemed to have some pep in their step despite the exhaustion they must have been feeling from the weekend with lots of activities and little time for sleep. It didn't even seem to matter that there wasn't something delicious waiting for them.

I went into the Lodge, which was mostly empty except for the cardboard cutouts of Jordan offering tidbits of his wisdom. I was relieved to get a whiff of delicious smells coming from the café. Since the Blue Door was closed on Sundays, Cloris had called in some of the kitchen help from Vista Del Mar. Jordan had made the kitchen and dining hall off-limits for the weekend, but the two workers had used the facilities in the café. When I walked in, they were just pushing a couple of tables together and laying out the food. The glass bowl of cut fruit was visually appealing with a selection of melons and berries. One of the workers was turning out waffles and putting them in a covered tray to stay warm. There was butter and pure maple syrup. Instead of the usual scrambled eggs, there was a baked frittata and a selection of toast and croissants. My mouth was watering just looking at it.

I heard the sound of someone at the entrance and looked up ready to great my people, but it was Diana with Tyler behind her. They were both trying not to look at the food.

"Do you suppose you could score me a coffee drink?" Diana said. "I'd kill for a cappuccino, foam only."

"Hey, get one for me," Tyler said, waving his hand to get my attention. "Make mine a latte with a shot of espresso." He gave me a smile. "No Lyla to jump out of nowhere and shake a finger at us." He caught himself and muttered something about her resting in peace.

I grabbed a couple of paper cups and wrote their orders on them and their names and handed them to the barista. He gave me a disparaging shake of his head but started making the drinks while the pair waited, trying to stay hidden.

My group started to file in and I took their drink orders, writing them on the cups along with their names. The two Jordan people's drinks were ready first and they stood in a corner downing them. I saw them both take a longing look at the food, but then they left.

As the drinks came up, I was glad they had names on them as I handed out the cappuccinos, lattes, Americanos and even a couple of coffee chocolate drinks capped with whipped cream.

Without Lucinda or Tag to act as host, it was all on me. Once I had the drinks delivered it was basically just making sure they all knew to help themselves. I was thinking about snagging one of the waffles. My eating for the weekend had been pretty sporadic and I hadn't gotten the sumptuous dinner that Dane had promised. I was about to grab a plate when Cloris tapped me on the shoulder.

"There was a message from Sammy," she said. "He needs some help and wants you to meet him in that escape thing on the lower floor of Hummingbird Hall." She saw me looking over my group. "Don't worry about them. I'll stand in for you."

I would have rather stayed with my group and made sure breakfast went well and gotten something to eat myself, but I was sure that Sammy wouldn't have summoned me unless he really needed my help.

I walked past the dining hall and heard the clatter of dishes and the hum of conversation, but once I went on a little further, it got very quiet. This whole area around Hummingbird Hall and beyond felt isolated from the rest of the grounds and seemed darker because of the shade from all the trees.

The door was open to the auditorium and I glanced inside. Chairs had been brought back in after the dance frenzy the night before. There was still a Jordan talk session before the Elite group went through the warren of rooms. The cap to their achievement was learning how to make a paracord bracelet, or arm-wear as Jordan had called it. I'd made sure to wear my samples.

I went around the building and down the slope to reach the lower floor. I could barely see the sauna almost hidden by the trees. It was practically on the edge of the property. I thought about the wedge of wood and whether Lieutenant Borgnine would agree with my conjecture.

I wanted to be done with whatever Sammy needed quickly. I called out his name as soon as I went into the lower level. He'd said something about how they'd attempted to soundproof the rooms, so when I got no response I figured he was inside somewhere working on something.

I went through the door marked *Enter*, expecting to breeze through the rooms until I found him. The door clicked behind me. I rushed through the clown room and went to push the door open, but it was locked. Luckily I knew where to find the code, and as soon as I punched in the numbers, I was able to go through into the next room. I ignored the walls covered in jiggling bugs and grabbed the code off the tarantula's leg. I moved through the snake room quickly, calling out Sammy's name, with no response. The claustrophobic room was harder to get through and I felt my heart pounding as I got to the end and squeezed through the small doorway. At last, I reached the final room as I came out on the step above the floor. There was still no Sammy and I realized he must have been ahead of me and probably had moved on to the final illusion. It would have been a lot easier if he'd been more specific where to meet him. It didn't matter now. All I had to do was go through this room and catch up with him. I took a deep breath and batted the cardboard cutout of the scary-looking clown out of my way. I looked ahead and saw that the view to the last door was blocked by a partial wall that had the tunnel. I really didn't look forward to going through it again, but even though the wall only went partway up, it was too high for me with my limited athletic ability to climb over.

The projections on the wall were easy to ignore, but my heartbeat did an uptick as I approached the entrance to the tunnel. I pushed myself to crouch, hoping to get through it quickly. I'd forgotten about the bottom being covered in the plastic snakes, which made it harder to move fast. I let out my breath in a gush as I came out on the other side and jumped up to standing. Now there was just a short distance to the door leading out. But then I heard an ominous noise. It sounded like a rattle and I thought it was merely a sound effect, but when I looked down at the floor littered with plastic snakes, something was moving. My eye went to the enclosures on either side of the exit and I saw that they were both open.

I could almost hear Frank saying he'd warned me about things coming in threes. Then he'd scold me for letting myself get set up. It was obvious now that there was no Sammy anywhere in the vicinity. Someone wanted me out of the way. I started to try to figure out who it was, but then ordered myself to snap out of playing detective. All my attention needed to be on finding a way to get out without encountering my slithering companions. My first impulse was to rush forward to the door, but I stopped myself, realizing I'd never make it without getting up close and personal with a couple of angry snakes.

I took a step backward and felt the end of the tunnel. Maybe I could backtrack and go back through the rooms and leave by the entrance. If going forward through the tunnel was bad, going backward was worse. I felt a moment of relief when I stood up on the other side. But it only lasted a moment as I realized the snakes could get through the tunnel with ease.

I got back up on the step and tried pushing on the door that led to the preceding room, but it was locked. It came back to me that Sammy had said something about Jordan making sure there would be one-way traffic.

I regretted that I'd left my tote bag in the café, not that my phone would have helped anyway since there was no signal. I took more deep breaths trying to chase the anxiety from my brain so I could think straight and figure things out.

Growing up in a high-rise with an incredible view of Lake Michigan hadn't done anything to prepare me for dealing with rattlesnakes. But maybe in my assorted professions there was something that would help.

I heard a rattle echoing in the tunnel and shivered knowing the snakes were coming toward me.

Think, I told myself. Easier said than done as a hot panicky feeling set in. I forced myself to take some more slow deep breaths and the panicky feeling began to subside as I tried going through my life experiences to find something that would help. What did I know about snakes besides being slithery and scary? Okay, during my stint as a teacher, there'd been a lesson on reptiles. I searched my mind for what had been said about rattlesnakes. They weren't like cobras, who could stand up and look you in the eye before they sunk their fangs in. As I recalled, they shook their rattles and hissed as a way to scare off predators. Most bites occurred when someone got too close. So the answer was to get across to the door without stepping on the ground.

I looked up and saw the two wooden slats running the length of the room. They would never hold my weight, but then looking at them I got a view of the ceiling of Hummingbird Hall. This lower space of the building was used for storage and maintenance and the ceiling was painted black, which almost hid the pipes running along it. I flashed back to my teacher days and thought of the kids hanging from the bars of the jungle gym in the schoolyard. Wasn't this pipe above me sort of like that? Only there were two problems. It was too high for me to grab onto, even from the step I was standing on, and how could I get my hands around it. Well, maybe three problems, the third being my lack of athletic ability.

I was back to getting sweaty and used the back of my hand to wipe away the moisture. That's when I saw a potential for a way out.

It was called a survival bracelet. "Let's see if you really work," I said out loud as I slipped the arm-wear off. In its current state the best I could do was play ring toss and hope it landed on the snakes' heads. I thought back to what Crystal had said. It was the cord that held the promise. I undid both bracelets and had two lengths of fluorescent pink nylon cord. Using what I'd learned from the yarn craft, I tied them together and made loops at each end. I tried waving them over my head cowboy style, hoping to launch them over the pipes with no luck. The cardboard clown banged into me, and as I went to push it away, I had an idea. I ripped it free of the thick wire hook that had attached it to the slat. I was able to wiggle the wire free and used it to ferry the cord over the pipes.

Now came the hard part—my lack of athletic ability. I was never very good at gym and wished I'd paid more attention to the exercises we'd had hanging from the rings or taken Dane up on the offer of karate lessons. Hoping for the best, I put my hands through the loops I'd made with the cord, and doing a Tarzan yell to give me power, I propelled myself off the step. My feet swung above the ground in the first section and up to the top of the partial wall. It might not have worked as a way to circumvent the crawl space, but there was enough for me to push off of and glide over the last part of the room. I let go and landed with a thud right in front of the door. Without even taking a breath, I punched the code in the keypad and the door swung open.

There was a cheer, applause and a shower of glitter and a sign that said *Congratulations*. When I looked up, Lieutenant Borgnine, Kevin St. John and Jordan were staring at me.

"Ms. Feldstein?" Lieutenant Borgnine said, sounding surprised. Neither Kevin St. John nor Jordan seemed happy to see me.

"What were you doing in there?" Jordan said in an angry voice.

"How about dodging rattlesnakes in that escape thing of yours," I said. The story tumbled out about getting a message that Sammy needed my help and the loose snakes. "It was clearly a setup. Probably by you." I pointed an accusing finger at Jordan.

"That's your version. More likely you were mucking around where you didn't belong and you let Rex and Rita loose." Then he looked to the lieutenant. "Will you please arrest her? She had no business going into my trademarked final challenge. She was trespassing." He glared at me. "I never should have agreed to let your lame yarn group have their retreat. You have undermined our whole structure." His eyes flared with annoyance. "I know you have helped some people give in to their cravings." He shook his head in disgust. "I could smell the coffee and sugar on their breath."

I looked at him as an image of him having coffee and cake at Maggie's popped into my mind. He must have remembered at the same time and turned on the charm. Instantly he changed from the man berating me to the one who went in front of the crowd. "The point is for our people to break old habits and addictions to sugar, coffee and excess food. We can't have them see the staff doing otherwise."

I got it—Jordan was covered because he'd had his caffeine and sugar out of sight of everyone. Kevin St. John turned to me, his expression twisted in annoyance. "You did what? How could you have interfered with Jordan's instructions?" He looked back to Jordan and started apologizing for me and at the same time making it clear that he had no idea what I'd been doing or he would have absolutely stopped it. Jordan was barely listening. He'd pulled out a walkie-talkie and was calling for help with the snakes.

"What Ms. Feldstein did isn't the issue," Lieutenant Borgnine said, giving Jordon an angry stare. "What's this about rattlesnakes?"

Jordan rocked his head as if the cop had said something ridiculous. "Don't get all worked up. They're normally safe and sound in their containers. It's just for show."

The lieutenant seemed unconvinced. "First it's poison mushrooms, someone stays too long in a sauna and now snakes."

"Those two were accidents. That's life. There's risk and things happen," Jordan said. He was going into his pitch mode and looked at me, when one of his security people showed up with a hook and a cloth bag. "The snake escape is all on her," he said as he waved for the security guy to go inside. Though Jordan tried to lose the rest of the entourage, the lieutenant insisted on seeing the inside of the escape challenge. Not to be left behind, Kevin St. John announced he had to inspect it as well.

Not one of them had even asked if I was all right.

Chapter Twenty-five

There was nothing to do but keep on going. I turned and walked up the slope, following the path as it led back to the Lodge. The Jordan people were still in the dining hall. They were all standing by their chairs and doing weird moves, and I figured it was an exercise class, probably to warm them up for his last pitch session.

"What happened to you?" Hanna said when I came into the café. They were just finishing their breakfast and the rest of them looked up when they heard her comment, and asked me if I was all right. I hadn't really thought about my appearance until then. All that crawling and swinging from pipes must have done some damage. I patted my hair and realized that some of it had gotten loose from the scrunchie I'd used to pull it back with. A tendril or two could look nice, but it felt like more than that and I knew without even seeing a mirror that I look disheveled and probably a little deranged. My shirt had come untucked on one side only. I pulled my hair back into the scrunchie, straightened my clothes and my mind. I was okay and nobody could say I wasn't a problem solver and resourceful. *Take that, whoever had set me up.*

Cloris came in from the main area of the Lodge. As soon as she saw me, her face took on a guilty look. "I know I said I would stand in for you." She let out a heavy sigh. "That police lieutenant showed up and Mr. St. John had to accompany him and Jordan to the scene of the problem." She checked my expression to see if I understood she meant the sauna.

I didn't explain that the three had made a detour and told her it was no problem about leaving my people. They seemed to have done just fine on their own. I suggested they go to our meeting room.

Suzy! hadn't even looked up. I could see she had her phone in her lap and was looking at the screen as if it was somehow comforting to stare at the icons even if she couldn't connect to anything. Vonda seemed concerned and suggested Suzy! try a piece of gum.

"It doesn't work and it got stuck in my bag and made a mess," she said in an annoyed voice. She shoved the phone in her bag and got up to join the others. As soon as they were gone, I asked Cloris how'd she gotten the message that supposedly came from Sammy. When I explained why I was asking, she started to come unglued, which wasn't like her.

"I'm sorry," she said. "This weekend with these Jordan people and all their crazy stuff and the accidents and now what you just went through—" She shook her head as if she hoped it would clear everything away. "It's just too much. Mr. St. John has been impossible. Even when I knew that I hadn't made a mistake with the tote bags for the foraging, he kept acting as if it was my fault since he'd put me in charge of the dining room." She made a face. "I felt terrible overseeing such awful meals. I don't care if that's part of their plan." I eased her back to my original question about how she'd gotten the message.

"One of the part-time people at the desk gave it to me. It must have been a phone message."

"Which would have been impossible," I said. "There's no way Sammy could have called from Hummingbird Hall with no cell service. Whoever it was either called from somewhere off the premises or from one of the phone booths."

"Well, who then?" she asked.

I shrugged as an answer, not wanting to tell her that after the way Jordan had behaved, he was the number-one suspect. But what was his motive? Was it punishment because I'd fed his people sugar and caffeine or was it way to keep me busy nursing a snakebite so I wouldn't interfere with his grand finale. Cloris started to gather up the dishes, but she'd done enough already. She seemed relieved when I told her I'd take care of it. Even so, she said she'd go to the meeting room and check to make sure everything was as it should be.

Seeing her leave, the barista announced he was taking a break and walked out.

I was carrying a pile of plates behind the counter when the door opened and Lieutenant Borgnine walked in. He walked up to the counter, and apparently not realizing who was behind it, asked for a cup of coffee.

"Oh," he said in surprise when I poked my head up.

"The barista took a break, but I think I can handle getting you a cup of coffee," I said. He glanced toward the little buffet we'd set up and lifted one of the metal serving dishes. "Help yourself." I pulled out a clean plate and handed it to him over the counter. "It's been quite a morning for all of us."

He took the plate and started loading it with eggs and a waffle. He had his usual gruff expression as he looked up at me. "Don't think offering me some food is going to get me to think of you as a colleague."

"Fine," I said with a shrug. "Then I won't share what I found."

He stopped pouring the syrup over the waffle. "That's withholding evidence," he said as he took the plate of food to one of the tables.

I brought him a mug of coffee and purposely didn't join him, instead standing next to the table, knowing that it gave me a power position. "I certainly don't want to be accused of keeping anything from you," I began, before telling him about the piece of wood and that I thought it had been used as a doorstop.

"Suppose you show me where it is." He looked longingly at the plate of food. "We better go now."

We became part of the crowd heading for Hummingbird Hall. The Jordan people were sleep-deprived and probably on the edge of hunger even though they'd just left breakfast, but they seemed enthused, or maybe it was just wired. I picked up some bits of conversation, all filled with Jordanisms.

When they reached the auditorium, they split into groups,

heading to different doors depending on their status. I guessed they had gotten value for their money because the group going in the closest door to the front seemed the most energetic.

It got a lot quieter as the lieutenant and I moved into the more remote area. He watched me with an eagle eye as I went ahead through the undergrowth and seemed almost disappointed when I stopped outside the area cordoned off with the yellow tape. I surveyed the underbrush until I saw the piece of yarn I'd used to mark the spot. I waved him over and he separated the dry-looking plants with a pen until the pale piece of wood was exposed. "I suppose you probably touched it," he said.

"I didn't know that it was evidence at first," I said. "But I put it back just where I found it."

"Why exactly do you think it's evidence?" he asked.

"You really don't know?" I said.

There was a flicker in his eyes and I got it. He wanted to see what I'd say. It had been a long weekend and I was pretty wiped out by now and wasn't up for any games. I would just tell him what I thought and let him do with it what he wanted. "It means the incident in the sauna might not have been an accident," I said as a finish. No expression showed on his face so I continued. "Someone could have stuck the doorstop in the door from the outside so that the victim couldn't get out. The controls were on the outside and they could have upped the time it stayed on. And they came by later and removed the piece of wood so it would appear to be an accident." I started to tell him what I'd learned about the difference between dry heat and steam, but his expression made it clear that he wasn't interested in extraneous information. He poked around where the wedge had been found and uncovered an old tennis ball, a flip-flop with the toe strap pulled loose and the skeleton of a rodent. I suggested he see if the wedge would actually jam the door shut. Reluctantly, he crossed the yellow tape and put the wedge under the door and then tried to open it. There were no congratulations or telling me it was clever thinking. He just nodded noncommittally.

"I suppose you've come up with a motive, too," he said. I'd expected him to find a way to dismiss what I'd said and was knocked off my heels when he seemed to be taking what I'd said seriously.

"Lyla Konker didn't seem to be popular with the staff. She was too rigid and hyper-critical of anyone who strayed. I already told you about the way she went after me for getting a couple of cups of coffee for some of the Jordan people." Then something came to me, and it must have shown on my face.

"How about you share," he said.

"As I said, Lyla said something like she'd seen what I'd done and she was going to tell. At the time, I took it for granted she was talking about the coffee, but what if it was aimed at who I'd gotten the coffee for and they were worried she'd tell Jordan and make sure they'd lose their job?"

He seemed disbelieving. "You think someone killed her over a cup of coffee?"

"It was a number of cups of coffee and there were cookies involved too. Lyla was a real stickler for the rules and she seemed to view herself as the one in charge of keeping the integrity of the retreat."

The lieutenant let out a weary sigh. "And what if it is just what it seems and the woman used bad judgment and stayed in the sauna too long. Those people have some strange ideas." He shook his head. "Rattlesnakes." He seemed ready to depart. "Just remember, conjecture isn't enough. You have to have proof."

• • •

My people were sitting around the table busy with their projects, but the energy was different. It was always that way on Sunday. They were finishing up and already thinking ahead to going home. When I looked at the tote bags on the table, I regretted again being talked into the blah-colored bags even with the touches to personalize them. They were dull compared to my blood-red bags with *Yarn2Go* in big letters on the front.

Crystal pulled me aside and said Kevin St. John had come in and told her they didn't want us to do the bracelet activity after all. "He said Cloris would be doing it," my colorful helper said.

"I think I know why," I said and told her what happened and how well the bracelets I'd made had served me. "I'm sure Jordan made a big fuss to Kevin and he's still foolish enough to try to please him, hoping they'll come back here again."

"Not if I have anything to say about it. But I am glad the bracelets were useful to you. What kind of idiot has rattlesnakes for show? I bet the animal rights people don't know about that."

We both felt for Cloris getting stuck in another bad position and Crystal volunteered to offer the assistant manager a quick lesson and to turn over the materials we had. "I'll be back as soon as I can." We'd been talking in the corner and I went back to the table. They were all intent on their knitting and crocheting in an effort to do as much as they could on the switched projects before it was time to give them back.

I was still thinking about the tote bags and decided to show off the one of mine that was hidden inside the ones we'd used. I always ended up with a bunch of extraneous stuff in my bag by the end of the weekend and I had to do a certain amount of cleaning out to get to the red bag. This time it was worse than usual. Not only did I have the paperwork for my group, but also all the pages for the Jordan group Kevin St. John had given me so I could keep my group separate from them.

I flipped through their schedule with a whole different perspective now that the weekend was almost done. At the end there were bios about the staff. I flipped through those too and then something made me stop and look up. I began to cycle through the things that had happened over the weekend. There were incidents that seemed to be unrelated, but now I saw a connection. Could the answer have been right in front of me all along? I thought about running to find the lieutenant, but unless I had something to prove I was right, it would go nowhere.

I could practically hear Frank's voice ordering me to think, telling me that the solution was out there waiting for me to find it.

I picked up the scrunchie I'd been working on. Sometimes when I worked with my hands it cleared my mind. It was repetitious and easy. I glanced up at the others. Suzy! had her phone in her lap again. Vonda looked over at her with a disapproving expression and Suzy! slammed the phone on the table. "Okay, I admit it. I'm Suzy! and I have a phone addiction. There, are you satisfied?"

"You need to calm down," Yolanda said, putting her hand on Suzy!'s arm. "How about I get you a cup of chamomile tea?"

And then suddenly I understood how everything fit together. And best of all, I knew how to get the lieutenant his proof. I did a great job of holding it in, even though I wanted to scream Eureka! I excused myself from the group and speed walked across the grounds back to the Lodge. With all the Jordan people getting pumped up for their last challenge, the cavernous room was empty. Cloris was moving around the room putting away board games and straightening the cardboard cutouts of Jordan that had gotten knocked askew. Kevin St. John was behind the registration counter and didn't even look up when I passed. I rushed into the café and saw that the barista was back from his break and was leaning on the counter, reading. I rushed around him looking for the trash bin with my fingers crossed it hadn't been emptied.

"How could you have emptied it?" I wailed when I saw the empty can.

"Geez," the barista said, looking up, "Usually I get grief for the opposite. If you want it so bad, go check the Dumpster."

I rushed out without a word and circumvented the dining hall. The big blue monstrosity sat against a fence with a gate that opened onto the street for the pickups. The cover was down, but it didn't keep in the garbagy smell. I approached it with trepidation. "You can do this," I said out loud to myself. It felt like more hype than truth. I lifted the lid and the smell instantly got worse. But dealing with all that stink fish had been like training to deal with this. I held my nose and pulled myself up to climb in. I pushed the lid back so it would stay open and give me access to fresh air as I tried to get my balance on the mountain of ick below me. I started sifting through what was around me hoping that what I was looking for was near the top.

It was impossible to keep my balance and I fell backwards into a seated position just as one of the housekeeping people went to empty a trash can into the Dumpster. I can't really blame her. Seeing something moving in the Dumpster had to have scared her and I can only imagine what she must have thought was in there. She certainly didn't look, just threw in the whole can and ran off screaming. The lid fell down as she fled.

I went back to my hunting, oblivious to what was getting all over me while trying to hold the lid up. I knew I had to hurry. A moment later I heard the whine of sirens. There were flashing lights as the fire department arrived along with a police cruiser. I took one last look among the trash and there was the needle in a haystack I was looking for. This time I did yell out Eureka!

Chapter Twenty-six

"Is this your new look?" Dane said, suppressing a smile as he reached up to pull something out of my hair. He was in uniform and surrounded by firefighters holding assorted equipment. Lieutenant Borgnine and Kevin St. John showed up a moment later. I couldn't even begin to describe their reactions to seeing me sitting in the Dumpster with some of those black beans Jordan had been serving smeared all over my shirt.

"Are you going to help me out of here?" I said to the crew standing there. They all looked at each other to see who was going to volunteer.

"You guys are all wimps," Dane said. He got a stepladder, and when he was on top of it, hoisted me up, and before I could object, threw me over his shoulder firefighter style. "Really?" I said and he just laughed, realizing he'd just done what he'd promised not to.

In all that I didn't let go of my found treasure. I barely had my feet on the ground before I was calling for Lieutenant Borgnine, waving something in my hand. "Remember what you said, conjecture wasn't any good without proof? Well, here it is."

We all looked at the cup full of garbage in my hand. Kevin St. John started trying to pull the lieutenant away as the firefighters went back to their trucks. "I'm telling you it's evidence," I said.

To humor me, he had Dane put it in a bag he'd pulled out of his pocket. Then he looked at me with distaste. "Take a shower and then we'll talk about it," he said.

"I know what happened and who is responsible," I said. "We need to do something now before everybody starts to leave."

"Ignore her," Kevin St. John said, positioning himself to block the lieutenant's view of me. "Hasn't she caused enough trouble disturbing the Jordan retreat? She has crime on the brain. The two deaths were accidents. I'm sure the Jordan people will take steps so nothing like that happens again." I stepped around the manager and was back in full sight of the cop. There seemed to be no way that he'd listen to my explanation of what I was sure had happened, so I just offered a name.

Borgnine's expression was unreadable and I thought that meant he was considering what I'd said. Dane stepped closer to his superior. He glanced back at me for a second, giving me an almost imperceptible nod of support.

"She's been right before," Dane said.

"You're hardly an objective party," the lieutenant said, shaking his head. He turned back to me. "I'm not talking to someone with apple peels in their hair."

To further make his point, he walked away. Kevin St. John stuck to him like glue. Dane had to follow, but looked back with a sympathetic nod. Once I was alone I really got a whiff of myself. I really stunk.

I ran to my place, jumped over Julius as he tried to direct me to the refrigerator. I showered, washed my hair and got dressed in fresh clothes in record time. My hair was still dripping as I jogged back to Vista Del Mar, formulating a plan as I went. I saw the car with its motor running parked by the Lodge. The clatter of wheels on the pavement drew my attention away from it as a figure hidden by a hoodie was almost running as they pulled a suitcase behind them. The person was too intent on getting to the car to notice me.

Oh, no, I mumbled to myself. Thank you, Lieutenant Borgnine, for taking your time. He was so sure that the killer wouldn't try to get away. Well, he was wrong. Glad I was wearing sneakers that made no sound and that I had dressed in khaki pants and an olive-green jacket that thanks to the cloudy sky blended in with the trees and brush, making me almost ninja invisible. I slipped down the driveway and came up behind the figure trying to make an escape. A short length of crocheted red yarn ending with a tassel hung off the handle. It was meant to make the black suitcase stand out from all the others that looked the same, but I now hoped it would be something to stop an escape. The person pulling the suitcase was laser focused on getting to the rideshare car as they rushed along. I reached out for the crocheted piece and gave it a tug. It pulled the suitcase backward. As it fell, it took the person pulling it with it as well. They'd barely landed on top of the suitcase before they tried to get up. I threw myself on top to end their escape. It was the first time I got to see a face and confirm I'd been right.

Chapter Twenty-seven

The rideshare driver sensing trouble when he saw me tackle his customer ran inside the Lodge for help. A moment later, Lieutenant Borgnine came outside holding a cup of coffee. "What's going on?" he said, seeing the two of us on top of the suitcase.

"She was making a run for it," I said as Hanna pushed me away and stood up.

"You better do something about her," Hanna said, dusting herself off. "She tried to assault me."

The lieutenant looked back and forth between the two of us. His gaze rested on my face long enough for me to be able to read his expression. He was betting on me.

But he kept a poker face as he dealt with Hanna, asking if she needed first aid before sending her off to an empty meeting room with the uniformed officer who'd ridden with him. He made it seem she was just going to be waiting to give a statement. She looked back as they walked away. "What about her? You're not just going to let her go," she protested.

"Of course not." And then out of nowhere he produced a pair of handcuffs and put them on me. "See. She's not going anywhere."

When it was just the two of us, he glared at me. "For the moment the person most in trouble is you since you appeared to have assaulted her and there's nothing illegal about leaving Vista Del Mar."

"Unless you committed a crime, or maybe two," I said.

He looked at the coffee cup in his hand. "How about we find someplace where I can drink this while you tell me your story." He made a face as he said *story*, as if he couldn't wait to poke holes in it.

I wiggled my hands. "You weren't serious about this?" I said.

"It was for show. If she thinks I'm arresting you, there's less chance she's going to try to bolt." He took out the key and unlocked them. All the maneuvering had meant he'd had to keep putting down his cup of coffee on a fence post and then picking it up again.

"Let's find a place nearby where I can drink this before it's completely cold," he said, holding up the paper cup. "The barista made me a special mocha drink with a whipped cream finish."

We found a bench near the grass circle that was private. Once we were situated, he tested the drink to see if it was ruined, and when he'd realized it wasn't, he turned to me.

"How about telling me how that cup of garbage you forced me to take as evidence has to do with Hanna Schultz?" Lieutenant Borgnine said, trying to keep the consternation out of his voice. I could tell it was hard for him to say it because it was admitting that I might know things he didn't, but his responsibility as a cop superseded his ego.

I took a moment to collect my thoughts. I wondered if I should start off by explaining that Suzy!'s fuss about the gum coupled with seeing the name on Hanna's tote bag after I'd looked at the Jordan staff list was what triggered my understanding of what had happened and who was responsible. But while I didn't want to gloat, I did want to show off my process of detecting and so decided to give him the whole story instead of answering his question directly.

"It's not what was in the cup that's the evidence," I said, "but I'll get to that in a minute." His mouth twisted in displeasure at having to wait, but he must have realized he had no choice and waved his hand for me to proceed.

"It started with the tote bags," I said. "Kevin St. John insisted that my group use the same tote bags the Jordan group had. The first night the Jordan staff and Elite group had to forage for their dinner. Even though there was a session detailing what plants to look for and more importantly what to avoid before the group went out, the contents of each of the bags was checked by Lyla Konker just to be sure everything each of them had gathered was okay to eat. It was only a group of about thirty, so the bags were left hanging on the chairs in the dining hall. All of them had the name of the owner written on them, and as Lyla okayed them, she put a check mark on each bag and then hung it back on the chair." I looked at the bulldog-like cop. "When you were investigating the victim's death, you had a tote bag with the victim's name on it and a check mark. The way you knew what had poisoned her was that there was a death cap mushroom still stuck inside the bag." That wasn't altogether true. All I'd seen then was the tote bag for a moment before he'd slipped it behind his back. I hadn't seen the name and check mark until Dane showed me the picture he'd snapped when he'd snuck into the evidence lockup. I held my breath for a moment, wondering if the lieutenant would catch it, but there was no change in his expression so I continued.

Lyla insisted that she couldn't have made a mistake and let the poison mushrooms slip through. I met one of the Jordan people who said she'd foraged with the victim and that they'd deliberately not picked any mushrooms." I gazed directly at Borgnine again. "And yet the victim ingested the poison mushroom and there was one still in the bag you found. Lyla Konker seemed like a very rigid perfectionist sort of person and at first I thought she simply couldn't deal with the thought that she'd made a mistake. But then I began to realize there was another option. What if she'd planted the mushrooms in the victim's bag when she went through it? I'd found out she viewed the victim as a weak link in the staff who was responsible for an accident in a previous retreat because she'd been distracted by her cell phone. But then Lyla died in another so-called accident before I could pursue it." I stopped to take a breath and could tell by his eye movements that the lieutenant was getting impatient, but I was not going to be rushed.

"But something had stuck in my mind. Cloris had mentioned there'd been a few people milling around in the dining hall while the bags were being checked. It was early on in the retreat and too soon for them all to know each other enough so that they would notice someone who didn't belong."

Borgnine leaned forward. "I get it, you conjectured that someone came in and switched bags after they'd been checked," he said. He started to wave his hand and suggested he didn't need all the details, but just any proof I had. But I wasn't going to skip to the end.

"A comment one of my people made stuck in my mind. She'd said something about replacing one habit with another. You probably don't know this, but a number of my people are trying to get over habits, well, actually addictions—"

"Drugs?" he said, interrupting as he sat forward again.

"Not illegal ones," I said. "John is getting off pot, Suzy!'s facing that she has a phone problem, and Hanna recently quit smoking. I was looking through the bios of the Jordan people around the same time I happened to look at Hanna's tote bag. She'd put her name on it with some decorations around it claiming that it made it easier to pick out from the others' bags. But I suddenly realized that wasn't it at all." Borgnine gave me a blank look, not understanding.

"I'd assumed the victim spelled her name M-e-g-a-n, but when I saw her bio it was spelled M-e-g-h-a-n." I took another look at the lieutenant to see if he got it now. He was almost smiling as if he'd caught me going off on some needless tangent.

"Hanna took her tote bag, which had no name on it, and wrote Meghan's name on it along with a check mark. I'm guessing she got the mushrooms from the samples Lyla had and added some plants she grabbed from around here. Then she left it on the back of the chair and took Meghan's actual bag with her. All it took was some time with a black marker to draw a sunflower over the M-e-g and to add an n-a, so that now it read *Hanna*. She made the check mark into the stem of a flower and added daisy petals to the top. To balance it all off, she drew another sunflower after her name. It probably seemed like a perfect plan, but she made one mistake. Remember I said replacing one habit with another? Fern, one of my retreaters, said Hanna may be doing that by replacing smoking with chewing gum. I saw her wrap up a chewed piece and drop it in her bag when she first arrived. The thing about chewing gum wrapped in paper is that it always seems to get free of the paper an end up stuck to something. When she took all of her things out of the tote bag before she transformed it to Meghan's, she must have missed the gum stuck to the inside of the bag." I checked the lieutenant's expression to see if he was still listening.

"If you recall, a mushroom was stuck to the bag that you took in as evidence."

"Stuck with chewing gum, hmm," he said. "For now that's just conjecture," he added and glowered. "The lab people will have to confirm it." He was doing his best not to make it seem like a done deal, but after what I'd said, I sensed he believed it was accurate. He put his hand to his forehead as the meaning of the cup of trash became apparent.

"As I'm sure you know, there would be the DNA of the gum chewer in the gum from their saliva. The cup you so reluctantly took as evidence is Hanna's coffee cup from this morning. You'll see her name written on the side."

"And her DNA is on the lip of the cup and can be matched to the DNA in the chewing gum," he said, as if it was somehow partly his idea. I waited to see if he'd add anything like *clever catch*, but he didn't. "So what about the death in the sauna?"

"Lyla was making such a fuss insisting that she couldn't have made a mistake. Like I said, I started to wonder if she was trying to cover up something she'd done since I'd heard that she was no fan of the victim. But now I see she was trying to clear herself of making a mistake by finding out how the victim had ended up with the poison mushroom. It was common knowledge that Lyla was doing some meditation and preparation in the sauna. All Hanna had to do was wait for Lyla to go in and slip the wedge under the door from the outside. Then she could have added to the time it was set for on the controls. And then later come back and pull out the wedge so it would look like an accident."

"I suppose you have the motives all figured out, too," he said.

"You caught me," I said. "I don't know what the story was with Meghan, but I think Lyla Konker had figured out what Hanna had done with the tote bags. Like I said, she was obsessed with proving that she hadn't made a mistake. And as I already explained, it seemed like she was talking to me when she said that she knew what I'd done, but when I thought back to it, I realized she might have been talking to someone around me—and Hanna was in that group. She must have been afraid that Lyla would turn her in." I put my hands up. "And that's all I know."

There was no apology for not listening to me when I'd first done the Dumpster diving. "Thank you," he said, as if it was hard to get the words out. "I'll take it from here." He got up and went to the door. "You can come if you want to," he said in a half-hearted tone.

I was on my feet in no time. "You're including me?" I said, surprised.

"Considering the lengths you went to to get the cup, you earned it." Even so he admonished me to stay silent.

"Remember, she thinks I want a statement about you tackling her," Borgnine said as we approached the door of the other meeting room. "The officer was supposed to be there to get her basic information. If she tried to leave, he was supposed to radio me."

Hanna looked up when we walked in. She appeared nervous and was pressing her lips together as if she was trying to keep silent. The officer was sitting across the table from her and filling out a form. The lieutenant introduced himself and made no mention of me.

I was surprised to see his usually gruff face relax into a more friendly expression. He asked her a few questions, making sure she didn't need any first aid after my attack. Then oh, so casually he asked if he could see her tote bag. She was in a trap. She didn't want to show it to him but probably figured if she refused he'd ask why. She seemed uneasy, but pulled it out of a pocket of her suitcase and put it on the table.

He asked if it was okay if he picked it up and looked inside. She swallowed hard before she nodded. He examined the front and it was just as I'd described it. Seeing it up close, her changes and additions seemed a little more obvious.

She threw me a hopeless look as her eyes became hollow and the color drained from her face. "I'm sorry," she said in almost a whisper. "I didn't mean for Meghan to die. I just wanted her to suffer after what my sister went through thanks to her carelessness. People recover from eating poison mushrooms all the time. There's no way I could have known she had some kind of underlying condition that made her more susceptible."

Borgnine knew enough to keep quiet and let her go on. Hanna's distraught expression turned to anger. "When I heard how she shrugged off the mistake she'd made when the Jordan people called her out on that first day . . ." She stopped to swallow and take a breath. "My sister came to a number of Jordan retreats. She was always sure the next one was going to turn everything around for her. During the last one she attended something happened. She didn't tell me the details, just that she'd fallen and hit her head during one of the challenges. The Jordan people convinced her that she was okay. After she came home she started getting horrible debilitating headaches. It made all her issues with depression and anxiety worse." Hanna looked from the cop to me. "She couldn't take it anymore and overdosed on pain pills. I tried to contact Jordan to find out what happened to my sister, but I just got the runaround. I knew he was having another retreat this weekend. I wanted to confront him and find out what really happened."

She shook her head with distress. "I found out what happened all right, but not from him. That first day when I heard the Jordan people talking about Meghan, I knew they were talking about my sister. That stupid woman was so obsessed with her smart phone that she didn't turn it off. It rang and she was distracted and wasn't there to do her part in catching my sister. It was a trust exercise." She threw up her hands in frustration.

"And Lyla figured out what you'd done," I said. The words had slipped out before I could stop them and Lieutenant Borgnine gave me a sharp look. She nodded and the story poured out just about exactly as I'd presented it. She'd come undone when Lyla confronted her and acted out of panic. When she got to the end, she crumbled and whaled. "What have I done?"

• • •

I was standing outside the meeting room after Hanna had been taken away. Figuring it out didn't feel like a triumph anymore. I asked the lieutenant what he thought would happen to her.

"You know everything else, but not that," he said with a world-weary sigh. "Unless an attorney can convince her otherwise, I'm guessing she'll plead guilty and they'll make a deal. Whatever happens, she's probably facing a long time in prison." He put his pen and notebook away. "The worst is when something pushes good people to do bad things."

• • •

The group was still in the meeting room when I returned. I had gotten so wrapped up in diving for clues and dealing with the lieutenant that I'd lost track of time. The room was in the middle of a transition. Crystal was packing up everything she'd brought for the weekend. My retreat people were clearing the table of their projects and tote bags, while Tag hovered, swooping in to gather up any scrap of yarn left behind.

Lucinda was opening containers on a metal cart. I was really grateful that although the Blue Door was closed on Sunday, they had arranged with the cook to come in and create the final meal for my people. It was going to end with everyone passing the switch project back to the original owner.

The whole crew stared at me when I came in, probably wondering where I'd been. I was glad they weren't seeing me in my Dumpster-diving clothes. I'd gotten a little disheveled when I tackled Hanna, but had already done repairs. All they knew was that Hanna was somehow missing from the group and I knew I was going to have to give them an explanation.

As expected, they were all shocked and saddened. I noticed that Daisy seemed to be taking notes. I waited until I got the whole story out before I asked what she was doing.

Her first move was to hide the small notebook and deny she was doing anything, but when they all said they'd seen her with a pen and paper, she relented.

"I kind of left out a few facts when I said why I'd come," she said with a guilty look. "I mean, it's true that I wanted to go someplace alone where I'd be in a group. But it was less about learning how to crochet and more about getting material to write an article about gurus like Jordan. Are they real or charlatans? How much do they really care about the participants? Do things happen?" She took the notebook out of hiding. "Between what I saw and what you just said, I got a lot of material."

"So what are your findings about Jordan?" John said.

"It's clearly a mixed bag." She went on about the lack of oversight and said that Jordan's plan seemed a little cavalier. "For the stable person who wants to tweak their life it's okay. There seemed to be quite a few of those. People who seem to have everything but feel like something's still missing," she said with a shrug. "But I'd worry for anybody with heavy-duty issues. Jordan makes it sound like if they go along with the program and do the challenges, their lives will be transformed. This retreat costs a fortune and some people have run up credit card bills to pay for it. The Elite group gets a five-minute one-on-one with him and he gives them all the same message about letting go of their fears. I don't think they know enough about the individuals who come for a transformation."

Yolanda got up and hugged her sister. "I love you," she said. "I'm sorry for saying I wanted to take my own vacations from now on." She turned to the rest of us. "I can understand why Hanna was so upset. I don't know what I'd do if something happened to Vonda like that." She paused to think it over. "Okay, I don't know what I would do, but I know I wouldn't kill anybody. We believe in forgiveness. So, I guess I'd try to change the situation for the future."

"And I'm sorry for being so judgmental about how you live. I am a little uptight and I should be a little more like you. I'm starting with joining you in dessert."

Fern seemed distraught. "It's been great with you guys, but now I just want to go home and hug my kids. I know I said it was overwhelming with three of them and how it was up to me to be their everything, but it's partly my fault. I demand too much of myself. I'm going to take some of the help my family's offered."

The table was officially clear and Tag came around setting up each place. It didn't take long before everyone was getting a little crazy as he kept repositioning silverware and such until it was just so, and then someone knocked it askew and Tag had to do it all again.

Lucinda was trying to speed things up by putting platters of food on the table while Tag was doing his ritual. John sat back in his chair and let out a sigh. "It's really a shock about Hanna. I knew she had something on her mind. I wish I'd gotten her to talk about it. Maybe she wouldn't have done what she did."

"I don't think you could have stopped her," Daisy said. "She was looking to blame someone for what happened to her sister."

I thought of how I thought I'd seen John arguing with a woman in the Jordan group. He'd denied it, but I asked him about it again.

"Oh, that," he said, looking as if he wished he could disappear. "I'm afraid I wasn't totally honest. My wife isn't dead, more like she's an ex. That was her. I've been trying to get her to sign some papers and I thought if I had a chance to talk to her directly rather than through an attorney, I could get it done. I attempted to sign up for the Jordan retreat, but it was full. So, I found this. It was my assistant who got me into knitting when she saw how stressed I was. I even went to a couple of her knitting club meetings. I'm not very good, but the needle pushing does work." He held up the scarf he'd gotten in the switch that he'd finished. It looked a little uneven. Crystal snatched it and began to play with it to make it look better. He looked over the table and had a small smile. "Even without her signing the papers, the knitting and company really helped. I feel more centered than when I came."

Suzy! had been quiet, but she suddenly burst into tears—loud look-at-me tears—and then she blew her nose so it sounded like a foghorn. She stood up and took out her phone, glaring at it. "My son was right. I admit, I'm addicted to it. Even when there was no signal, I needed to be able to see it, touch it, scroll through old emails. I admit it—I did sneak off the grounds and found a signal. I don't want to be like the dead woman, so connected to my phone that I let bad things happen."

As Tag finally finished and the food began to get passed around, they all offered support for Suzy!. "It's not a black-or-white proposition," John said. "Like everything else, you need to learn moderation. I know I had to cut the umbilical cord to mine. I started small, putting it out of sight for a while. No one says we have to be accessible twenty-four-seven. People can leave messages. You can answer emails later. You don't have to keep checking the news or social media."

"It's about being here now," Fern said. "I'm anxious to see my kids, but I'm grateful for this weekend and meeting all of you. To you guys, I'm Fern, not Sonny's widow or my kids' mother."

True to her word, Vonda accepted dessert. Yolanda was ecstatic when she saw it was apple pie. They all lingered and then went off to pack up their things. We still had one last get-together to pass back the switched projects.

Tag and Lucinda had their cart all packed up and I thanked them for all the help in pulling off the retreat despite the Jordan group. They made a memorable pair. He with his bushy brown hair and her in her Ralph Lauren outfit and perfect makeup. Tag had been too wrapped up in dealing with the silverware and food to focus on what I'd told the group about Hanna, but Lucinda had heard it all. She gave me a big hug. "You did it again. Nice that Lieutenant Borgnine is finally recognizing your skill."

"Sort of, anyway," I said with a smile.

We parted company when we reached the heart of Vista Del Mar. Cloris was walking with a group of people showing off their survival bracelets to the bigger crowd who'd only observed the making of them. She looked drained, but the people around her seemed amped up by the weekend despite the lack of food and sleep.

Diana was walking on her own and came up to me. She showed off her bracelet and let out a tired sigh. I asked her about the escape thing and she shrugged. "It was like a bad Halloween horror house." She seemed different than the others, and different than she'd been at the beginning of the weekend when she'd talked about being stoked when she'd finished the previous retreats.

"You made it through," I said in a cheerful voice.

"Yes, but this will be the last time I come to one of these," the dark-haired woman said. "Next time, I'm coming to one of yours. I finally got it. It's not Jordan or completing the challenges. It's like Dorothy in *The Wizard of Oz* movie. The power is in yourself, not in some guy in blue jeans. I just had to see it." I made sure to give her my card and told her I was arranging for my next retreat already.

"Spots are going fast," I said with a grin.

I stopped inside the Lodge and saw that the large room was busy with people milling around the cardboard cutouts of Jordan. BB was manning a table with a crowd clustered around it. I moved in to see what was going on. She was pitching people on becoming one of Jordan's Gold members. It sounded expensive and offered access to his lectures, special events, and some one-on-one time. She was also taking sign-ups to his next retreat while there was still room.

When I walked out onto the deck, I was surprised to see Tyler talking to Daisy. He shot a guilty look my way as I approached them.

"What's up?" I asked.

"Don't tell anyone," Tyler said in a whisper. "But I'm leaving the organization. I finally saw the person behind the guy on the stage and I didn't like what I saw. He's a fraud. All that nonsense about him being on a juice fast and meditating—the only juice he had was probably in his mimosas. He's eating cake and forcing us to eat beans. I heard his pitch enough times that it sounded like a recording. But mostly, it's just how he doesn't really care about anybody. He only kept Meghan around because he literally couldn't get rid of her. She was stuck to him like Velcro and she probably knew details he didn't want to get out, like he wore women's underwear or something. He barely blinked an eye when she and Lyla died. It was all about the image." He gestured toward Daisy. "I'm helping her with inside dope."

I didn't know what to say. He thanked me for the coffee and cookies that helped him keep his mind sharp. People were starting to come outside and he and Daisy slipped off.

I moved on to Hummingbird Hall and went to the lower floor to see what was going on with the escape challenge. Sammy was helping them disassemble the illusions at the end.

"Quite a weekend," he said.

"You can say that again." He started to repeat what he'd said as a joke, but I batted him on the arm and then told him about my morning adventure looking for him.

"Wow, Case, I had no idea. I just heard the snakes got ixnayed at the last minute." He looked down at my legs. "They didn't get you, did they?" He seemed relieved when I shook my head.

I had confronted Hanna about the snake meetup just before the lieutenant took her away and she'd admitted it was her doing. She thought if I was nursing a rattlesnake bite, I'd forget about passing along what I'd figured out.

"It's just one and done as far as I'm concerned. I'm not interested in being on Jordan's medical team or an illusion specialist for him," he said. "I'd much rather do magic shows with you as my comic sidekick." He reached out and magically a flower seemed to appear from my hair. I didn't say anything, but I wondered how long that would really continue. He'd taken a leave of absence from his medical practice in Chicago and was taking over for someone here. But that couldn't go on forever. He'd created a unique magic-comedy combo. I bet he could get gigs in Chicago and a real assistant. It was time for him to stand up to his parents anyway.

I left him to his work and retraced my steps. The doors were open to the auditorium on the upper floor. I peeked in, curious to see what was going on. The chairs were still set up and Jordan and his team were huddled in the front. Lieutenant Borgnine was talking to them. I slipped close to the doorway near where they were, curious to hear what was being said. He was basically telling Jordan that if he ever intended do another retreat in Cadbury, there'd be no poisonous anything.

Jordan got defensive but agreed and then quickly changed the subject and said he'd already been thinking they needed to be better able to deal with the fragileness of some of the attendees. Did he mean it, or did he think that would pacify the cop?

It was time to head back for the last get-together of my group. The dining hall was empty as I passed and a housekeeping crew was doing a cleanup. I cut through the Lodge and saw Kevin St. John, Cloris and Crystal off in a corner. Crystal waved me over. "Mr. St. John wants to tell the Delacorte sisters that the problems were caused by your retreat and you." Her eyes went skyward at the absurdity of it. He looked at me with his usual hostility.

"Are you really trying to blame everything on me?" I said, incredulous.

"It was one of your retreaters that did all the damage," he said.

"But you were the one who agreed to a retreat that featured rattle-snakes."

Crystal looked directly at Kevin St. John. "I hope your mantra is live and learn."

I made a quick detour home and then Crystal joined me as we went to meet up with the group. The room was clear and everyone but Hanna was sitting in their usual seat with the switched project on the table in front of them. I handed out the tote bags they should have gotten from the beginning and then they returned the project to its owner. Hanna had left the one that belonged to Fern behind, but Daisy was at a loss of what to do with the scarf that she had finished for Hanna.

Someone suggested we walk to the beach and let the tide carry it out. It seemed a little melodramatic, but somehow a fitting end.

And then it was time for them to leave. As I waited with them, they were all trading emails and text info. I watched from a step away and thought about how at the beginning of the weekend they had just been a list of names, and as in all the other retreats I'd done, now I knew the people behind the names with their backstories and secrets.

The airport van came and farewell hugs were shared all around. Those going to the airport got on and Vonda and Yolanda went to their car. As I watched the van and car go up the driveway, I wondered if the weekend had left them changed for the better, but I was pretty sure like every experience it had in some way changed them for good.

Julius was waiting when I got home and this time he wasn't going to let me jump over him and avoid his stink fish treat. I was just doling it out when my landline rang. It was Frank. "Feldstein, you left me hanging. How did it all turn out?"

"How about I had to zip line over a pair of rattlesnakes," I said before launching into how I had solved the whodunit and presented it to Lieutenant Borgnine.

"Sounds like that lieutenant is softening up," he said when I'd finished the story. "Is there something going on between you two?"

I choked on a laugh as I tried to speak. "I don't think I've ever described him to you," I began.

The afternoon faded into darkness and I wondered how I would have the wherewithal to do the baking, but the Blue Door needed their desserts and the coffee drinkers of Cadbury their muffins. I packed up the supplies for the biscuit muffins and hauled them out to my yellow Mini Cooper. The lights were on in the guesthouse, which meant Sammy was home. How long before his place was fixed so he could move back?

I let myself into the closed restaurant and took the bag to the kitchen. I went back to turn on the radio to the soft jazz hoping it would soothe away the rough edges. Dane was standing outside the window on the door and knocked when he saw me.

No uniform this time, instead he was dressed in jeans and a pocket T-shirt. "You sure look better now," he said with a grin, glancing over my hair as if there might be some garbage still stuck to it.

"Did you just come here to comment on my cleanup?" I said.

He held out his palms. "I know you had quite a day. What are we making?"

I gave him the list of desserts for the Blue Door. "And I want to do something for the lieutenant. I thought I'd make a sweet version of the biscuits in a cup, or as I call them, biscuffins."

"Sounds good." He began to help unload the bag of supplies. "I'm here to help and to show you how I've got your back."

I felt a huge sense of relief. "Thanks for the help. I didn't know how I was going to manage. I've always been in charge of watching my own back," I said.

"That's what a relationship is about, give and take," he said.

"So you make me delicious spaghetti and watch my back and I—"

"Provide muffins and give me someone to care about who keeps saying she's going to leave," he said as he began to help me set up the ingredients for carrot cakes.

"It hardly seems like a fair trade. Are you sure that's enough?" I said.

"Well, now that you mention it, maybe it isn't," he joked. "I'll have to come up with a list of expectations." He pulled out the cinnamon. "I'm sorry our Saturday plans got ruined. I wasn't expecting there to be a murder at Vista Del Mar and to be put on the night watch. We could try again next Saturday. The candles are still good, but the rose petals are wilted."

"And I gave away the chocolate fondue," I said.

"That's right, you did." He gave his best impression of being crushed.

"I still have the fondue pot. I could get more chocolate and strawberries," I said. I stopped what I was doing and looked at him. "But do we really need all that?"

He laughed as he measured out the brown spice. "I knew it. You want me. You really do." His eyes danced with good humor.

"Maybe after we drop off the muffins," I said tentatively.

"Sounds good to me," he said

"But I'll be expecting a hot breakfast," I said in a teasing voice.

"With pleasure," he said and squeezed my arm.

Sweet Biscuffins

Makes 12

2 cups flour
1 tablespoon baking powder
1 teaspoon salt
2 tablespoons sugar
1¼ sticks of cold butter cut in small pieces
1 cup buttermilk

For topping:
1 tablespoon melted butter
1 tablespoon sugar mixed with ½ teaspoon ground cinnamon

For glaze:
½ cup powdered sugar
2 tablespoons milk
½ teaspoon vanilla

Preheat oven to 450 degrees F.

Line muffin tin with paper baking cups.

Mix flour, baking powder, salt and sugar in a large bowl.

Cut in butter using pastry blender or two knives until the dough resembles crumbs.

Add buttermilk and mix until just blended.

Drop with tablespoon or small scoop into baking cups. Brush the biscuffins with melted butter and sprinkle cinnamon sugar. Bake for 12–15 minutes until golden and a toothpick comes out clean.

Make glaze by mixing powdered sugar, milk and vanilla. Cool the biscuffins slightly then drizzle glaze over the top.

Crochet Scrunchies

Supplies:

100 percent cotton, like Peaches & Crème or Sugar n' Cream. One skein will be more than enough to make both styles of scrunchies.
Elastic hair bands
H/8-5.00mm hook for Scrunchie #1
J/10-6.00mm hook for Scrunchie #2
Tapestry needle for weaving in ends and sewing together the ends of Scrunchie #2

Scrunchie #1

Using H hook, make a slipknot and make 26 sc around the elastic hair band.
Sl st to first sc, ch 1 and make a sc in each stitch around, sl st to first sc.
Ch 3 and sc into the next st, Repeat * to* around sl st to first st.
Fasten off and weave in ends

Scrunchie #2

Using J hook, make a slipknot and chain 12, loop around the elastic hair band and sl st to first chain to make a ring. Chain 3, counts as first dc, dc around the loop. Do not join to first stitch but continue with dc making a tube around the elastic hair band until it's ruffly. Fasten off and leave a long tail of yarn to use to sew the ends together. Sew the ends of the tube together.

Acknowledgments

Bill Harris wears a lot of hats as editor and more. He wears them all very well and is a pleasure to work with. Jessica Faust continues to help me navigate the world of mystery writing. Dar Albert keeps coming up with such great covers that capture the Monterey Peninsula location so well.

I want to thank Burl, Max and Jakey for once again being my recipe taste testers and giving the Sweet Biscuffins a thumbs-up.

About the Author

Betty Hechtman is the national bestselling author of the Crochet Mysteries and the Yarn Retreat Mysteries. Handicrafts and writing are her passions and she is thrilled to be able to combine them in both of her series. She also writes the Writer for Hire Mysteries, which are set in her Chicago neighborhood of Hyde Park and have a touch of crochet.

Betty grew up on the South Side of Chicago and has a degree in Fine Art. Since College, she has studied everything from improv comedy to magic. She has had an assortment of professions, including volunteer farm worker picking fruit on a kibbutz tucked between Lebanon and Syria, nanny at a summer resort, waitress at a coffee house, telephone operator, office worker at the Writer's Guild, public relations assistant at a firm with celebrity clients, and newsletter editor at a Waldorf school. She has written newspaper and magazine pieces, short stories, screenplays, and a middle-grade mystery, *Stolen Treasure*. She lives with her family and stash of yarn in Southern California.

See BettyHechtman.com for more information, excerpts from all her books, and photos of all the projects of the patterns included in her books. She blogs on Fridays at Killerhobbies.blogspot.com, and you can join her on Facebook at BettyHechtmanAuthor and Twitter at @BettyHechtman.